THE COMPLETE TALES OF DOCTOR SATAN

THE COMPLETE TALES OF
DOCTOR SATAN

BY
PAUL ERNST

WITH AN INTRODUCTION BY
JOHN PELAN

ALTUS PRESS • 2013

© 2013 Altus Press • First Edition—2013

EDITED AND DESIGNED BY
Matthew Moring

PUBLISHING HISTORY
"Introduction" appears here for the first time. Copyright © 2013 John Pelan. All Rights Reserved.
"Doctor Satan" originally appeared in the August 1935 issue of *Weird Tales* (Volume 26, Number 2).
"The Man Who Chained the Lightning" originally appeared in the September 1935 issue of *Weird Tales* (Volume 26, Number 3).
"Hollywood Horror" originally appeared in the October 1935 issue of *Weird Tales* (Volume 26, Number 4).
"The Consuming Flame" originally appeared in the November 1935 issue of *Weird Tales* (Volume 26, Number 5).
"Horror Insured" originally appeared in the January 1936 issue of *Weird Tales* (Volume 27, Number 1).
"Beyond Death's Gateway" originally appeared in the March 1936 issue of *Weird Tales* (Volume 27, Number 3).
"The Death's Double" originally appeared in the May 1936 issue of *Weird Tales* (Volume 27, Number 5).
"Mask of Death" originally appeared in the August/September 1936 issue of *Weird Tales* (Volume 28, Number 2).
"Writing Weird Tales" originally appeared in the February 1935 issue of *Writer's Review*.

THANKS TO
John Locke, John Pelan and Christopher Roden

ALL RIGHTS RESERVED
No part of this book may be reproduced or utilized in any form or by any means, electronic or mechanical, without permission in writing from the publisher.
This edition has been marked via subtle changes, so anyone who reprints from this collection is committing a violation of copyright.
Visit altuspress.com for more books like this.
Printed in the United States of America.

TABLE OF CONTENTS

INTRODUCTION 1

DOCTOR SATAN 1

THE MAN WHO CHAINED THE LIGHTNING 32

HOLLYWOOD HORROR 65

THE CONSUMING FLAME 98

HORROR INSURED 134

BEYOND DEATH'S GATEWAY 166

THE DEATH'S DOUBLE 197

MASK OF DEATH 230

WRITING WEIRD TALES 264

JOHN PELAN

THE MAN BEHIND THE MAN IN THE MASK

GREAT VILLAINS ARE always more interesting than the hero.... After all, who would offer up more interesting conversation, Hannibal Lecter or Clarice Starling? Victor von Doom or the dry as toast Reed Richards? The suave cosmopolitan Dracula or the British corporate flunky Jonathan Harker? You get the idea.... A great villain can carry a novel, film, or comic book far easier than the hero. After all, in most cases we *know* the hero is going to be around for the next installment, but the villain might not be... unless of course, we're talking about one of those rare instances where the work in question revolves around the villain and in most cases, these instances are short lived.

Probably the first and best known series that "starred" the villain was Sax Rohmer's Fu Manchu... (At least I don't think anyone read those stories because of Dr. Petrie or Nayland Smith). Russell Thorndike's Dr. Syn proved so popular that Thorndike was obliged to go back and expand one novel into several books in order to satisfy reader demand for more of the pirate-turned-vicar. Comic books had the Claw getting the best of Daredevil for several issues of *Silver Streak* until they realized that their lead character was being made to look foolish on a regular basis, so they gave the Claw his own superhero to kick around in the person of the *Ghost*. (The Ghost did eventually prevail, but no one remembers him and everyone of a certain age knows who the Claw was, even if they have never read a comic book in their life.

The pulps tried out several fiends in their own magazines, but had limited success with Dr. Yen Sin or Wu Fang (both of whom were obviously modeled on Rohmer's much more interesting character, Fu Manchu). The Octopus and the Scorpion only made it for a single issue each, while Dr. Death managed to stick around just a bit longer. (Actually the good doctor could work today, as he was basically an eco-terrorist long before the term was coined). The most successful recurring villain had to be Mr. Chang back in the 1920s in the pages of *Detective Fiction Weekly*, but a decade later Paul Ernst had the chance to have a long-running series with Dr. Satan; it was just in the wrong venue as we shall see....

Paul Ernst is best remembered today for his work under the house name of Kenneth Robeson, a byline most frequently associated with Doc Savage. Of course, Lester Dent penned the Doc Savage novels leaving Ernst to be assigned the task of creating a new pulp super-hero, which he did with Richard Benson, the Avenger. While Ernst's creation is not nearly as well known as Doc Savage, the stories proved popular enough to run for several years and were reprinted in paperback in the 1980s, with SF author and pulp aficionado Ron Goulart adding several volumes to the series. In the last few years a new publisher has begun issuing the series in handsome trade paperback format.

Matt Moring and I are both of the opinion that Ernst should be known for a lot more than merely laboring on a Doc Savage knock-off. As with many of the wordsmiths of the day, Ernst wrote widely on a variety of subjects and by his own estimate was successful in placing 90% of his output; a rather remarkable achievement for any writer, the more so as Ernst was cranking out over a million words a year at the time. What Paul Ernst did best was write supernatural or horror fiction.... And *Weird Tales* proved to be a ready market for the type of material he most enjoyed doing. His first story "The Temple of Serpents" appeared in the October 1928 issue of *Weird Tales* and is remark-

INTRODUCTION

able for the level of craftsmanship shown by a novice, so much so that it was reprinted by the magazine in the 1950s when editor Dorothy McIllwraith was mining earlier issues for "classics"; the same is true of his third sale to the magazine "A Witch's Curse." Between 1928 and 1930 Ernst placed several additional tales to markets including *Weird Tales* and *Ghost Stories,* culminating with the sale of a novel to *Weird Tales (The Black Monarch),* which was to be serialized in five parts. This last sale was a sufficient confidence builder to allow for Ernst to take the plunge into full-time freelancing.

Now established as a reliable wordsmith, when it came time to launch a new feature in *Weird Tales,* editor Farnsworth Wright came to Ernst. The concept was simple: readers seemed to enjoy weird detective stories. After all, Seabury Quinn's Jules de Grandin had been a reliable staple of the magazine for several years. What about combining a weird super-criminal sort of an anti-Shadow or anti-Spider with a detective equally equipped with science and the arcane arts *a la* Donald Wandrei's Frost?

The result was Dr. Satan. Debuting in the August, 1935 issue with a stunning Brundage cover (that looked nothing like the author's description of the character), the "world's weirdest criminal" leered at readers from behind his red mask. The initial story introduced both Dr. Satan and his nemesis, Ascott Keane. Wright was definitely interested in pushing the character as frothy blurbs appearing before and after the publication of the story show. Dr. Satan was described thusly, "he is no madman, but sane as you and I..." If a mass-murderer who looted and killed primarily for the sheer thrill of it is an example of mental health, I'll be quite happy to be labeled crazy.

Every good super villain has his henchmen and Dr. Satan was no exception, he started off with three: Bostiff, a legless giant with incredible arm strength; Girse, a small man described as possessing a "monkey face;" and Monroe, an dissolute aristocrat who runs afoul of his employer in the very first story with predictable results.... However his two more grotesque helpers stayed around for quite some time.

The Dr. Satan stories follow a pretty strict formula, and I would advise readers to sample the tales one at a time, interspersed with other reading so as not to spoil the effect. Remember that the stories appeared in a magazine with companion pieces that ranged from the Cthulhu mythos to ghost stories to interplanetary adventure, and as such they were allowed to shine. Reading them all at the same time would ruin the effect.

Dr. Satan's career lasted only one year, eight novelettes of each coming in at approximately 10,000 words. Paul Ernst was a fine writer and excelled when he was given what others might consider to be a restrictive formula. It was in situations like that where Ernst's creativity shone through and *Terror Tales, Dime Mystery, Horror Stories* and *The Avenger* all profited as a result. His work for *Weird Tales* including Dr. Satan was top-notch, but Dr. Satan was hardly welcomed with open arms by the readers, who were vociferous in their denouncing of the new series. It's odd, but my personal experience with *Weird Tales* consisted of buying the 1934–1936 run with paper-route money when I was twelve and I felt that the Dr. Satan stories fit perfectly and were more interesting than the de Grandin yarns by Seabury Quinn.... However, the more sophisticated readers of the mid-1930s did not share my viewpoint and every new Dr. Satan story was greeted with cries of outrage that the magazine was being "ruined" or was turning into a detective magazine.... Quite frankly, *Weird Tales* published a lot of material that was much worse than the Dr. Satan stories, all of which are quite good.... Unfortunately, Dr. Satan was in the wrong place at the wrong time. A year or two later in the pages of *Dime Mystery Magazine* or *Strange Detective Mysteries,* Dr. Satan and his foe, Ascott Keane might very well have been the cover feature month after month. However *Weird Tales* readers never warmed to the series and with the Aug–Sept issue of 1936, Dr. Satan joined Wu Fang, The Scorpion, Dr. Death, Dr. Yen Sin, and the Octopus in the ranks of super-villains that were unable

INTRODUCTION

to build up a following.

One of the central things that many writers ignore when constructing a character of this type is that the most important characteristic is that *the villain does not think of himself as a villain!* Whether operating under a false sense of entitlement, trying to right wrongs either real or imagined, or suffering from the monomaniacal viewpoint that they are the only person that has the answers, the villain *must* consider their particular cause to be just. The great villains in literature from Guy Boothby's Dr. Nikola to E.R. Eddison's Lord Gro in *The Worm Ouroboros* clear back to Shakespeare's Richard III have one characteristic in common: they fully believe that they're right and everyone else is wrong.

Had Paul Ernst thought the character through in more depth there's no reason to think that the reader response would have been anything but positive.... As it was, the rationale that Dr. Satan was the scion of a wealthy family and committed horrendous crimes just for the thrill of it is not a motivation that any sane person can identify with.

Contrast if you will the motives of Dr. Death, who is basically an eco-terrorist years before the term came into vogue. We can certainly be appalled at his methods, but there is a small spark that says his heart is in the right place.... The completely sociopathic behavior of Dr. Satan wasn't going to endear him to readers. The only thing that could have saved the series would have been a more interesting antagonist. This is also a difficult feat for a writer to pull off, the hero must not be made to seem a total buffoon, yet the villain manages to elude capture in every installment. Unfortunately, Ascott Keane was a pretty generic type without any standout characteristics that would compel readers to follow his exploits month after month.

So, despite what could have been a long-running series, just a few years later when the strange detective tale as a genre came into vogue, editor Wright pulled the plug on the masked man after only eight installments, (which is still more appearances than any of his contemporaries at Popular Publications). However, we have these eight novelettes collected together for the first time in over seventy-five years. They may not be great literature, but they are a hell of a lot of fun and another solid reason that Paul Ernst should be remembered as one of pulpdom's very best authors.

John Pelan
Winter Solstice 2012
Midnight House
Gallup, NM

DOCTOR SATAN

BUSINESS WAS BEING done as usual in the big outer office of the Ryan Importing Company. Calls came over the switchboard for various department heads. Men and girls bent over desks, reading and checking order blanks, typewriting, performing the thousand and one duties of big business.

Yet over the office hung a hush, more sensed than consciously felt. The typewriters seemed to make less than their normal chatter. Employees talked in low tones, when they had something to communicate to one another. The office boy showed a tendency to tiptoe when he carried a fresh batch of mail in from the anteroom.

The girl at the switchboard pulled a plug as a call from the secretary of the big boss, Arthur B. Ryan, was concluded.

The office boy looked inquiringly at her as he passed. "How's the old man?"

The girl shook her head a little. "I guess he's worse. That last call was important, and he wouldn't take it himself. He had Gladys take it for him."

"What's the matter with him, anyhow?"

"A headache," said the girl.

"Is that all? I thought from the way everybody was acting like this was a morgue, that he was dying or something."

"I guess this is something special in the way of headaches," the switchboard girl retorted, smoothing down the blonde locks at the back of her head. "And it came up awful sudden. He walked past here at nine, two hours ago, and grinned at me like he felt great. Then at ten he phoned down to the building drugstore for some aspirin. Now he won't take a call from the head of one of the biggest companies in the city! I guess he feels terrible."

"A headache!" snorted the office boy. "Well, why don't he go see a doctor?"

"I put through a call for Doctor Swanson on the top floor of the building, ten minutes ago. He was busy with an appointment, but said he'd be down soon."

"A headache! And he can't take it! Wonder what he'd do if he got something serious the matter with him."

He swaggered on, and the hush seemed to deepen over the office. A premonitory hush? Were all in the big room dimly conscious of the sequence of events about to be started there? Later, many claimed they had felt psychic warnings; but whether that is a fact or imagination will never be known.

A hush, with a drone of voices and machines accentuating it in the outer office. A silence, in which the doors of the executives, in their cubicles along the east wall of the office space, remained closed. A quiet that seemed to emanate from the blank, shut door marked Arthur B. Ryan, President.

AND THEN THE hush was cracked. The silence was torn, like strong linen screaming apart as a great strain rips it from end to end.

From behind the door marked President came a shriek of pain and horror that blanched the cheeks of the office workers; a yell that keened out over the hush and turned busy fingers to wood, and which stopped all words on the suddenly numbed lips that had been uttering them.

Ryan's secretary, pale, trembling, ran from her desk outside the office door and sped into Ryan's office.

"Oh, my God!" the shriek came more clearly to the general office through the opened door. "My head… oh, my God!"

And then the screams of the man were swelled suddenly by the high shriek of the secretary. "Look—look...."

There was the thud of a body in Ryan's office, telling the plain message that she had fainted; an instant later the agonized shrieks of the man in there were stilled.

For a second all in the general office were gripped by silence, paralyzed, staring with wide eyes at the door to the private office. Then the sales manager stepped to the open door.

He glanced into Ryan's office, and those outside saw his face go the color of ashes. He tottered, caught at the door to keep from falling.

Then, with the air of a man dazed by a physical blow, he closed the door and stumbled toward the switchboard.

"Phone the police," he said hoarsely to the girl. "My God... the police... though I don't know what they can do. His head...."

"What—what's the matter with his head?" the girl faltered as her fingers stiffly manipulated the switchboard plugs.

The sales manager stared at her without seeing her, his eyes looking as if they probed through her and into unplumbed chasms or horror behind her.

"A tree growing out of his head," he gasped. "A tree... pushing out of his skull, like a plant cracking a flower-pot it outgrows, and sending roots and branches through the cracks."

He leaned against the switchboard.

"A tree, killing him. Hurry! Get the...."

He lunged for her, but was too late; the switchboard girl had slid from her chair, unconscious. Blindly, with fingers that rattled against the switchboard, the man put through the call himself.

THAT WAS AT eleven in the morning of July 12th, 193—, a day that made criminal history in New York.

At eleven-ten, in a great Long Island home, the second chapter was being written.

The home belonged to Samuel Billingsley, retired merchant.

It was a huge estate, high-walled. In the walls a new iron gate glistened, closing off the front driveway. It was a high gate, heavily barred—the kind of a gate that would be installed by a man afraid for his life. Beside that gate two men lounged. Each was big, heavily muscled, with a bulge at his armpit speaking of a gun in readiness.

At the front door of the house another man was stationed; and there was one at the rear, and still another patrolling the grounds. This last one carried a rifle.

The summer sun gleamed bright over the estate. The silence of the suburbs enveloped it, yet danger lowered like a black veil over the place.

A long low roadster slid to a stop before the closed iron gate. A young man, dark-haired, with dark gray eyes, sounded the horn. Reluctantly the gate was opened. The man drove the roadster in and started toward the house, but was stopped by the two guards who stood before the car with an automatic apiece covering its driver.

The young man glared. "Well?" he snapped. "Who the devil are you? What are you doing here?"

"Same to you, buddy," rasped one of the men, coming closer. "What's your business here?"

The young man glanced at the new, high gate and back to the guards.

"I'm Samuel Billingsley's nephew," he said. "My name's Merton Billingsley, I've been away for a month—and I come back to be stopped at the point of a gun at my own uncle's house...."

"Take it easy," said the man gruffly. "We're the old—I mean we're Mr. Billingsley's bodyguards. Hired us two days ago. Orders were to investigate everybody driving in here. Have you got any proofs that you're his nephew?"

The young man showed letters. His annoyance was giving way to curiosity—and alarm.

"Bodyguard!" he exclaimed. "Why a bodyguard? Is my uncle's life in danger?"

The man shrugged. "I wouldn't know, but I guess it is or he wouldn't have hired us. He didn't tell us anything except to keep everybody out of the grounds."

Merton Billingsley clutched at the man's arm. "Is he all right now? Have there been any attempts on his life so far?"

"None yet," said the man, holstering his automatic. "And I guess he's all right—except he's got a headache."

"A headache?"

"Yeah. His high-hat butler came down here a half-hour ago, and said a doc had been called and we were to let him through. The old—Mr. Billingsley had a bad headache. The doc came ten minutes ago and is up in his room with him now. But aside from the headache, he's all right...."

Through the golden summer sunlight, like jagged lightning impinging on the ear-drums instead of the optic nerves, a scream lanced out. It was a thin, high shriek that drove the color from the faces of Merton Billingsley and the two guards. It came from behind a shaded window in the front corner of the great house.

"My uncle's room," breathed Merton. "What...."

He swallowed, and jerked his head to the two guards. "On the running-board," he snapped. "We'll get to the house...."

The whine of gears drowned his words. With a guard on each side, the roadster sped down the graveled driveway and to the house.

The door opened as Merton got to it. A gray-headed butler faced him.

"Willys!" exclaimed Merton. "My uncle... what in God's name is the matter with him?"

The man shook his head. "I don't know. He complained of having a terrific headache, sir. And I phoned for Doctor Smythe. Then, Just a minute ago he screamed...."

Down the curved marble staircase to the front hall a man was stumbling—a middle-aged man whose features were distorted.

"Smythe!" said Merton. "Uncle Samuel… tell me! Quick!"

The doctor stared at him. He moistened his lips. "Your uncle is dead."

"Dead! But what happened to him? He was an old man, but he was in good health. What killed him?"

"A plant," whispered the doctor. "A kind of bush. Thornbush—God knows what! That thing, blossoming from his head…."

Merton shook his shoulder savagely. "Are you insane? Pull yourself together! What's this talk of bushes?

"A bush… growing out of his head!" whispered the doctor, moistening his pale lips again and again.

MERTON STARTED UP the stairs. Smythe, rousing himself, grasped his arm. "Don't go up there, Merton! Don't!"

Merton wrenched his arm away. "My uncle lies up in his room, dead—and you tell me not to go up to him!"

He took the stairs two at a time.

"I'm warning you," came the doctor's shrill voice. "The sight you'll see…."

But Merton went on, around the curve in the staircase, down the hall at the top.

The door to his uncle's room was closed. Impetuously he opened it and leaped inside the big bedroom. It was dim in there, shaded against the sunlight; but after a few seconds he saw it—his uncle's body.

It lay beyond the big bed, the corpse of a man of seventy, thin, clad in a silk robe. The body was twisted and distorted, but it was not the body that riveted the gaze of the dead man's nephew; it was the head.

The head was turned so that, though the body lay on its side, the face was pointed toward the ceiling. And from the top of the skull something was protruding. Merton's hands crept toward his throat as he looked at it.

A sort of bush, with leafless, sharp-pointed twigs branching out in all directions, grew from the top of the skull. It was like a hand with many small sharp fingers that had thrust up through the bone, with its thick, wrist-like stem rooting in the brain beneath.

A tree, quick with life though rooted in death! Quick with life? As Merton stared with glazing eyes, he saw the leafless, sharp little branches crawl out a little farther. The thing was growing even as he watched it!

With a low cry, he turned and ran from the room.

2.

In a Park Avenue penthouse two men were seated in a great room fitted out as a library. The room was lined with books, in sections which were unobtrusively but precisely labeled as sections of shelving in public libraries are labeled. Science, one of the largest sections, crammed with books, was tagged. Another read, Mythology; a third, Occult. Then there were Psychology, Engineering, Biology, many others, each containing dozens of volumes.

The focal point of the big, lofty chamber was a huge ebony desk. It was at this desk that the two men were seated, one in a leather chair beside it, the other leaning back in a swivel chair from before it.

The man in the visitor's chair was about fifty, expensively dressed, a typical big business man with the suggestion of a paunch that comes with success and a striving after more millions instead of physical fitness. But there was one thing about this business man that was not typical. That was the expression on his face.

Fear! The blind terror of an incoherent animal caught in a trap beyond its comprehension!

His face was gray with fear. His lips were pallid and his hands were shaking with it. The sound of his ragged breathing was clearly audible in the almost cathedral-like hush of the great library.

The man sitting proprietorially at the desk watched his visitor with almost clinical detachment, though sympathy showed in his deep-set eyes. A man to attract attention in any gathering on Earth, this one.

He was a big man, but supple and quick-moving. His eyes, deep under coal-black eyebrows, were light grey; they looked calm as ice, as if no emergency could disturb their steely depths. He had a high-bridged, patrician nose, a long chin that was the embodiment of strength, and a firm, large mouth.

His mouth moved, clipping out words with easy precision. "You say you got the note yesterday, Walstead?"

Thus casually he addressed Ballard W. Walstead, one of the richest men in the city.

"Yes," said the man in the visitor's chair.

"Why did you come to me with it?"

"Because, said Walstead, raising a trembling hand in a repressed gesture of pleading. "I thought if anyone on Earth could save me it would be you. Oh, I know about you, though I realize that not a dozen people in the world are aware of the real life of Ascott Keane. These few know you as one of the greatest criminal investigators that ever lived—a man whose achievements have something almost of black magic in them. They know that you've raised a hobby of criminology into an art that passes beyond the reach of genius."

Ascott Keane's calm, steely eyes stared steadily into the frantic depths of the other man's pale blue ones.

"I am a dilettante," he murmured. "I inherited a fortune, and

I loaf through life playing with first editions, polo ponies and big game hunting.

"Yes, yes, I know. That's the picture the world has of you. The picture you've deliberately painted; but I tell you I know your capabilities! You've got to help me, Keane!"

Keane's long, strong hand went out. "Let me see the note."

Walstead fumbled in his pocket and drew out a folded sheet of paper. Handling it as though if were a deadly serpent, he handed it to Keane, who spread it out on the desk.

"Ballard Walstead," Keane read aloud. "You are hereby given a chance to purchase a continuation of your rather useless life. The price of this continuation is the round sum of one million dollars. You may pay this in any way you please—even in checks, if you like, for if ever you attempt to trace the checks you will die. And if you refuse payment you will die even more quickly.

"You will disregard this as a note from a crank, of course. But by noon tomorrow you will know better. You see, I have given two other men, Arthur B. Ryan and Samuel Billingsley, a choice similar to yours—and I believe they are going to defy me. Read in the afternoon papers what happens to them, Walstead. And believe me when I say that the same thing will happen to you if you do not meet my price. Directions will be given to you tomorrow noon as to where and how you are to pay the money. Your obedient servant, Doctor Satan."

KEANE LOOKED UP from the paper.

"Doctor Satan, he repeated. Into his steel-gray eyes came a hard, relentless glint. "Doctor Satan!"

"You know him?" asked Walstead eagerly.

"I know of him. A little. You read in the papers this afternoon of what happened to Ryan and Billingsley?"

"Yes," whimpered Walstead. "My God, yes! And that's what will happen to me Keane, if you won't help me." He shuddered as though drenched with icy water. "A tree—growing out of a man's head! Killing him! How can such things be done?"

"That is something only Doctor Satan can answer. Did you get instructions about where to pay the money this noon, as is promised in this letter?"

IN ANSWER, WALSTEAD drew out another bit of notepaper.

"Walstead:" Keane read. "Leave the money either in thousand-dollar bills or in checks up to twenty thousand dollars apiece, in the trash can at the corner of Broadway and Seventy-Sixth Street, tonight at nine o'clock. If checks, make them payable to Elias P. Hudge. Signed, Dr. Satan."

Keane's eyes searched Walstead's again. "Are you going to do it?"

"I can't!" exclaimed Walstead hysterically. "I'm a wealthy man, but my affairs are in such a state that to take a million dollars in cash from my business would bankrupt me! I can't!"

Keane's long, powerful fingers formed a reflective pent-roof under his long, powerful chin.

"You're going to defy Doctor Satan, then."

"I must!" cried Walstead. "I have no choice."

Keane's fingers moved restlessly.

"This Doctor Satan must have known your affairs were such that you couldn't meet his order. And he must have foreseen that you would have to refuse his demand… Were you in your office when the second note was delivered?"

"Yes."

"Who delivered it?"

Walstead shivered again. "That is one of the deepest mysteries of all. No one delivered it."

Keane stared.

"Nobody delivered that note!" Walstead repeated. "I was alone in my office, reading over some papers. I turned away from my desk a moment, when I turned back, the note was there, on top of the other things. No one had come in. The window was closed and locked. Yet the note—was there. It—it was like witchcraft, Keane!"

Keane's fingers, stilled for a moment, moved restlessly again. "You may be speaking more truly than you know, Walstead. After you received the note, what did you do?"

"I stayed in my office till four-thirty. Then I went down to the building lobby, and saw the afternoon papers. Screaming headings about the deaths of Ryan and Billingsley. After that I came here as fast as my chauffeur could drive me.

"Did anything unusual happen to you on the way?" Walstead shook his head. "Nothing. I got into my car at the office building, was driven straight here, and got out in front of your building.

"No one said anything to your? Or, perhaps, jostled you?"

"No one," said Walstead. Then his lips tightened. "Wait a minute. Yes! A man bumped into me just as I was coming into this building entrance."

Keane's eyes narrowed till all that was apparent of them was two gray glints. "Can you describe him?"

"No. I didn't pay any attention to him at all, after I saw he had no weapon in his hand and meant me no harm. His shoulder brushed against my neck and cheek, and then he was gone, after apologizing."

KEANE GOT UP from his desk. He eyes were more inscrutable than ever. "I'll do all I can to help you," he said. "Suppose you run along now, Walstead."

Walstead jerked to his feet with frenzy and perplexity in his face. He was almost as tall as Keane, but didn't give the appearance of being nearly so big.

"I don't understand, Keane. Are you throwing me over? Aren't you going to act with me against this Doctor Satan?"

"Yes, I'm going to act against Doctor Satan." Muscle ridged out in Keane's lean cheeks."You go along home."

"I'd hoped you would let me stay here, with you, till the danger was past...."

"You will be in no more danger at home than you would be here," replied Keane, with odd gentleness in his tone. "My man will show you to the door."

With the words, Keane's man appeared; a silent, impassive-looking fellow who handed Walstead his hat and stick. Walstead, with many protests, went out....

"Beatrice," Keane called softly, when he was alone in the big library again.

A section of the shelving, lined with books, swung smoothly away from the wall, forming a doorway. Through it came a girl with a shorthand notebook and a pencil in her tapering hands. She was tall and beautifully formed, with dark blue eyes and hair that was more red than brown.

"You sent him away!" she said, eyes at once accusing and bitterly disappointed. "You wouldn't help him. You sent him away."

"He is past help," replied Keane. "The stranger that jostled him in front of the building—that stranger was death. Perhaps Doctor Satan himself, perhaps a helper."

"How can you know that?"

Keane breathed deeply. "Doctor Satan must have known in advance that Walstead could not pay his demands. Hence he must have planned to use him from the start as a sacrifice—a third horrible example of what happens to wealthy men who defy him. The man who jostled him planted death's seeds in him. He will die within the hour, with one of those unearthly shrubs forcing its way up through his skull."

"Still—you sent him away."

"I did, Beatrice. Suppose he died here. The police! Many questions! Detention! And I don't want to be delayed; I have work to do now that makes any of my former tasks seem like unimportant games. Doctor Satan! With three rich men dead, no others will defy him. He'll loot the city—if I can't stop him."

The girl, Beatrice Dale, Keane's companion as well as secretary, fingered the notebook in which was recorded the talk between him and Walstead.

"Who is Doctor Satan, Ascot? she said. "I don't seem to remember that he has figured in any of your former work."

"He hasn't; Doctor Satan is a new phenomenon. I've been expecting to hear from him ever since I heard the first whisper of his existence a month ago. Now, with these three fantastic murders, he makes his bow. Who is he? Where does he hide? What does he look like? I don't know—yet."

He began pacing up and down before his big ebony desk.

He chanced to be looking at the chair when it happened. The chair, also ebony, was pushed a few feet back from the desk. It was tilted back a bit, with the felt pad slightly away from the movement of his body as he had left it.

It squatted there, a dark inanimate thing at one instant. At the next there was a soft pouff of sound—and the chair leaped into blue incandescence. Lambent flame played over it, so hot that it blasted the faces of Keane and Beatrice five feet away. For perhaps four seconds the blue flame persisted. Then it died out as suddenly as it had appeared.

And the chair was no longer there. In its place was a little heap of fine ash, smoldering on the carpet.

Keane gazed slowly into Beatrice's horrified eyes. "I don't know about Doctor Satan yet," he repeated coolly, "but apparently he knows a great deal about me!—Well, what is it, Rice?"

Keane's man stood in the library doorway, staring first at his master and then at the tiny heap of ash that was all that was left of the ebony chair.

"Mr. Walstead just died, sir," he said. "It was in the lobby of the building, Just as he was about to step into the street. He's lying down there now." Rice's eyes flashed bleakly. "There's something pushing up through his head, sir. Little sharp spikes of something, like branches of a little tree, or bush."

3.

THREE MILES AWAY, in a windowless, black-draped room, a figure bent over a metal table in the attitude of a high priest bending over an altar.

The figure looked like one robed for a costume ball, save that in every line of it was a deadliness that robbed it of all suggestions of anything humorous or social.

Tall and spare, it was covered by a blood-red robe. Red rubber gloves swathed the hands. The face was concealed behind a red mask that curtained it from forehead to chin with only two black eyes, like live coals, showing through eyeholes.

Lucifer! And to complete the mediaeval portrait of the Archfiend, two horned red projections showed above the red skullcap that hid the man's hair.

Before him, on the metal table, a thin blue flame died slowly down into a sprinkling of yellowish powder from which it had originally been born. The blue flame was the only light in the room. By its flicker could be seen three other men, crouching around the walls and watching the flame with breathless intensity.

One of these three was a young man with an aristocratic but weak face. The other two were creatures like gargoyles. The first was legless, with his great, gorilla-like head, set on tremendous shoulders, coming up only to a normal man's waist. The second was a wizened small monkey of a man with bright, cruel eyes peering out from a mat of hair that covered all his features.

The blue flame on the metal table died out. The red-clad figure straightened up. A gloved hand touched a switch and the room was illuminated with red light.

"Ascott Keane," said the man in Satan's costume, "has escaped the blue flame."

The three men around the walls breathed deeply. Then the younger, with the weak face, scowled. "How do you know that, Doctor Satan?"

"If the flame had consumed him," Doctor Satan said, "the blue flame fire would have burned red while his body was devoured. It did not burn red."

The younger man walked toward the table. He moved with a curious air of ringing defiance. "How do you control the flame, Doctor Satan?"

The coal black eyes burned into his through the eyeholes in the red mask.

"It is all in here," Doctor Satan said at last, pointing to an ancient roll of papyrus spread flat on a stand near the metal table. "The ingredients of the flame were compounded first in Egypt, five thousand years ago. To these ingredients are added powdered bits of the person of the one to be consumed by the flame. Fingernail parings, hair, bits of discarded clothing, for instance. Then when the powder is burned, the person burns, though a thousand miles of distance separate him from the blue fire."

"Yet Keane escaped," said the young man, watching Doctor Satan narrowly.

"I had no bits of Keane's person to place with the chemicals. He is too shrewd to have allowed hair or nail clippings to be smuggled from his home. I had only a sliver of the chair in which he customarily sits. Obviously he wasn't in the chair when I touched off the fire, and so escaped death."

THE YOUNG MAN lit a cigarette. The frightened defiance of his every gesture was heightened by the manner in which he lit it. "The death tree, Doctor Satan. How do you work that?"

"It is a species of Australian thornbush," Doctor Satan said without hesitation. "Rather, it was, till with a certain botanical skill I altered it into a thing that flowers in two hours or less, rooting in a man's brain. The only drawback is that the seed, a tiny thing that floats in air, must be inhaled by the victim, to lodge in the nasal passage and later work its way up to the brain."

"You have more seeds of this tree?"

"Yes," said Doctor Satan. His manner was strange, his voice almost gentle, but there was a deadliness in the very gentleness. The monkey-like little man with the hairy face, and the legless giant with the huge shoulders, stirred restlessly in their positions by the wall.

"Why didn't you use the flame on Ryan and Walstead and Billingsley?" questioned the young man. "That would have been easier than killing them with your thornbush."

"Easier," conceded the grim figure in red, "but not quite so spectacular. I wanted those three to die as fantastically as possible, so the requests I make on other rich men will be more quickly granted."

Doctor Satan walked to the stand on which the papyrus rested. He pulled out a drawer and took from it ten bundles of currency. In each bundle were thousand dollar bills. And the band around each bundle proclaimed that each contained a hundred such bills.

"The first contribution," Doctor Satan said. "From William H. Sterling, the philanthropic manufacturer of automobiles. One million dollars."

The young man stared at the heap of currency with glistening eyes. A fortune, in such small compass that it could be concealed under a man's clothes!

But now, at the same time, he seemed suddenly to sense the mockery of Doctor Satan's geniality, and of his apparent frankness in disclosing his affairs. Color drained from his face, and more drained from it at Doctor Satan's next words. "You know a great deal about me, don't you, Monroe?"

Monroe swallowed painfully, then straightened his shoulders.

"Yes, I know a lot. I know your real name—a family name familiar to everyone in the United States. I know your philosophy of life; how you, an enormously wealthy man, tired of all the thrills that money can buy, have turned to crime. I know you intend to make your crimes pay as part of your game. I know you have studied the occult and the scientific, in preparation for this debut. And now I know how you control two of your murder tools—the blue flame and the tree of death."

Doctor Satan's eyes bored into Monroe's till the younger man gripped the edge of the metal table for support.

"Yes, you know a lot, Monroe," he crooned. "More than anyone else living. You wouldn't think of betraying me, would you?"

"Not if you treat me fairly, Doctor Satan. But if you try to double-cross me, you are lost. In a safe deposit box which is to be opened by my lawyer in case an 'accident' happens to me there is a full account of yourself...."

His voice trailed off into a frightened squeak at the look in Doctor Satan's coal-black eyes. The red-clad figure appeared to loom taller and taller, till it almost filled the room. And now all the defiance was gone from Monroe's posture, leaving only the fright.

"What are you—going to do?" he panted. "What...."

Again his voice trailed off, but this time it ended in a thickness like that of beginning sleep.

Doctor Satan's eyes, glittering, ruthless, held Monroe's eyes. Doctor Satan's hand passed slowly before Monroe's face. The monkey-like man and the legless giant watched from the wall.

"You are asleep." Doctor Satan's voice sounded somnolently in the silent, windowless room.

"I am asleep," breathed Monroe, wide, glassy eyes fixed on the red mask.

"You will tell me all you know and all you hope to do."

"I will tell you all I know and all I hope to do."

"What are your plans concerning me?"

For a second, Monroe's still features twisted, as though even in hypnosis his will fought to avoid answering that question. Then his lips moved mechanically.

"I am going to inform the police how to find you when you collect your next looted million. Then I am going to take the money, and the seeds of the death tree and the chemicals for the blue flame, and collect more money myself."

"It is enough," said Doctor Satan, still in that almost gentle voice.

The monkey-like man and the legless giant looked at each other. Doctor Satan had pronounced a death sentence.

Doctor Satan spoke to them, eyes never leaving Monroe's face. "Girse. Bostiff." The two moved toward Monroe. The monkeylike man known as Girse hopped like a deformed ape. Bostiff hitched his giant torso over the floor with his thick arms, using his calloused knuckles as feet.

"The iron box, Bostiff."

Bostiff hitched his way to one wall, pushed back the stable drapes and drew from a three-foot niche a coffin-like box that gleamed dully in the red light.

Doctor Satan's hand went out. He plucked three hairs from Monroe's blond head. He laid the hairs on a small pile of the yellowish powder on the metal table.

"You will lie down in the box, Monroe," he droned.

The blond young man walked with jerky steps to the metal coffin and lay down in it.

"The lid, Bostiff."

Picking up the massive iron cover of the coffin as easily as though it were a pot lid, the legless giant put it on the box. Then, without further orders, he dragged the metal coffin back to its niche in the wall and slid it home in the surrounding stonework.

DOCTOR SATAN PICKED up a pinch of the yellowish powder and crumbled it sharply in his fingers. The tiny heap on the table burst into blue flame. The three blond hairs writhed and were consumed.

The end of the metal coffin, showing from the niche, was suddenly red-hot, then glowing with white incandescence. Slowly it faded to deep, hot red in color, and back to black.

Girse and Bostiff watched stolidly. If ever an investigator opened that box nothing would be found but a pinch of ashes. A pinch of ashes that had been a man, planning to betray the master.

Doctor Satan's voice sounded, calmly. "Danger has been eliminated from within. Now no one on Earth knows my real identity. It remains only to eliminate danger from without."

Bostiff spoke, his dull eyes fixed on Doctor Satan's mask. "The danger from without, Master?"

"Yes. The danger that lies in Ascott Keane. There is the only danger I recognize. The Police? Ludicrous! Private detectives? Bodyguards hired by wealthy victims? They are children! But in Ascott Keane lies a threat."

The red-gloved hand touched the light-switch. Slowly the red bulbs faded out, bathing the room in a lowering darkness like that of a lurid rapid sunset.

"But the threat of Ascott Keane is to be removed at once. Walstead saw him. Walstead showed him the note. Keane will act on that knowledge—and with that action he will be trapped."

4.

IN FRONT OF a triple mirror before which was a bench holding hundreds of tiny pots and jars, Ascott Keane worked deftly. His fingers flew from jar to features, pot to face. And as they flew his face subtly altered. Already it was no longer the face of Keane. It was a countenance which to Beatrice Dale was vaguely familiar—though she could not yet name it.

"That hideous death shrub!" she said. "I can't see how it is used by Doctor Satan."

"You've seen Indian fakirs make a tree grow in a pot, haven't you?" said Keane. "Usually it's a miniature orange tree. They make it grow before your eyes, and pick an orange from it. Well, Doctor Satan's wizardry is something like that; only he utilizes a form of thornbush that flowers in human substance instead of earth."

He reshaped his lips with a collodion-like red lacquer, and the girl cried aloud. Keane's face was that of Walstead. Line for line it was Walstead's slightly puffy countenance that was reflected in the mirror. A close friend of the dead millionaire would have been deceived.

"What are you planning to do, Ascott?"

Keane began pinning thin pads to the lining of his coat to give his lean strong body the bulk of Walstead's puffy body.

"Doctor Satan said in his note to Walstead to put the money in a trash can at Broadway and Seventy-Sixth Street. Very well, I'm going to take Walstead's place. Made up as him, I'll drop a package in that can—and wait to see who picks it up."

Beatrice shook her beautiful, coppery brown head. "Walstead's death isn't out in the papers yet, but surely Doctor Satan must know that the man is dead. Or are you hoping to fool him? "

"Doctor Satan," said Keane dryly, "hardly has to wait to get his information from the newspapers."

"Then he'll know that the man who looks like Walstead, and who drops the package in the trash can, can't possibly be Walstead."

"That's right," said Keane, drawing on the padded coat and scrutinizing himself in the triple mirrors.

"But he'll know it's you! And he'll most certainly try to kill you!"

"That's what I'm hoping, said Keane, putting on a hat of the type worn by Walstead.

"But Ascott...."

"It's like this," said Keane. "Doctor Satan hasn't met me yet. I want him to underestimate me, so I am rather stupidly disguising myself as Walstead and going to the place where Walstead was to have gone, in the hope that Doctor Satan will trap me. In that event—his jaw squared—"I think he'll be sorry."

He stepped away from the mirrors. And it was not Keane who moved—it was Walstead!

In an antique Italian cabinet there was an extra wide drawer. Keane pulled this out. In it was a rolled papyrus that closely resembled the papyrus that had been spread wide in Doctor Satan's black room. Beside the papyrus was a little stone jar.

Keane opened the jar and took from it a bit of greenish paste, which he touched to his forehead, the soles of his shoes, and the palms of his hands.

"Marvelous beings, the ancient Egyptians," he said softly. "I recognized the blue fire that burned my chair—and would have consumed me if I'd been in it. The fire burned in many a temple along the Nile, but what the Egyptian wizards concocted they usually made fruitless by further research."

Beatrice caught his arm, her eyes fearful.

Keane pressed her hand. "Don't worry about me, my dear. I'll be back soon, and I think I'll be back with news that this Doctor Satan, new peril to a city at yet ignorant of his existence, has passed on to the hell he should have reached long ago."

He walked to the door, moving as Walstead had moved. His eyes met the girl's deep blue ones. Then he was gone.

NINE O'CLOCK! UPPER Broadway was crowded with night shoppers and movie-goers. Among the crowds near Seventy-Sixth Street moved a tall, slightly paunchy man who kept his face shadowed by the brim of his hat, a face that many in the city would have sworn was that of a ghost—of the dead

Walstead.

On the northeast corner of Broadway and Seventy-Sixth Street a trash can showed. The man disguised as Walstead crossed to the can. Under his arm was a small parcel done up in newspaper. He dropped the parcel in the can, and walked on. Without a backward glance he rounded the next corner.

But once around the corner, Keane stopped and went back, moving like a shadow. He peered through the double angle of a corner plate-glass window at the trash can.

The can was of wire, with interstices in its walls through which the contents could be seen. When Keane has tossed the package into it, the can had been half full of refuse. Now the old papers and odds and ends of trash seemed to be melting away, like water draining down through a hole. Lower and lower the contents sank—till finally the can was empty.

Keane shook his head a little, eyes gleaming like ice. "Transmission of substance through empty air!" he breathed.

None in the crowds so close to the can had noted the way the refuse slowly disappeared from within it, but Keane had caught it all. Moreover, he had seen that the trash had disappeared first from the north side of the can, as though it were flowing in that direction, melting into thin air as it flowed.

The north side of the can. Toward him.

Keane slunk into a doorway. His quick eyes roved over the Broadway crowd, and in a moment they rested on a figure that tensed his body. A tall, shambling man, across the street from the trash container, was walking slowly toward the Seventy-Second Street subway entrance. Under his arm was held a parcel done up in newspaper.

Keane's lips thinned. Doctor Satan was making sure he saw the parcel and followed the carrier!

He stepped unobtrusively from the doorway and into the Broadway crowds, where he followed the tall, shambling figure to the subway entrance. Was the tall figure that of Doctor Satan himself, or one of his helpers? Keane did not know; but he did know that he would have shot the man down in cold blood, had he not been fully aware that no weapon as crude as an automatic could prevail over an opponent like Doctor Satan.

The tall figure got off the subway at a Greenwich Village station. Keane followed, a block behind, his body was taut as a stretched tendon. He knew he was to be trapped, to be brought to a carefully devised death. He knew that, for the moment, Doctor Satan had dropped all other plans to concentrate on removing him.

He was prepared for violence as he walked along the dark Village street after the tall figure. He was ready for anything from a bullet or knife in the dark to an attack and abduction by masked men springing on him from dark area-ways; but he was not prepared for the thing that actually did happen.

At one moment he was following the tall figure. At the next the figure ahead had disappeared—and Keane was still moving forward, though he had willed his body to halt while he gazed around to see where the figure could have gone.

Keane strove to stop, to walk to right or left. He count not; his muscles were driven by another's will. And now another thing happened—a thing even more frightening. He began to lose his sight.

The dark street, the partly lighted buildings lining it, the sidewalk before him, all slowly, faded from his sight. But his body kept moving slowly, surely forward.

In a moment he was blind. He could see not one thing. But his feet seemed able to see. They bore him on without a stumble, raising for curbs, lowering him for gutters. Thus with no man forcing him, apparently, blindfolded as surely as if thick cloths were tied over his eyes, Keane moved to the will of Doctor Satan, toward the trap.

He felt himself turn. Under his hand was an iron railing. He felt himself going down steps. A door creaked open in front of him. He walked on, totally blind, and heard the soft creak, and a slam, behind him.

More stairs downward. Hands outstretched to scrape along the moist walls of a passage like a low tunnel. Steps again. A clang over his head as though a stone trap-door had been battened down above him. Finally a swish of drapes and a gentle, yet deadly-sounding voice that made every nerve-end in his body twitch.

No need to speculate on the ownership of that voice! The arrogance that lay behind the softness of it told him. It was the voice of Doctor Satan himself.

5.

SLOWLY KEANE'S EYESIGHT returned to him, to telegraph to his mind weird, nightmare pictures.

Black-draped walls closed him in. Lounging against one wall were two men—a man with a giant's torso and no legs, and a creature with a hairy, ape-like face in which were set bright, cruel little eyes.

Across from them was a metal brazier, set on a high tripod, in which a small flame flickered. In the center of the room was a metal table, bare save for a small pinch of yellowish powder. And over this table was bending the man who had spoken—a figure that set the blood to leaping in Keane's veins as his heart thudded with sudden acceleration in his breast. A tall figure robed in red, with a red mask over the face, red gloves on the hands, and a red skullcap from which protruded small mocking imitations of Satan's horns.

Doctor Satan turned from the metal table. His black eyes burned at Keane through the eyeholes of the red mask.

"Welcome, Ascott Keane," came sardonic words. "We are honored that you should have gone to such trouble to visit us in our modest lair."

Keane's face, looking, in the red glare that illuminated the room, like something cast in bronze, remained impassive. Wordlessly he watched the diabolical figure in red.

The cultured tone was edged with steel as Doctor Satan continued.

"You committed suicide when you resolved a month ago to devote your life to destroying me. Oh, yes, I knew of the resolve the instant it was made. I have ways of knowing what is in men's minds; though I concede that you were able, shortly after that, to shield your brain from me. Tell me, Ascott Keane, what warned you of my existence?"

Keane stood straight and tall before the red-robed figure. His resemblance to Walstead faded, in spite of make-up, with the altering of his expression. He was Keane again, regardless of collodion-painted lips and padded clothes.

"A month ago," he said, "I talked with the son of a bankrupt friend of mine. The boy, a wild and not very strong character, said nothing significant. But I too can read a little of what is in men's minds; and in his I caught a glimpse of a figure in Satan's masquerade. I got a hint of the man's background and motives: a rich man, still young, jaded with purchased thrills, with no more humanity in his heart than a snake—out to become the world's leading criminal. A man whose whimsical choice of a name, Doctor Satan, could not have been more apt in expressing his purpose. A sleek beast, playing a monstrous game. A thing to be stamped out as soon as possible."

The black eyes gleamed through the satanic mask. "Young Monroe, you are talking about. Fortunately he did not know my identity at that time. And now no one will ever know. Monroe is no longer in a position to talk. And some papers he left behind with his lawyer have been destroyed within the hour."

Now the arrogant voice was gentle again.

"So you decided to be the one to annihilate me. Noble Keane! But the roles will be reversed. It is you who will be annihilated.

I marked you at the start as a nuisance to be eliminated. Wealthy yourself, with a fairly analytical mind, you have entertained yourself for years by scotching crime. But your career ends, with me, Keane. It ends now, in this room."

Girse and Bostiff slowly left the wall they had been lounging against. Girse came with quick, small steps to Keane's left side. Bostiff hitched his great body, with swinging movements of his huge arms, to Keane's right side.

Keane still stayed motionless. Futile to attempt to overpower Doctor Satan physically: it could not have been done even had the gigantic Bostiff and the agile Girse not been there in the blackwalled room. The walls of the trap he had entered were strong walls; and its teeth were sharp teeth, from which there seemed no escape.

Doctor Satan repeated an order he had given once before on that day. "Bostiff," he said softly, "the iron box."

The legless giant hitched his way to the wall, drew back a sable drape, and pulled from the niche in the stonework the coffin-like metal box.

Doctor Satan stared at Keane with green-glinting eyes. The stare held, minute after minute. Keane's eyes slowly glazed.

"You are asleep," droned Doctor Satan at length.

"I am asleep," breathed Keane.

Girse and Bostiff stared at each other with savage expectance on their face.

"You shall do whatever I command." Doctor Satan said.

"I will do whatever you command," said Keane, like an automaton.

DOCTOR SATAN'S RED-GLOVED hand went out toward Keane's head. He plucked three hairs and laid them over the small mound of yellowish powder on the table. Act for act, he was duplicating the scene in which a treacherous disciple had been reduced from a man to a pinch of ashes.

"Take the lid from the box, Bostiff."

The legless giant lifted the iron cover from the coffin. Within it could be seen scattered fine ash.

"Keane, lie down in the box."

The black eyes gleamed with a feral light as Ascott Keane slowly walked to the box and lowered his body into it. Keane lay there, gazing up with wide, glazed eyes.

Bostiff placed the lid back on the box.

His dull eyes went from the box to the niche in the wall.

"No," Doctor Satan answered his unspoken question, "we'll not put the box in its crypt. Leave it where it is. I want to watch this."

The red-gloved hands clenched with eloquent triumph; the red-robed figure towered in the room. Then Doctor Satan turned to the metal table.

He picked up a bit of the yellowish powder and crumbled it between powerful fingers. The tiny heap on the table burst in to clear blue flame. The eyes of Doctor Satan and his two servants turned toward the metal box in which lay Keane.

Swiftly the box glowed dull red, cherry red, white-hot. Its rays beat against the faces of the three, set the sable drapes to billowing a little. And in that white-hot metal coffin a thing of flesh and blood was lying—or had been lying when the blue flame began to burn.

The metal box lost its fierce white glow. The heat rays beating from it faded in intensity. Doctor Satan's red robe stirred with the deep breath he drew.

"And so ends Ascott Keane," he said vibrantly. "The one obstacle in my path. I can be a king, an emperor, now, in time."

He turned to Girse and Bostiff.

"Go. I have no more need of you."

Bostiff hitched his huge body silently toward an end wall. He drew aside a drape and opened a door. Girse followed him out of it.

Alone, Doctor Satan went to the cabinet and drew from a drawer the ten bundles of currency containing one hundred thousand dollar bills apiece. The bundles disappeared beneath the red robe. His hand went toward the switch that controlled the red illumination of the room.

But his finger did not touch the switch. His hand remained suspended in the air, while he watched the iron coffin. And his red-robed body was as immobile as that of a statue.

The lid of the coffin was moving.

Slowly, steadily, it raised, to slide from the box and clang against the floor.

A hand and arm appeared above the edge of the box, which was still black-hot. The hand was unharmed. The coat sleeve above it was charred a little at the cuff; that was all.

Another hand and arm appeared, and then the body of Ascott Keane from the waist up as he sat in the coffin.

Silently, rigidly, Doctor Satan glared at him, and Keane got out of the coffin and stood beside it. Wisps of smoke rose here and there from singed garments, but his flesh was not even reddened by the fierce fire, and his gray eyes bored steadily at the black eyes behind the mask.

"What the Egyptians discovered," he said softly, "they rendered fruitless by succeeding discoveries. I read the origin of your blue flame in your first attempt on my life, Doctor Satan, and I took the precaution of using as armor some of the green paste the old priests used against the consuming fires of their enemies."

He took two slow steps toward the red-clad figure.

"You should have watched your flame, instead of the iron coffin, Doctor Satan. You would have seen then that the flame burned blue throughout; it should have burned red if any body was devoured."

The breathing of the red-masked man sounded in the tense hush of the room.

"Now we are alone, Doctor Satan. You have considerately sent your men way, as I hoped you would do. We'll see if your powers are as strong as you think they are."

The glare faded from Doctor Satan's eyes, leaving them glacially cold.

"I'll not underestimate you a second time, Ascott Keane! The death shrub—the blue flame—you are armed against those. But I have other weapons."

"You'll never use them," Keane growled deep in this throat.

And then his hand shot up.

Around Doctor Satan's red-robed body a softly glowing aura suddenly formed. It was like a ball of pale yellow light which enclosed him, a lambent shell against the red rays of the room's illumination.

A snarl came from Doctor Satan's lips, sounding muffled, as though the lambent shell had actual substance and could stifle sound. He straightened, with the aura moving as his body moved.

His hands moved, weaving strange designs in the yellowed air. And slowly the aura faded a little from around him.

Tendons ridged up on the back of Keane's outstretched hand. Perspiration studded his forehead with the intensity of his effort to overwhelm the figure in red.

That aura which he had flung around the red-robed body was one of the most powerful weapons known to occultism: a concentration of the pure form of electricity known as the Life Force. Mantling a living thing as it mantled Doctor Satan, it should drain out life, leaving behind nothing but inanimate clay. Yet it was not harming this man! Slowly, relentlessly, the aura continued to fade. And then Doctor Satan's hands rose and leveled toward Keane.

Strange duel between two titans—two men who probably knew more of Nature's dark secrets than any others on Earth. Odd battle, with Keane, the force of good, gradually being beaten down by the force of evil.

For now Keane's rigid arm was sinking as the yellow aura almost disappeared from around Doctor Satan. Slowly he sank to his knees, as if a great weight oppressed him. And, as though this great weight was that of some intangible sea which could suffocate as well as weigh down, he began to gasp for breath. Louder and louder his agonized breathing sounded in the room. Doctor Satan's black eyes glowed with triumph.

Keane could see nothing—could feel nothing. Yet it was as if some colorless, invisible, tremendously heavy jelly were gradually hardening around him.

The red lights grew dimmer, though Doctor Satan had not touched the switch; Keane felt that he was almost lost.

With enormous effort he brought his arms up, spreading them wide at his sides. "Mother of God!" he whispered.

Like a living cross he was, in that position; with trunk and head the upright, and arms the horizontal bars.

"Mother of God!"

Doctor Satan's snarl was that of a beast. His eyes took on their feral green light, with a fiendish disappointment embittering their depths.

And the great, invisible sea that was beating Keane down gradually receded from around him. But as it receded, so dimmed the red lights, till the two men were in blackness.

"This time you preserve your life," Doctor Satan said, in the darkness. "Next time—you leave your life behind!"

There was a thud of sound, like a soft explosion.

"Next time," began Keane, struggling to his feet and forcing his body forward through the last traces of the deadly, unseen sea.

He stopped. He was alone in the black-walled room. Slowly the lights came up again, as though shining ever more clearly through a psychic, thinning fog. Keane began wrenching the black drapes from the walls.

He found a door and opened it. Ahead of him he saw a low passage with steps at the end. He ran down the passage, up the steps. In a moment he was in the street, clutching the iron railing he had felt when he came here blinded.

Cursing softly, he looked up and down the sidewalk. There was, of course, no sign of the red-clad figure. Doctor Satan had made good his escape. And with him had gone one million dollars, fruit of his first fantastic crime.

Keane's wide shoulders sagged, but only for a moment. Then they straightened.

The first round was Doctor Satan's. But there would be another time. And then, knowing a little more of the manner of being he was pitted against, he could fight more effectively— and win.

THE MAN WHO CHAINED THE LIGHTNING

THE WIND PLAYED an eerie chorus among the dank leaves of the trees lining the wealthy residential street. Far off, the flickering of lightning split the black September night in 193—.

From behind the high wall bordering the Weldman estate came a hoarse cry. It was not a shout so much as an exclamation; but in it was packed a horror that could not have been more vividly expressed had the person yelled at the top of his voice.

With the low cry, the wind seemed to die down as if to listen. In the lull the slam of a small gate in the high wall rang out.

A man sped through that gate. His face was white in the light of the street lamp fifty yards away. His eyes were wide and staring. His mouth was half open and twisted as if for another cry.

He began to run down the street toward the town section. He pounded through puddles and mud, with his head straining forward and his breath tearing in sobs from his throat. He was slight, bald, middle-aged, and fear lent such speed to his feet that he ran as a youth might run. But only for an instant did he speed through the night.

The end of the Weldman wall was still a hundred feet in front of him, when suddenly he stopped. This time a piercing scream echoed down the midnight quiet of the street like a banshee wail.

The man began to dance, as if grotesque, horrible music

sounded from somewhere near. And as his feet beat clumsily on the muddy sidewalk, he struck himself with his clenched fists. Against his chest his fists beat, and then against his throat, as though he had gone mad and was attempting to punish himself for some recent transgression.

His screams ripped out in an almost unbroken flow of sound while he struck at his throat and chest. But only for a few moments did he dance there, and swing his arms. Abruptly his screaming stopped, as though cut across the middle with a knife-blade. His arms ceased to move.

He stood in the center of the sidewalk, staring up beyond the end of the Weldman wall. A patrolman was running toward him, drawn by the frightful screams; but the man did not seem to see him. He simply stood there, silent now and motionless, as if turned to rock. And then, with the policeman still a dozen yards away, he fell.

Full length to the sidewalk his body crashed, stiffly, like a thing of wood rather than of yielding flesh. And like a rigid thing of wood he lay in the water and mud of the walk.

The patrolman reached his side and bent over him.

Glaring, sightless eyes turned up into his face. The man's lips moved stiffly.

"What?" said the policeman, raising the man's head. "What's that you said?"

The middle-aged man's voice sounded again, muffled and thick: "…master… shaving…."

The patrolman almost shook him in his anxiety to hear what was wrong.

"What is it?" he snapped. "Are you sick? Have you been hurt? What's happened?"

But the man said no more. His face was blackening and swelling. His lips were parting over bared teeth, while between them his breath rattled with ever more difficulty and agony.

Then the agonized breathing stopped. The man's eyeballs

rolled up so that only the whites were visible. And the patrolman lowered him to the sidewalk and blew his whistle.

The man was dead.

Instinctively the policeman crossed himself as he stood looking down at the body.

A SQUAD CAR screamed to a stop beside the dead man and the cop. A detective jumped out from beside the driver and ran forward. One look he took at the dead, blackened face; then he shook his head and whistled.

"Weldman's valet! He was on his way to the station house to tell us something. I was standing near when the desk sergeant took the call. Something terrible, and too important to be told over the phone, the guy said. Something about his employer, John Weldman. Some danger hanging over him, I gathered."

He stared at the agonized dead face.

"Well, whatever it was he was going to tell us will never be known now. But it must have been something big for him to have been knocked off like this to keep him from spilling it!"

"Hey, he wasn't knocked off," said the policeman. "I saw him keel over. There wasn't anybody else in sight."

The detective stared somberly at him.

"It doesn't matter whether anyone was in sight or not. This guy was murdered!" He touched the curiously rigid body with the toe of his shoe. "If only he'd said something before he died...."

"He did," said the policeman.

"What?" The plainclothes-man's hand shot out and clutched the cop's shoulder. "What did he say?"

"Just three words. And they don't seem to make sense at all. He said 'master... millions... shaving....'"

The detective relaxed his tense grip.

"'Master. Millions. Shaving.' That doesn't mean anything to me. I guess the valet's secret died with him."

But the detective spoke too soon.

So far as the police force went, the dead man's secret might have died when he did. And the three words muttered by the dying lips might never be made clear to them.

But the night was alive with an intelligence far beyond theirs; an intelligence which was aware of things reaching back beyond this death of a servant, and which was already moving ahead of the death toward the apprehension of the cause.

Across the street from the two men who bent over a blackened corpse was an unusually large tree. In the branches of the tree a shapeless shadow clung.

The black figure slowly and silently descended while the plainclothes man and the patrolman waited for the coroner and the ambulance. Under his arm was what appeared to be a small square box.

The figure got to the sidewalk, faced the men unseen for a moment, then moved silently off into the night.

FROM A SQUARE black box in a pitch dark room came a beam of light, spreading from a half-inch opening to cover a six-foot-square silver screen. On the screen showed a high white wall—the wall of the Weldman estate.

In the blank white wall could be seen a dim oblong which was a small gate. The gate opened suddenly and a man leaped forth. Even in miniature, on the screen, his face could be read: an expression of stark terror was on it, twisting the partly opened mouth and glinting from the wide eyes.

Faithfully the movements of Weldman's valet were reproduced on the screen. Slight, bald, middle-aged, he ran through the night along the white wall. Then the picture showed him stopping and beginning his clumsy, inexplicable dance, and beating insanely at his own neck and chest.

But the picture revealed something more—something which made the halt and the self-punishment only too logical!

Just before the man stopped, something moved at the top of the high wall ahead of him. The something was a hand. The hand curved out over the wall with fingers contracted as if to pluck something. But the hand did not gather anything in. Instead, it released an object—a tiny object which did not show in the rather dim moving-picture until it had hit the unfortunate valet. Then it showed on the whiteness of the valet's throat.

It was a tiny blur, too small to be described by the camera lens. But it moved.

In the picture it showed for just an instant on the running man's throat, and then disappeared under his collar. It was just after that that the man stopped and began beating himself.

"An insect," a deep, brooding voice split the blackness of the room. "A poisonous insect! Carried into the Weldman home, no doubt, for the death of the valet there. But the man had left the house on his way to the police station. He nearly escaped…."

The picture went on , showing the valet's sudden immobility, showing him fall and lie like a log in the mud.

Then—it showed something else, at the top of the wall where the hand had appeared.

The hand was withdrawn now, and a face looked over. It was turned toward the dying man and it was a face to haunt the soul in nightmares.

There were no features to it. Only a blank expanse showed from forehead to chin, with black holes for eyes. A face masked as though for a masquerade; but there was in the masquerade no suggestion of humor.

Over the masked, terrible face was a low-brimmed black hat, and the top of the shoulders showing over the wall also showed black; some sort of cloak.

Evil emanated from the masked face as, like the covered face of a ghoul, it bent over the top of the wall toward where the valet lay dying. Calmly, terribly, it watched the man twitch and lie still. Then, leisurely, indifferently, it disappeared.

"Doctor Satan…" a girl's half-stifled cry sounded in the darkened room.

THE MAN WHO CHAINED THE LIGHTNING

There was no reply to the exclamation. The picture continued, revealing the movement of the man's numbing lips.

A hand slowed the projector. The picture, running at a slower tempo, showed the formed words on the man's lips: "…master… millions… shaving…."

Then the lips stopped moving and the figure of the patrolman edged into the film. The projector stopped. There was a click, and light flooded the room.

2.

IT WAS A huge room, a library, with books running from floor to ceiling of all four walls, crowding windows and the one door of the chamber. The books were all volumes of learning—a library such as few universities have, and containing some yellowed tomes dealing with the occult which no universities would have permitted on their shelves even had they the wealth with which to purchase them.

In the center of the library was a great ebony desk. Standing beside this was a girl, lovely, tall, lithe, with dark blue eyes and hair more red than brown. The sudden light revealed in her dark eyes, as they rested on a man next to her, a look of perplexity, vague horror, and something soft and glowing and shy, which faded the instant the man's gaze answered hers.

The man was one who had brought a glow to many a woman's eyes. For this was Ascott Keane, interesting to the mercenary for his large fortune, and to the unmercenary for his looks. His face, under coal-black hair, with steely gray eyes shaded by black eyebrows, had been reproduced in many a rotogravure section. To readers of those society sections he was a wealthy young man who idled when he was not playing games, a fellow without a serious thought in his head. But the girl beside him, Beatrice Dale, his more-than-secretary, knew better.

She knew that Ascott Keane's playboy character was a cloak under which was a grim seriousness of purpose. She knew that he was one of the world's most learned men in all the sciences—and in those deep arts known, for want of a better name, as Black Magic. She knew that he had devoted his life to the running-down of such super-criminals as could laugh at the police and rise to the rather lofty altitude of his own attention.

And she knew that the masked, terrible face that had peered over the top of Weldman's wall for an instant belonged to a criminal who was perhaps, more than worthy of his attention. A man known only as Doctor Satan, from the Luciferian costume he chose to wear when engaged in his fiend's work. A man of great wealth, who had turned to crime to stir his jaded pulses. A man whose name and identity were unknown, but whose erudition, particularly in forbidden fields of learnings matched Keane's own.

That was the veiled personality which occupied Keane day and night now, to his own great danger. That was the devil who had killed the valet with a poison insect—and who had done other things in the last few weeks at which Keane, till now, had been able only to guess.

The telephone on the ebony desk buzzed softly. Keane picked it up.

A soft voice sounded. "Ascott Keane, you are meddling again!"

Beatrice Dale heard the voice as well as Keane. "Doctor Satan!"

Keane's eyes glittered. He dropped the instrument as if it had turned into a serpent in his fingers.

"I've told you death would strike if you interfered with my plans again," the soft voice continued, sounding from the floor where the phone lay. "And I always keep my promises...."

The words ended, swiftly and dramatically. With their ending, the telephone on the floor jumped like a live thing, while from transmitter to receiver, in a thick blue arc, crackled a stream of

THE MAN WHO CHAINED THE LIGHTNING

electricity that would have killed a dozen men.

The crackling arc streamed just as far lightning flickered in the skies south of New York, and died as the lightning died.

Keane stared at Beatrice, who had gone white as death.

"He can harness the lightning!" he breathed. "That I cannot do myself! If I can't stop him soon, God knows what will happen to this city—to the whole country...."

He stared at the instrument. The metal was half melted. The hard rubber had been utterly consumed. Then he shrugged and turned toward the screen again, where, dimmed now by the lights in the room but still showing, was the picture of the dying valet, showing motionless with the stoppage of the projector.

"But I *will* stop him!" Keane's voice came bleakly. "Doctor Satan, hear that, wherever you are now."

He stepped across the melted telephone with a gesture that brushed into a past of forgotten dangers the fate he had just narrowly escaped, and stared at the lips of the pictured man.

"Shaving," he repeated, while Beatrice gazed at him with the fear in her dark blue eyes almost buried by that soft glow which she never, never allowed him to see. "Shaving. I think in that word lies the key to the problem we've been working on for the last few weeks. The problem ending with the death of Weldman's valet.

SWIFTLY KEANE REVIEWED the problem, one which he alone had become aware of; a string of events which singly had been noted by several people but which in their entirety had been remarked on by no one.

One by one over the past two weeks four wealthy men in New York had done odd things. Each had disappeared from his office without warning, in three cases breaking important business appointments. Each had then been seen neither at home nor in any accustomed haunt for many hours. Following that, on his return, each had seemed to avoid both his home and his office, appearing only now and then at either place and letting his business take care of itself.

Each, in those two weeks, had personally drawn large sums in cash from the United Continental Bank of New York—always that bank, never any of the others in which they kept money. Each of the four was living alone in his great home with only the servants, his family happening to be away at the time. And each, in the few times he was in home or office, did odd things which seemed to indicate a suddenly faulty memory.

These things Ascott Keane, alone in the city, had noted and pieced together into a pattern he felt sure had sinister meaning. More, it was a pattern behind which he thought he could sense the figure of Doctor Satan in his red robe, with red rubber gloves hiding his hands, and red mask and cap hiding face and hair.

John Weldman, copper magnate, had been the last to go through the queer antics. So to the wall outside Weldman's estate Ascott Keane had taken his special moving-picture camera, which recorded movement in dark night by means of an infra-red ray attachment he had invented.

And the camera had recorded the death of Weldman's valet—which Keane had been too far away to prevent—and the movement of his dying lips: "... master... millions... shaving...."

Beatrice peered into Keane's steely gray eyes. "What does it mean?" she whispered. "Do you know yet, Ascott?"

"I think I do," said Keane slowly. "I–think–I–do!"

THE FLICKERING LIGHTNING to the south of New York lit with its rays a small graveyard in the heart of the downtown section of the city. It was a curious little cemetery, less than a hundred yards square. Long unused, it was dotted with crumbling tombstones over which long grass grew.

On two sides of it a great factory, built in an L-shape, made a pitch-dark, five-story wall. On the third side an old apartment reared its height. On the fourth side, the street side, a high, rusty iron fence closed it off.

A curious, forgotten place of death in the heart of New York, encroached on by the factory and the apartment building. But more curious yet was a figure which furtively approached the rusted gate in the fence and paused a moment to make sure no person was near.

The figure was tall and gaunt. A low-brimmed black hat hid its head and most of its face. The rest of the face showed masked—a blank expanse covered by red fabric. A long black cloak covered the figure from neck to ankles, making it blend into the darkness.

The gate creaked open and the figure glided in among the moldering tombstones.

Beside one which lay prone in the rank grass, the figure stopped. Then it stepped on the six-foot slab—and the slab sank under it. A yawning hole appeared where the slab had been; a dark pit into which the figure disappeared.

After an instant the slab rose and settled into place, apparently as it was before, looking as though it had lain there solid and undisturbed for a dozen years.

Under it the black-cloaked figure went down a passage that slanted yet lower into the earth. The passage was lined with broken rock, and through the cracks occasional bits of rotted wood projected. They were remnants of ancient coffins, and with them now and then could be seen bleached white fragments. Bones.

The figure opened a door at the end of the passage and stepped into a chamber as bizarre as it was secret.

It was a cavernous room twenty feet square, lined with the broken rock as was the passage. It was very dim, with a small red lamp in the corner near the door as its only illumination. Along the far wall were cages, small, about the size of large dog-houses. In these cages four white figures squatted like animals. In the dim light their species could not be determined. They were simply whitish, distorted-looking beasts which seemed too large for their small cages.

Leaning against the wall near the light were four figures that looked at first like sleeping men. But a glance told that they could not be that. Fully clad in expensive clothes, they leaned there like sticks, without flexibility or movement, more like dolls than men, perfectly fashioned in the images of Man but seeming to want motive power and direction.

In the center of the room, drawing themselves to attention as the black-cloaked figure entered the weird chamber, were two creatures that would bring a chill to the spine of any man. One was an alert, agile little man with pale eyes shining through a mat of hair over his face. And this one, apelike in movement and thought, was Girse, Doctor Satan's faithful servant. The other was a giant with no legs, who supported his hugely muscled torso on his hands, swinging it along on his knuckles as he moved. This was Bostiff, the second of Doctor Satan's servants.

The figure that had entered the room stood straight. Its shoulders moved, and the black cloak dropped. With a sweep of a hand, the black hat was removed. A red robe sheathed body and limbs. Red rubber gloves were over its hands. The face was masked in red, and the head was covered with a red skullcap so that even its hair did not show. From the skullcap, in mocking imitation of Satan's horns, two small red knobs projected. Lucifer! Someone going robed as Satan to a costume ball! But instinct whispered that this was no mere costume, that the man under the makeup was as malevolent as his garb was mocking.

"Master!" breathed Girse. "Doctor Satan!"

Bostiff scraped his calloused knuckles along the floor uneasily and stared at Doctor Satan out of stupid, dull eyes.

DOCTOR SATAN GLANCED at the cages in which were dimly to be seen the curious, whitish animals. "Have they been fed?" he asked, his voice soft, almost gentle.

"They have been fed," replied Girse.

"They have given no trouble?"

"None, Master," said Bostiff, grinning significantly.

A feeble groan sounded from one of the cages.

"One is ill?" asked Doctor Satan.

"One is near death," retorted Bostiff. "The cold down here...."

"No matter. All have their duplicates, so that any may die without hurting my plans. Any save the last to come here. And I intend to remedy that now...."

The voice of Doctor Satan was drowned by a shriek from the cage in which the groan had sounded a moment before. The strange white animal in it suddenly reared up, or tried to, beating its head against the top of the cage. It rattled the bars for an instant, and then fell.

There was deathly silence in the chamber under the graveyard. Then Doctor Satan strode to the cage.

"Dead," he said, indifferently.

At the word, the other three animals in the adjoining cages set up a wailing and howling, chattering noises that sounded oddly like words.

"Silence!" said Doctor Satan, little above a whisper, yet a whisper that penetrated. The chattering ceased. "Bostiff."

The legless giant hitched his torso toward the cage.

"Take this one into the next chamber." Doctor Satan's red-gloved hand went under his robe. It came out with an odd thing like a crystal tube an inch in diameter and nearly a foot long. "Place this against the body, with the free end slanting toward the south where the lightning still plays."

Bostiff visibly paled.

"But that draws the lightning in here, Master. The walls and roof will collapse...."

"Do as I bid you! The walls and roof are safe. But the fires of heaven will consume that carcass, and so we are rid of it."

Bostiff grunted and nodded his great head. He opened the cage in which the white beast had fallen, and dragged it out. But now as the carcass was drawn nearer the light, it could be seen that it was not a beast at all. It was a man, elderly, naked, hideously scarred and emaciated. And so the other three left alive in their cages were men, penned up like animals in spaces too small to allow them to lie or stand at full length. Dumbly, cowering behind their bars, they watched the red-robed fiendish figure.

Doctor Satan went to a chest as Bostiff dragged the dead man through a door leading to another underground room like the first. He took from the chest a small object looking prosaic in this dimly lit chamber. It was a checkbook, on the United Continental Bank of New York City.

Doctor Satan walked with the checkbook to the end cage. He handed it, and a pen, to the shadowy white figure within.

"Make out five checks," he commanded. "Three for a hundred and fifty thousand dollars apiece, two for a hundred thousand."

The cowering figure in the cage straightened a little, and refused to take book and pen through the bars.

"Bostiff," called Doctor Satan. His voice still soft, soft, but there was in it an essence that made Girse shiver.

The legless giant came from the next chamber, leaving the door open. The doorway was suddenly flooded with light that beat at the eyeballs like whips. Through the portal could be seen the dead man who had been taken out of the cage. But when the flash was over, only charred remnants of the corpse were left. That was all. The crystalline rod in their midst waited to bring the next lightning flicker from the south to consume even the remnants.

"Yes, Master?" said Bostiff dragging his great body forward.

"This man does not want to do as he is ordered. You will kindly reason with him."

"I'll write them!" screamed the man suddenly. "My God, don't let that legless fiend get me—I'll write them!"

Doctor Satan's red mask moved slightly, as though beneath it his lips shaped themselves to a smile. He handed pen and book through the bars to the naked creature in the cage.

THE MAN WHO CHAINED THE LIGHTNING

3.

IN THE MORNING, which was flooded with calm sunlight after the night's storm, Ascott Keane paused a moment before the impressive stone facade of the United Continental Bank.

The bank building looked like a fortress, with thick walls and bronze doors that could have withstood an army. It spoke of comfortable, prosaic wealth, and the power to hold it indefinitely from marauders. It spoke of a world of skyscrapers and giant industrial plants and motor cars.

It seemed to give the lie to the possibility of the existence anywhere of a person capable of looting it—a person like Doctor Satan who could laugh ironically at bronze doors and stone walls.

Keane passed through the guarded entrance of the bank, and went to the rear of the great room within, past marble and glass counters, cages in which shelves of money changed hands, and desks at which transactions involving millions were being accomplished.

At the rear was a private elevator which went up to a big office on the fourth floor of the building. The office was marked, President.

Keane's name gave him instant entrée to the president of the bank. For Keane was known to this man not only as a wealthy citizen whose business would be useful, but also in his more secret role of marvelously capable criminal investigator.

"Keane!" said Mercer, the president. "It's good to see you. What brings you here?" He glanced at the electric clock on his desk. "Only nine-thirty in the morning! That's practically dawn for you. At least that's what you like to let people think."

Keane did not smile in return. He studied the man.

Mercer was a small man, lean and leathery, with prim nose-glasses like a school teacher. One might be tempted to dismiss him as prim and fussy—till the jaw was noted. Mercer had a jaw like a steel trap, and blue eyes that were shrewd, capable, and honest-looking.

"I'm here to ask about a few of your customers," he said.

"I think I know which ones," said Mercer, the smile fading from his leathery face. "Sit down and tell me about it."

Keane took a chair at the end of Mercer's desk. It was an enormous desk. On it there was no welter of papers; it was bare save for a large onyx electric clock which was at the back and end of the desk between Mercer and whoever sat in the visitor's chair.

"The men I wanted to talk to you about," Keane said, "are Edward Dombey, Harold Kragness, Shepherd Case and lastly, John Weldman, all rich, and all depositors here."

Mercer leaned back in his chair, putting the tips of his fingers together and saying nothing, letting Keane talk before he told what he himself knew.

"I've learned," Keane went on, "that all four of these men have been making heavy withdrawals of cash here lately. For some reason each of them has found it necessary to have hundreds of thousands of dollars in bills with him. Yet here's an odd thing.

"Each of the four has deposits in other large New York banks. Between the four of them, indeed, they have large sums in no less than six of the biggest banks in the city. Yet they always have come here to draw their cash."

Mercer stirred. "I didn't know that," he said thoughtfully.

"Well, it's true. So I came here to see if I could find out why. And I think I have." Keane glanced at the onyx electric clock. "That is, I believe I have—if the checks happened to be made out in this office."

Mercer nodded. "They were. All of them."

"All right, tell me about them," said Keane, leaning back to listen in his turn.

Mercer cleared his throat.

"Those are the four men, and that's the business, I expected you to ask about when the girl announced your name," he said. "Because there's something damned queer about it, although I haven't been able to puzzle out what it is.

"It started two weeks ago. Harold Kragness came up here. He talked pleasantly enough with me for a moment or two and then said he wanted to cash a rather large check. A hundred and seventy-five thousand dollars. He thought I'd better put my initials on it so the teller would pay the money without question.

"That was queer—both his desire to get the sum in cash, and his idea that I should countersign his check. I wouldn't have had to do that. He could get anything up to half a million downstairs without special arrangement. But I scribbled my initials on the check and...."

"Just a minute," said Keane. "Did he bring the check here already made out?"

Mercer shook his head.

"He wrote it out here on my desk, before my eyes. He waved it a minute or two to dry the ink, disregarding a blotter I passed him and then handed it to me."

"It was his signature, all right?"

"Oh, yes! No doubting it!"

"Go on."

"Kragness went out with the check and cashed it downstairs. I thought about it a lot. Why should he want all that in cash? The obvious idea was that he might be blackmailed or something. But he didn't look like a man under a strain; he was cheerful, laughing. And I certainly couldn't question the genuineness of a check made out here in front of me.

"I THOUGHT NO more about it, then—till two days later. Then Dombey came in and went through the same rigmarole, only with a check for two hundred thousand dollars. After that the flow started.

"Kragness came in again, and Dombey, and then Case, and finally Weldman. All well known to me. The four of them cashed check after check, all for big sums. Never did any of the four seem worried or terrified, as they would have been if they were buying their way clear from some sort of danger. Yet—all those checks!

"I was certain something was wrong. But I couldn't put my finger on it. In each case the check was written here in the office by the man himself. Each man denied that anything was wrong, when I exceeded my rights and asked them bluntly.

"I went so far as to put a private detective on the trail of one of them, Dombey—though for heaven's sake don't ever let anybody know that. The detective reported that Dombey met no suspicious characters. He went home with his money, where he seemed cheerful and unalarmed. His wife and daughter are away in Europe, you know...."

"I know," said Keane grimly. He glanced at the clock again. "Each man made out each check here, before your eyes, so that you could testify that nothing could possibly be wrong...."

"Testify?" said Mercer quickly.

"Let it go," said Keane. "We'll put it this way: each check is beyond suspicion, and you, the president of the bank, could swear to it. Which is an important part of the game."

"Game? Come, Keane! Tell me what's wrong?"

"It's too soon, Mercer. Tell me one more thing. You say each of these four men is known to you personally. You couldn't possibly be fooled by somebody made up to represent them?"

"Not possibly!" said Mercer. "Besides, there were the checks, made out in their handwriting while I watched."

"The four seemed absolutely normal to you?" Keane persisted.

Mercer hesitated for a full minute before he answered that. Then his voice was a little strained, a little chilled.

"Normal? That's a hard word to define. Each of them was undoubtedly the man he said he was. The four who came in here, and between them have drawn several millions in the last two weeks, were certainly Dombey, Kragness, Case and Weldman. And each seemed cheerful and without worries. And yet...."

"Well?" prompted Keane as the man stopped.

"Well, in spite of all that they didn't seem what I would call 'normal'. It's hard to describe it. And I can't, as applied to them. I can only tell my own reactions."

He moistened his lips, and stared past Keane at the blank office wall.

"There *was* something the matter with those men, Keane! All the time I talked to each of them, I could feel it. A sort of chill along my spine—a feel of horror." He tried to laugh. "I used to feel that way when I was a boy and passed near a cemetery at night. That's all I can tell you, Keane. I'm afraid it isn't much."

"It's a lot," contradicted Keane. He got up, eyes icy with growing knowledge. "A lot! Thanks, Mercer."

He left the bank. Four men who seemed without worries—but who cashed large checks as though being bled by some criminal ring! Four who seemed normal at first glance—but who made the bank president feel as he had felt when near a graveyard as a boy!

Keane went to the presidents' offices of the five other big banks in which the four men had large deposits, but from which none had drawn money in the past two weeks. He found what he had thought he would find.

On the desks of none of the five executives was there anything corresponding to the onyx electric clock on that of Mercer. Their desks were bare of all but papers.

IN HIS BIG library, to which none gained admittance save after searching preliminaries, the frosted glass television screen on his ebony desk glowed softly. The face of Beatrice Dale was reflected.

He pressed a button and the door swung open. Beatrice came in. He stared inquiringly at her. She was dressed in street clothes and had evidently just come in.

"I've just come from Mr. Weldman's home," she said. "I talked to a maid there. The servants are terrified, of course, at the death of the valet."

Keane nodded impatiently. "They would be, naturally. But Weldman! How about him? How does he act?"

Beatrice caught her red lip between her teeth.

"He acts cheerful, absolutely normal. In fact, he seems almost too cheerful after the murder of his man. Certainly he seems in no danger, nor does he act like a man who is being blackmailed."

"Did you see him?"

"Yes, I saw him for a moment from the servants' wing. I got just a glimpse. But, Ascott"—her voice sank—"I had the most uncanny sensation when I saw him! There's something about that man—something…" She stopped with a shudder.

"Go on," said Keane gently.

"It's impossible to put into words. He frightens me. I don't know why. And it isn't exactly fright—it's horror."

"Do the servants feel the same way about him?"

The girl touched her burnished, red-brown hair distractedly. "Yes. They're a little afraid of him without knowing why. Several are leaving, because of the valet's death, they say; but I'm sure that vague feeling of horror is part of their going."

Keane's large, firm mouth tightened. His strong fingers clenched a little. But his voice was even as he said; "The rest of the report, please. You saw the barbers I listed, and talked to the other valets?"

"Yes. I talked to the barbers in the four buildings where Dombey, Case, Kragness and Weldman have their suites of offices. And I talked to the valets of Kragness, Case and Dombey. None of them has shaved any of the four in the past two weeks."

Her face colored a little. "It seemed a silly question to ask them, Ascott. But I know you must have had a good reason for telling me to inquire about it."

"I did," said Keane. "The best. The answer to that question clears up in my mind almost the last of the mystery of Doctor Satan's latest crime methods—precisely how he is draining the fortunes of these rich men."

Beatrice shook her head, bewildered. "Perhaps it's clear to you. I certainly can't understand it! And I can't understand what it is that takes place in Doctor Satan's mind! He is master of a hundred secrets of nature unknown to all others, save perhaps you. He could get all the money he wanted, if he chose, without these dreadful crime plots."

KEANE LOOKED AT her with his gray eyes reflecting a knowledge of the motives of men that was far beyond the knowledge other mortals could glean from human contacts.

"You don't look at it from the right angle, Beatrice. Money? It isn't money alone Doctor Satan wants. He has more than enough of that without plotting for it. It's the game itself he is after. The grisly, stark game of plundering his fellow men of their fortunes and souls and lives—solely for the thrill of conquering them. Of course he must get the money, too; one of the rules of his game is that his crimes must pay. But the fact that he is not purely a money-grabbing criminal is what makes him so infinitely dangerous. That, and his learning."

His voice lowered, and into it crept the resolution that had tempered the steel of his nature since first he had heard of the ruthless, cold-blooded individual who chose to dress in the devil's masquerade and call himself all too appropriately, Doctor Satan.

"But I'm going to stop him, Beatrice! It may cost me my life, but the cost will come *after* the purchase—which is the destruction of Doctor Satan!"

He smiled, and his voice returned to normal. "However, histrionics won't catch him will they? It takes work and persistence to do that. Such work as the sifting of news items, for example. And I think I have one here that is to prove very, very important."

He took from a drawer a half-page cut from the society section. It pictured three people, a woman with a granite chin and gray hair like cast iron in a wave over her forehead; a girl who was a replica of her; and a foppishly handsome young man with a harassed look.

"Mrs. Corey Magnus, wife of the financier, is sailing at midnight tonight for England with her daughter, Princess Rimova, and her son-in-law, the prince, last of the Borsakoffs. They will be received at court...."

Keane stared long at the pictures and the text.

"Another wealthy man living without his family for a time. Corey Magnus. And all the others were left alone by their families before beginning their cash withdrawals...."

He put the clipping carefully away; and in his eyes was pity as well as stony resolve; he knew that another man had been marked by Doctor Satan.

4.

IN THE HOME of Corey Magnus at nine next evening, Magnus's private secretary opened the library door and almost tiptoed in. He walked softly to the fireplace, in front of which was standing a tall, heavy-set, imposing-looking man with gray hair and slate-gray eyes who stared with a frown at the leaping flames.

THE MAN WHO CHAINED THE LIGHTNING

The secretary's bearing expressed the deference due the man who was Chairman of the Board of the American Zinc Corporation, president of the New York & Northwestern Railway, president of the New York Consolidated Trust, and many other huge financial and industrial groups.

"Mr. Bowles, of the Gull Oil Corporation, is here to see you, Mr. Magnus," he said.

Magnus's slate-colored eyes turned on him. "Ask Bowles to wait for a moment. I don't feel very well… a touch of dizziness… But don't tell him that!"

The secretary nodded and went out, closing the doors of the library behind him. He was looking worried and perplexed. Asking a man like Bowles to wait! Even Corey Magnus might be sorry he had done that.

Behind him, his employer starred dully at the closed door, and then back at the flames in the fireplace. His eyes contracted as though he were in pain. He swayed a little, and caught at the mantelpiece for support.

The open French doors leading to his garden caught his gaze. He walked toward them, breathing deeply of the chill fall air. Small beads of perspiration studded his forehead, and his heavy face was pale.

He walked out of the doors.

His head was bent forward on his thick neck, and he looked intent, almost rapt, as though something called him from out there and he must find out what it was.

It was ten minutes later when his secretary came back into the library again, not daring to keep Bowles waiting longer. He saw that the room was empty, and went to the open French doors.

The garden was empty too. He rushed back to give an alarm—and saw something he had missed before. A note on the library table.

Send Bowles away, the note read. Tell him I'm ill and will see him

in the morning at his office. You may go home, yourself.
C.M.

The secretary bit his lip. No word in the note as to where his employer had gone so abruptly! No explanations of any sort!

But the brusk letter was indubitably in Magnus's handwriting. There was nothing for him to do but obey its commands.

UNDER THE LITTLE cemetery, in the rocklined chamber, Girse and Bostiff, servants of Doctor Satan were busy.

More lamps had been lit. Now the room was brightly illuminated with garish red light. In the brighter illumination the cages along the end wall showed plainly: the one empty cage, the occupant of which had been consumed by the trapped lightning in the next chamber, and the three occupied cages.

The figures in these cages, seen in detail under the better light, would have astounded the city in the heart of which this chamber was buried. Naked, disheveled, gaunt with hunger and mottled with cold, they were Edward Dombey, John Weldman and Shepherd Case, men among the two per cent who controlled four-fifths of the wealth of the country.

The empty cage had belonged to Harold Kragness.

Girse, with ape-like movements, was clearing out the empty cage. Bostiff, with a look of awe and fear on his bovine face, was stirring something in a large metal bowl.

It was curious stuff he stirred, faintly phosphorescent, like a colorless, opaque jelly. It clung to the pestle and, once, splashed sluggishly high enough to touch Bostiff's hand. When this happened, he exclaimed aloud and shook the stuff off his flesh, to land in the bowl and mingle with the rest.

Girse sneered at the exclamation. "What are you afraid of, you ox?"

"This—this stuff in the bowl," Bostiff rumbled. "It's kind of alive!"

"Sure it's alive," chuckled Girse, keeping his distance from the bowl. "It's this here proto—protoplasm, Doctor Satan said. The junk you're made of, and me, and everybody else."

"I don't like it," said Bostiff, leaving off his stirring.

"I do! Anything that brings in the cash that stuff brings, I like a lot. God, Doctor Satan's smart!"

" 'Smart'?" Even to Bostiff's limited intelligence the word seemed feeble; but he could supply no other. "Smart enough to know everything we think or say. And to kill us if we don't think the right thing."

Girse nodded, his ape-like grin fading. He had seen his red-robed master read treachery in one man's thoughts, and kill him in a blue flame the only materials for which were mysterious powdered chemicals in a little heap.

The ape-like man started to say something, then stopped. The red lamp near the door was winking on and off, on and off. He opened the door and went down the passage revealed.

"Bostiff!" The voice came from a distance.

The legless giant hitched his way out of the chamber and down the tunnel to join Girse. Beside Girse, at the foot of the shaft down which the broad tombstone slid as an elevator, was a motionless figure. A heavy-set, important-looking man who was breathing strenuously but was obviously unconscious.

"Corey Magnus!" Bostiff rumbled. "I've seen him many a time in his private car when I worked on the New York & Northwestern Railroad! That's where I lost my legs. So he's the next! It'll be a pleasure to handle *him*."

Even Girse paled a little at the dull ferocity in Bostiff's eyes.

The two of them dragged Magnus to the chamber and shut the door. There, working with the method of those who have performed the work before and know in advance every move, they began a strange series of tasks.

Girse hopped agilely to a box beside the metal mixing-bowl in which Bostiff had stirred the protoplasm, afraid of it, but having no conception of the marvel of it. From the box Girse took moistened, pulped papier-mâché.

He pressed a thin blob of it over Magnus's unconscious face. It slowly hardened there. As it did so, Bostiff stripped the man, leaving his slightly paunchy body bare and white in the cold underground chamber.

Bostiff moved with the clothes to the row of figures leaning against the wall near the door like life-sized dolls. And now it could be seen that there were five figures leaning there instead of four.

One of the figures was naked; and its nudity revealed a fact about itself and the clad four beside it that was the most startling thing about the underground room. These were not mechanical things—dolls the size of men and dressed in men's clothes. These were corpses; bodies; dead men, perfectly preserved but nevertheless as dead as last year's leaves!

Bostiff, handling the corpse as though it were a thing of wood, clothed it in the garments of Corey Magnus. And Girse, after feeling the papier-mâché sheet over the unconscious man's face to make sure it had hardened properly, carefully lifted it off.

He held in his hands a perfect mask of the millionaire.

THE RED LIGHT next to the door winked again. But it was a different signal this time. Instead of winking on and off at random, it blinked twice, hesitated, then blinked three times.

"Doctor Satan!" said Girse. "Is everything ready for him?"

"Everything is ready," said Bostiff, leaning the freshly clad corpse against the wall.

The door opened, slowly, as though no hand had touched it. A step sounded in the passage. Into the room came Doctor Satan, red-robed and gloved, with the crimson light reflecting dully from his red mask and the skull-cap with the mocking, Luciferian horns on it.

An instant Doctor Satan stood within the doorway, black eyes glaring at the two who served him so well. Then he swung the door shut behind him with an impatience of movement that made Bostiff and Girse glance apprehensively at each other.

Doctor Satan was in a rage. They knew the signs.

"Has all gone well, Master?" said Girse, timidly.

The coal-black eyes behind the mask narrowed as if their owner would ignore the question of an underling. Then the mask moved with words.

"You have the man, Magnus, whom I directed here in the little death of hypnotism. Doesn't that mean that all has gone well? And yet…."

Doctor Satan strode to the unconscious, stripped financier.

"All has not gone well," he said at last. "Keane escaped the lightning, and he was not in his home a while ago when I went there to deal personally the death he has avoided so far. Keane… A man in my own position—wealthy, learned, making an avocation of crime prevention as I have made a pastime of crime.

"The ancient Greek theory had it that every force that reared in the world soon found an equal, opposing force rearing against it as an antidote. Can that be true? Has some high Providence observed my rise, and in the observing prepared for me an antagonist like Ascott Keane? But, no! There is no God, no higher Providence. Keane is an accident—an opponent more dangerous than most, but still one to be destroyed by me almost at will!"

The red-clad figure strode to the cages. Doctor Satan stood with folded arms, staring at the three men who cowered within them at his near approach.

"And you are three of the world's great," Doctor Satan's quietly glacial tone lashed them. "Observe! Three who thought themselves all-powerful! Cringing here like animals in a cage! But I am more powerful than any other, though the world does not yet know that."

The three men cowered lower. Doctor Satan turned abruptly.

"The mask is prepared? The body matching Magnus's body in height and weight and build is prepared? But yes—I see it is so clad, and the garments fit it well. Bring me the mask, and the bowl."

He bent over Corey Magnus. Bostiff and Girse went to the corner and came back with the bowl of protoplasm, and the papier-mâché mask.

Working with deft, gloved fingers, Doctor Satan began a process of scientific sculpture the methods and materials of which transcended anything yet known in science, art, or plastic surgery.

5.

AT A NOD from Doctor Satan, Bostiff hitched his great body over to the newly clad corpse, dragged it down, and carried it to him with one huge hand under the dead man's belt.

He laid it beside the unconscious financier. Doctor Satan carefully placed the mask over the dead face, and thrust a small tube into the bowl of living substance. The other end of the tube was placed between the mask and the dead face.

No process of siphoning was begun as far as Girse of Bostiff could see. Yet the level of the protoplasm lowered steadily in the bowl as the jelly-like stuff flowed sluggishly up the tube and under the mask.

After a while the level ceased to sink in the bowl, and Doctor Satan stood up.

"It is done. Tomorrow another industrial giant shall go to the bank and draw out the first of many blocks of cash."

He removed the mask, and even Girse and Bostiff, who had seen such things before, gasped aloud.

The face of the dead man was the face of Corey Magnus!

Doctor Satan's coal-black eyes fixed themselves on the altered face of the corpse. His gaze was electric, compelling, mystic.

"Magnus," he said, "for from now on you are Magnus—rise!"

The man, lying there nameless in oblivion, was dead. That was beyond questioning. His flesh was cold and stiff. For many hours the heart had not beat.

But—the body rose slowly, stiffly, at Doctor Stan's word.

Doctor Satan's eyes impaled the dead eyes of the moving, standing corpse.

"Smile," he said.

The dead lips, altered with the protoplasm, moved in a smile. It was the wolfish grin of Corey Magnus, pictured many a time in cartoons.

"Speak. What is your name?"

"My name," spoke the corpse, "is Corey Magnus."

"I shall tell you silently what you are to do tomorrow," said Doctor Satan. "Then you shall repeat my instructions."

For several minutes, the glittering, coal-black eyes probed the dead eyeballs of the animated body. Then the stiff lips moved.

"I shall go to the United Continental Bank tomorrow. With me I shall have a check written out by the man who lies behind you. I shall take this check to the president's office...."

But now a new voice spoke in that underground room, a voice not heard before. One that made Bostiff grunt in amazement, as though he had been struck. One that stiffened Doctor Satan's red-draped body as if an electric shock had coursed through it.

The voice came from behind Doctor Satan. And its message was as electrifying as its presence in that chamber.

"Let *me* tell you what the corpse was to do for you tomorrow."

For the space of a heart-beat the silence that chained the room was more terrible than shrieking chaos. Then Satan whirled and stared at the man who had been lying behind him.

The man was sitting up now; and though body and features were those of Corey Magnus, there was something about the eyes… something….

"Keane!" Doctor Satan whispered. *"Ascott Keane! Here!"*

THE BLACK EYES glared at the head of the man, so different from the lean, hawk face of Keane. Glared amazement—and rage.

"You have altered your face and body with protoplasm! You blundered onto my method of using and creating it…."

Keane's voice, came again, amazingly, from Magnus's throat.

"That's only one of the many things I've discovered, Doctor Satan. I know all you've done and planned to do.

"Tomorrow that revivified corpse would take a check, made out in advance by Corey Magnus, to the office of the president of the United Continental Bank. Why to that one bank? Because only on that one presidential desk is there an object—such as an electric clock—behind which your puppet could write with a dry pen over the words and figures already made out by Magnus, and thus seem to write the check fresh 'under the very eyes of the president.'"

The coal-black eyes glaring at him from the red mask were like living jet, burning with hate. But, relentlessly, Keane went on, slowly getting to his feet as he spoke.

"A clever, if somewhat complicated, scheme, Doctor Satan. But like all complicated plans, it provided its own drawbacks as it went along.

"For one thing, your dead men roused an inexplicable feeling of horror and dread in the minds of observers. They seemed all right, and acted all right—but something chilled those they came in contact with, and that fact was remembered.

"For another thing, there was the matter of their queer actions at home and in their offices. Clever as you are, you couldn't know all the details of their private and business lives, so your masquerading corpses made mistakes sometimes.

"Again, there was the matter of shaving. Hair does not grow on the dead, contrary to superstition. And your mask of living protoplasm, of synthetic flesh, covered the facial hair of the dead who did your bidding. So there was no shaving to be done—to the bewilderment of barbers and valets. It was this that started Weldman's valet to spying around, as a result of which he started for the police, and his death.

"Finally, you had to pick rich victims who were not living with their families at the moment: No matter how marvelous the disguise, immediate relatives of course could not have been fooled. It was that fact which informed me, when Corey Magnus's family went abroad, that he would probably be next on your list. So I persuaded him to go away secretly while I took his place. An easy way to find you, wasn't it, Doctor Satan?"

WITH THE FIRES of hell glittering in his jet-black eyes, Doctor Satan had heard Keane out. They flamed like fire opals as he finally spoke.

"An easy way to get here, Ascott Keane. Very easy! But you may find it more difficult to leave."

"I'll take my chance on that," said Keane.

Doctor Satan's red-clad body quivered. "Seize him!"

Girse and Bostiff clutched Keane's arms and held him in apparent helplessness.

"Bind him!"

Rope was wound around Keane's arms and body and pulled so taut that it cut deep into the synthetic flesh with which Keane had built out his hard, firm body to resemble Magnus's pudgier one.

Keane stared at Doctor Satan—and smiled.

Doctor Satan's hand brought from under his red tunic the deadly, crystalline tube.

"The lightning tube!" muttered Bostiff, mouth open stupidly. "But Master, there is no storm tonight. The sky is clear...."

"Fool," said Doctor Satan gently, "there is always lightning, and storm, somewhere in the world. And distance makes no difference to *this.*"

He thrust the crystalline tube between Keane's bound arm and his side, jet-black eyes flaming with triumph.

"When the next lightning bolt splits the sky, somewhere on Earth," he said, softly, "you die, Keane. That may be in five seconds—it may be in ten minutes. But whenever it comes, death comes with it."

And still Keane smiled.

"You're so sure, Doctor Satan? Under this synthetic flesh on my body there might be something that would astonish you ...."

The sentence was never finished.

In some far distant place, lightning flared.

And suddenly the underground chamber was ablaze with blue-white light that dazzled the eyes even through closed lids. It was an inferno of light, a soundless, rending explosion of it.

In a blinding sheet it played over the body of Ascott Keane. Played over it—and as suddenly shot away from it at a crackling right angle!

Girse screamed and Bostiff roared like a lanced bull as a little of the tremendous current rayed into them. But Doctor Satan made no outcry.

The main stream of blue-white death was streaming from Keane's body—straight into the red-clad figure!

Doctor Satan's body convulsed at the touch. A smell of burning fabric filled the room, to mingle with the acrid odor of burned ozone.

And then Doctor Satan was down, with sheet after sheet of lightning bathing Keane in harmless radiance and streaming from him to plunge into the writhing red figure on the floor.

KEANE'S BONDS WERE burned away by the force he had redirected. Some of the synthetic flesh over his abdomen was charred from him, revealing part of a crystalline plate, like armor over his body.

He dropped Doctor Satan's tube, which smashed on the floor, and leaped over the moaning figures of Girse and Bostiff toward the cages in which three men screamed pleas for help.

From the walls and roof of the low room bits of rock and earth were falling, loosened by the lightning bolts. The very floor seemed to sway under his feet.

He opened the cages. "Run!" he shouted. "Run!"

The three staggered to the door and into the passage, with Keane behind them. At his touch on a concealed projection, the tombstone from the cemetery above sank down to get them....

With a soft roar the earth behind them caved in, burying many feet deep the passage between them and the room in which they had left Doctor Satan, Girse and Bostiff, and the five dead men who had served Satan's turn.

The passage shuddered and quivered. Air from the cave-in screamed about their ears. The four clung to one another for support.

Then, in the racking silence succeeding the pandemonium, they stared at each other in the faint light of the stars coming down the black pit.

"The end of Doctor Satan," breathed John Weldman at last. "Thank God for that!"

But Ascott Keane said nothing. He was remembering that in the burned patches of Doctor Satan's red robe he had seen some crystalline stuff; and he knew that was armor such as he himself had devised against the lightning's bolt. Not as impervious as his own, perhaps—letting some of the current through to convulse the man's body—but still saving him from death.

The cave-in? That could not have harmed Doctor Satan. He must have constructed the chamber to resist the lightning shocks, because he drew them there himself. Only the passage between the room and the end of the tunnel could have collapsed.

So Keane said nothing to Weldman. But he knew the truth; neither lightning nor cave-in had killed Doctor Satan.

HOLLYWOOD HORROR

THE CENTRAL SOUND STAGE on the lot of the R-G-R Motion Picture Company was almost ready for the shooting of the main scene in the company's latest production of 193—. Outside the square, windowless concrete building the massive doors were being closed. In a moment the red light would burn which would keep anyone from entering and ruining the sound effect. Inside, all was tense activity and bustle.

The inside of the sound stage had an eerie, cavernous look. One huge room, it was dark and shadowy at its outer fringes, and its high ceiling was lost in darkness. Shadows of people and things appeared like soundless prehistoric monsters.

Far above in the semi-darkness were shadowy platforms along which electricians were moving as they shifted scenic lights and equipment. An electric crane purred like a giant cat as it moved a heavy bit of scenery.

In the corner of the sound stage a set was being completed. It was for the picture, *Enchanted Castle,* in which the great star, Joan Harwell, had the leading role.

Men were hauling huge "sun-spots," incandescent globe spotlights, to platforms on three sides of the set. "Baby spots" also were being fixed in place to give a beautiful backlight effect on Miss Harwell's bronze hair.

All was prosaic, business-like, commonplace to the moving-picture industry. And yet...."

One of the electricians, who was trundling a baby spot into

position, shivered suddenly. He was a small man, partly bald, with a sensitive, thin face. He had wide blue eyes which, at the moment, glistened with something more than apprehension in the dusk of the great stage.

He paused beside another electrician, a burly, phlegmatic man, as he got the spot to the right position to play on Miss Harwell's head when she sat in the divan around which the forthcoming scene centered. His hand touched the burly man's shoulder.

"Bill," he half whispered, looking embarrassedly around to make sure he wouldn't be overheard, "do you feel it too?"

"Feel what?" grunted the big man.

The smaller man cleared his throat, plainly torn between a desire to speak what was in his mind, and a fear that he might be thought a fool. Desire won over fear.

"There's a kind of funny feel to this joint today," he muttered finally. "I've never noticed it in here before, but I can sure notice it this afternoon!"

"What are you talking about?" demanded the big man. "What kind of a feel?"

"I... don't exactly know how to describe it." The smaller man stared aloft at the spidery forms of workmen on the cat-walk, and then glanced almost fearfully at the set which had been constructed for the afternoon's shooting. "It gives me the willies, that's all."

The big man stared around, with his forehead wrinkling. "It's kind of quiet, like everybody was holding their breath," he said. "But it's always like that when we're about to shoot."

"No—it's more than that," babbled the smaller man. His hand on the big man's arm became a frantic clutch. "God, Bill, something's going to happen in here today. Something awful—something not on the director's program. I can feel it. I *know* it!"

He moistened dry lips.

"I remember once feeling like this when I was a kid. I've always been funny about feeling things—a spirit medium called me psychic, once. Anyway, this time I was just going into a picture show. I was about fourteen, I guess, and I went with a couple of other kids. When we got inside the theater I almost turned around and went out. I didn't know why. I just felt that something was going to—happen. I tried to get the others to leave with me, and they only laughed. I couldn't explain my feeling, you see. I said I felt that something terrible was going to happen in that theater, and we ought to get out before it did. But—they only laughed. We stayed."

Even in the half-light the whiteness of the man's face was perceptible.

"Bill, it happened, all right. That theater was the Mohawk Theater in Chicago. Everybody still remembers the name—and the fire that destroyed it and killed half the people in it. That was what happened, and I was the only one of the crowd of us who went in that got out alive."

He wiped sweat from his face.

"I feel now, today, just the way I felt that night, an hour before the fire! I feel now, this afternoon, that something awful is going to happen in this sound stage. Bill, should I say anything to the boss or the director—maybe get them not to shoot this scene today?"

The big man jerked his arm loose from the other's detaining hand. His phlegmatic face registered annoyance and contempt.

"Are you nuts? Sure, they'll put off shooting the scene for a day, with a forty-four thousand dollar payroll, just because you got a shivery feeling in your spine. I can just see them doing a thing like that!"

"But, Bill..." quavered the smaller man.

"You better get busy," said the other, briefly. "Come on, hop to it."

The two left the baby spot the smaller man had adjusted to

illumine Miss Harwell's bronze, silky hair. The big man was scowling, and a sneer shaped his lips. But the smaller man looked almost ill, and his eyes glinted like the eyes of a frightened horse in the dimness.

Neither of the two noticed something it was, in a way, their business to see:

Taped inconspicuously to the power cable trailing from the spot that was to throw its rays on Miss Harwell's head was a fine bare wire. It entered the shell of the light along with the big cable. It was soldered, with the other, to the incandescent globe socket. And before this globe there was a lens that differed just a little in color from the glass of the other lenses.

A trifling difference. One any man could be forgiven for not seeing.

A tall man with stoop shoulders adjusted a microphone at the end of a long boom. He stepped front of it, called: "One, three, five, six, seven…."

The voice of the monitor in the glass-enclosed booth came hollowly from a loud-speaker, like the voice of a ghost: "Okay on valve test."

Through the great outer doors came the director and the members of the cast who were to participate in the scene, two men who played minor roles, and Miss Harwell.

IT IS UNNECESSARY to describe the great Joan Harwell. Before her untimely end, she was familiar to two-thirds of the population of the country. Her silky, red-brown hair had dazzled millions of eyes with its soft sheen. Her large, brilliant eyes were the envy of the women of a nation. Her body, flawless in the delicate maturity of its curves, had stirred the pulses of a nation's men. A great beauty, she would have been outstanding in any period; one of those women who almost frighten the beholder by their perfection.

She was dressed in a creamy satin negligee which was to register white on the film. The negligee clung to her figure, accentuating its loveliness, and revealed perfect bare arms and throat. Above it her exquisite face and flame-brown hair were flower-like.

"Miss Harwell," said the director, a corpulent man with a bald head, "you know your lines?"

"Yes," she said, in the soft, well-modulated tone with which all the theater-goers in the world were familiar.

"We'll rehearse this living-room scene, then... What is it? Don't you feel well?"

The director looked anxiously at the star's rather pale face, spotting the pallor in spite of her exaggerated make-up.

Joan Harwell hesitated a moment, with her red lips quivering. Then she smiled. "I feel all right."

"You're sure? We've been working you pretty hard lately."

"I'm sure." The beautiful face continued in its smile, although the deep violet eyes were not smiling. "I felt a little cold for a moment, that's all. Not exactly cold—a little chilled, as though a cold, damp wind had touched me."

"I don't think there's any draft in here," said the director jovially, glancing at the solid walls. "Well, let's get on with it. I'll run over the scene again for you.

"You are to sit on that divan in the center of the set. You are to register happiness mixed with fear. The man you love is on his way to see you—but another man may reach him before he gets here with a malicious tale that may turn him against you. So you are in a fever of impatience, mad to hold him in your arms, ecstatic at one moment and at the next fearful that he may not come at all. Then the malicious tale-bearer comes in and announces that your lover is on his way back to the ship that will carry him out of your life for ever. You have lost. You go through the throes of grief and rage... But I think you know the rest well enough. Take your place, please."

Miss Harwell walked to the divan and sat down. Light in floods brought every detail of her face and form into relief as she reclined on the divan. She faced a little away from the bank of cameras.

"You're sure you feel all right?" persisted the director, staring at her violet eyes.

"Yes. I'm all right."

The director bit his lips, then shrugged. After all, this was only a rehearsal. The star's slightly strained look, for which he could think of no reason whatever, would not matter.

"More light on Miss Harwell's right cheek," he called.

The burly electrician moved a baby spot. The planes of the star's face leaped into higher relief.

"On the back of her head," said the director.

The man with the sensitive face and the wide, apprehensive eyes moved another small spot so that Miss Harwell's lustrous hair became a web of silky light.

And Joan Harwell shivered suddenly as that light touched her.

All noticed it, though none noticed that the last small spot to be moved was the one that had the fine bare wire subtly fastened to its power cable.

"Is the lens of that light clean?" snapped the director. "It seems just a shade off-color... No, I guess my eyes are playing me tricks. All right, Miss Harwell."

Absolute silence reigned in the great sound stage. In it, workmen and actors, property man and director, stared at the nation's most beautiful woman who sat on the divan in the lacy negligee that molded limbs and body a sculptor could not have equaled.

The star swung into her part.

"He's coming," she whispered, just audibly for the microphone to catch it. "He'll be here soon... after nearly a year...."

The director frowned. Her voice was strained, almost harsh. But her facial expression was all right. It registered happiness—mixed with fear. No, not fear. Horror! What ailed the girl?

The spotlights rayed on her face and body. The little spot that illuminated her hair seemed to burn with a faintly orange tint....

The director, seated in his camp chair, gripped the rough wooden arms and stared with eyes that protruded from their sockets.

Joan Harwell's hair! What in heaven's name?...

It seemed to be fading from her head like a cobweb mist, revealing the lines of her skull!

The director blinked rapidly, and stared again. Was he going mad? The slight rasp of his panting shivered in the air. He was going insane—or blind!

"He'll be here soon," Miss Harwell whispered, "unless Tim reaches him first...."

A sort of croak came from the director's throat, a rasping small sound of utter horror.

The beautiful lips that had murmured the words had become like the lustrous hair—misty, like substance of fog rather than of flesh. He could see her teeth through the lips!

THE SHIVERING SOB of the small electrician near him in a way reassured the director, though the reassurance was a dreadful thing. For it told him that someone else was seeing what he saw.

"If Tim tells me that lie, and kills his love for me!" breathed the star. "But he won't! Fate couldn't be so unkind."

And now in the sound stage there was a paralysis of silence more terrible than wild shouts. Every eye was riveted on the star with chains of horror. Riveted on her face and head.

Something was happening to the beautiful face—something terrible and impossible beyond description—something of which Joan Harwell still seemed unaware, though the tone of her voice had grown more strained and odd with each word she uttered.

Her face was disappearing!

Shuddering, whimpering silently in his throat, gripping the arms of his chair, the director glared at the girl on the divan. And now the metamorphosis, progressing ever more swiftly, was complete. And Joan Harwell no longer had a countenance that could move men to rapture and women to envy.

Gone were the violet eyes and the straight small nose. Gone the silky hair and the creamy skin of cheeks and brow.

On the star's lovely throat a skull rested!

With a scream the director leaped from his chair. And his wild shriek broke the awful silence that chained the others in the sound stage. As one, they ran for the great outer doors, hiding their eyes from the thing of horror that now sat on the divan; all but the burly electrician, who stood near the cameras and stared, with eyes that started from his head, at the thing that had been a woman.

A gorgeous body, seductively revealed by a cream satin negligee—but a body on which was nothing but a grinning skull!

"My God!" whimpered the one man who had stayed behind. "Oh, my God!"

"Harry!" shrilled Joan Harwell, getting up from the divan and turning toward the doors from which the men were hastening. "Harry—what is it? What has happened to me?"

The director did not answer. He did not turn back to look at her. Not for empires would he have gazed again at what had been sheer beauty. He ran from the doors and out into the afternoon sun. The star was alone with the shaking big man in coveralls who stared at her with twitching terror in his stupid face.

The thing that had been Joan Harwell walked toward the man. The negligee, trailing from the perfect body, rustled in the stillness. The blanched white skull on the slender, lovely throat turned toward him.

"You," Joan Harwell's voice came from between teeth that

chattered in their bony sockets, "for the love of heaven—tell me! What has happened?"

The man's nerve broke utterly at last. With a hoarse yell he turned from the glaring, hollow eye-sockets of the skull, and raced for the door to join the others.

The beautiful form in the clinging negligee stood beside the cameras. The ghastly skull turned this way and that.

"Gone! All of them! They ran from me. But what has *happened* to me?"

The lovely figure swayed. Then it walked unsteadily to a make-up box near the set, with the skull atop the creamy bare shoulders shining almost phosphorescently in the dimness. Death on lovely life! A pallid skull on a beautiful woman's body!

The thing that had been Joan Harwell stretched out a trembling arm and hand toward the make-up. Pink, tapering fingers opened it. In the lifted lid a mirror showed.

For perhaps ten seconds of frozen silence the glaring eye-sockets of the skull stared into the reflection of themselves. Then through the clenched and naked teeth scream on scream ripped forth.

People gathering outside the sound stage, drawn by the almost crazed director and workmen, heard those screams and shuddered. But none moved to enter the place. None dared!

And suddenly the frightful screams ceased. The pink fingers holding the lid of the make-up box slammed it down, shattering the mirror into a thousand pieces. In its place the fingers caught up a pair of shears, keen, thin, long.

Straight and tall the figure stood—lovely as few women's bodies are lovely. Then a bare white arm went up. The shears glittered in the dimness of the sound stage; glittered more as they swept down and in; ceased glittering as they were bedded in flesh.

Joan Harwell fell, the negligee half covering a breast from which crimson poured, but with nothing covering the thing of horror that had been a flawless countenance crowned by bronze hair.

And now in a far corner of the great stage a shadow moved. It had seemed nothing but a mound of debris covered with tarpaulin. But now it took on human shape.

A tall, emaciated-looking figure stood erect. A black cloak covered it from heels to head. A dark felt hat with a down-drooping brim hid the head and part of the face. The rest of the face was covered by a red fabric mask.

The figure walked to the body of the dead star, and stared down. From eye-holes in the red mask, black eyes gazed callously at the skull set on the creamy throat. Then the felt hat moved as the man nodded.

Silently the figure moved from the body to the small spot that had been trained on Joan Harwell's head. Fingers sheathed in red rubber gloves ripped the bare fine wire loose from the power cable. Then the figure moved toward a smaller door in the sound stage leading into the property warehouse—where a secret exit could be made with the fine wire which was all the clue that might have explained the method by which a flawless face had been turned to fleshless ruin.

2.

IN THE CONFERENCE room flanking the private office of the president of the R-G-R Motion Picture Company, eight men sat. They were the wealthiest men of the industry, titans of the picture business. But they looked like anything but titans as they sat there.

The eight were frightened to the verge of collapse, and they showed it. Their faces, whether lean or chubby, were paper-white. Their hands trembled. Several smoked, sucked in great drafts from cigar or cigarette and expelling them again without really knowing what they were doing. And the eyes of all were turned toward the door marked: *A.R. Stang, President.*

In the big private office behind the closed door, there was a sight to evoke the same dread as that inspired the day before in the sound stage when Joan Harwell gazed into a mirror and saw why men ran from her.

Stang, the president, shivered in a huge leather chair next to the big desk across which normally flowed the business of R-G-R. But no business was flowing now. The desk was bare. And beside it, a fantastic creature, cowered Stang. Or the thing Stang had become!

The president's corpulent body remained untouched. But his left forearm and hand were the hand and forearm of a skeleton! Like bony twigs his fingers writhed and clenched while he sat there gazing at them; gazing out of sockets as eyeless as Joan Harwell's had been yesterday! For on the thick neck of the man was no longer placed a head. A skull was there, blanched, pallid, naked bone.

No sound came from the fleshless mouth. Sounds had been worn out. For eighteen hours Stang had cowered in the office, unable to drag himself out of it to face the horrified stares of the rest of the world. For eighteen hours he had screamed and cursed, raving for those who knocked at the office door to go away.

Now the first person to come into the big room was pacing up and down before him and shaking his head while he said with stiff lips: "I don't know what to do. I've been a practicing physician for twenty-eight years, and I've never seen anything like it. You haven't any idea what caused the change?"

The skull on Stang's shoulder spoke.

"I have no idea at all. I was sitting at my desk, bent over. I was writing. Just a check, so I didn't bother to light my desk lamp—I sat with only the light from the overhead fixture shining down on my head and hand. Maybe that light… but how could a light do—this—to me?"

He raised his skeletal left hand and forearm. The doctor's nails bit into his palms as he repressed a shudder.

"I didn't feel anything much. I recall feeling cold, as if a dank wind had touched me. That was all. The first thing that told me of the change was my secretary's behavior. She came into the office, stared at me as though she'd suddenly been turned to stone, and fainted. And I've been in here ever since…. Doctor, for God's sake, do something!"

The doctor walked toward the door.

"I'll do everything humanly possible. But first I've got to try to find out what is wrong. I'll take this sample of your flesh down to the laboratory and report back as soon as I can."

HE OPENED THE office door, with a reflection in his eyes of the panic that had filled the eyes of those who had fled from Joan Harwell, and went into the conference room.

The eight executives in there surrounded him.

"Doctor—what causes it?"

"Is it some new disease? Is it contagious?"

"Is it controllable?" rasped one who held crumpled in his fist a sheet of notepaper.

The doctor brushed them aside with a weary wave of his hand. "Gentlemen, I know nothing yet. I can only tell you what I told Mr. Stang. As soon as I find out something I'll report."

"But what could strip the flesh off a human being's bones like that?" demanded a short fat man whose high voice was like a squeal. "And how can a person live in such a condition?"

"The flesh is not stripped off," said the doctor, moistening his lips. "That at least I have found out. I found it out by feeling of the affected parts. The flesh is still there, gentlemen. Mr. Stang's head is not a naked skull. Hair and flesh and eyes and features are still there. But in some unguessable way they have been made invisible, or transparent. The flesh is as it always was—but it is as translucent as so much spring water, so that all you can see is the bony structure underneath. Similarly with his left hand. So it is not as bad as we feared."

"Not as bad!" squealed the fat man. "Does it make it any the less frightful that the skull is not really a naked skull? To the eyes of all beholders, it is only dead bone!"

"An illusion," the doctor began shakily.

"Hell, man! In a case like this illusion is as ghastly as reality. Stang can never mingle in the world again, like that. At a stroke he has been made into a thing that is dead even though still alive. You've got to do something!"

The doctor shrugged, opened his lips as though to retort, and then went on out of the conference room. Behind him, the eight reseated themselves at the big oval table.

"Gentlemen, we're beaten," said the man who held the sheet of note-paper in his hand. "We will have to follow the demands of this outrageous letter."

He straightened the crumpled paper and read again that message which any of the eight could have repeated word for word from having read it so many times already:

Bertrand C. Phillips, President of Acme Pictures, Incorporated: You will arrange to pay me five hundred thousand dollars by tomorrow at midnight. You will also instruct your star, Dorothy Dean, to pay to me the three hundred and eighty thousand dollars she has invested in Government bonds. If the payments are not made, she will suffer the fate of Joan Harwell, and you shall become as A.R. Stang—whom I advise you to visit immediately in company with other motion picture heads. His appearance may be an object lesson.

Signed DOCTOR SATAN.

The man with the letter looked around the circle of faces.

"Bertrand Phillips," he said. "That's me. And if I don't pay, I'll have a skull for a head and enter into a life in death such as lies before Stang. If I do pay, and persuade Miss Dean to pay, it will be only a beginning of the schemes of this man who calls himself Doctor Satan. Every one of you will have to give in to the same threat in turn. And then all of us will have to keep on, paying millions to the fellow."

The little fat man shook his head like a scared, bewildered child. "But nobody can do a thing like that! Making flesh transparent over bone so that only the bone is seen, like a living skeleton! It can't be done."

"The only answer is that it *has* been done," the other man ground out. "I'm going to pay, personally. I'll pay Miss Dean's share too, if she should refuse to do as Doctor Satan demands. Her head is worth more than three hundred and eighty thousand dollars to me. Not to mention my own!"

"Is there no way out, then?"

"None, gentlemen, as far as I can see. A man who could perform such miracles of horror as were performed on Stang and Joan Harwell is a man far beyond the reach of law or the police." He sagged lower in his chair. "I repeat, we're beaten—"

The outer door of the conference room opened. A man stood on the threshold an instant, then calmly came into the room. He was tall, dressed in dark gray that masked the width of his shoulders and the muscularity of his athletic frame. Steely gray eyes peered out from under black eyebrows. The eyes, combined with a large but aristocratic-looking nose, gave him a hawk-like appearance.

"Who are you?" squalled the little fat man in feeble wrath. His fear and uncertainty in the last hours came out in a burst of rage against the intrusion. "What are you doing in this room? We left orders that no one was to come in here!"

The man's large, firm mouth moved in a grim smile.

"Your orders were observed by your office help," he said. "Or, they would have been observed—but I walked past them out there and came in anyway."

"Who are you, anyhow?"

"My name," said the man, "is Ascott Keane—"

"Keane? Keane! That means nothing to me. I never heard of

you—"

"Just a minute," the voice of the man with the letter cut across the little fat man's voice. "That name means something to *me!* Ascott Keane... Aren't you a criminologist? From New York?"

Keane nodded.

"You're a sort of undercover man, working for no one but yourself? You tackle the big crime cases, sometimes when the regular police don't even know the cases exist?"

Again Keane nodded.

"For God's sake," quavered Phillips, "sit down and talk this over with us. I don't know if you realize it, but a man like you couldn't have come here at a better time!"

Ascott Keane looked at the letter Phillips handed him. He didn't even bother to read it. The signature, Doctor Satan, was all he needed to see.

His steel-gray eyes turned toward Phillips. "I didn't come here by any accident," he said quietly. "I came knowing I would find some such thing as this in Hollywood. I saw the news flashes yesterday about the hideous thing that had happened to Miss Harwell. Within a half-hour I was on a plane, with my secretary, Beatrice Dale, headed this way. At the airport when I landed I overheard a man talking of what had happened to Stang here. The man was on his way out of California, afraid it might happen to him too. So I came here at once, to place my services at your disposal."

"If you will," babbled the little fat man, "if you only will—well, you can name your own fee."

Keane's grim smile appeared again.

"I happen to be fairly wealthy, gentlemen. I am not working against Doctor Satan for fees. I'm working"—his eyes flamed—"to rid the world of a monster that will be emperor of all crime if he can't be destroyed!"

Phillips clutched his trembling hands together. "A man who can do what he has done," he said, "could be emperor of the world, I'd think. Who is he, Mr. Keane? You seem to know of him already."

"I know very little. I don't know his identity, nor does anyone else. But I do know that his is a name that is internationally famous for family wealth and power. I know that he is a man in the prime of life, who has become jaded with the pleasures of wealth and has turned to crime of a sort so advanced and bizarre that nothing like it has ever been known before—crime, incidentally, that must pay, in the end. That is one of the rules of his game. Though he is perhaps richer than any of you here, he must get money from his crimes or they would not be successful and he would not get his thrill from his grim play."

The little fat man clutched his arm. "You can stop him, can't you?" he squealed. "You can force him to leave Hollywood? Money! Successful crime! He'll get all the wealth of all us if he can't be stopped."

"I can do my best," murmured Keane. "Can any of you men give me a hint or clue of how the change was wrought in Stang or Joan Harwell?"

The eight looked at each other. Finally Phillips said: "I don't think any of us can give you a bit of help. I doubt if Stang himself can." His voice sank to a tearful whisper. "I wonder where Doctor Satan is, here in Hollywood. And I wonder if he has prepared my fate, and that of Dorothy Dean, already."

3.

THE MOTION PICTURE industry was still a new one; and R-G-R was not a pioneer company. None of its buildings was very old. But one of them, the property warehouse, was old enough so that all but a few veteran workmen had forgotten one feature of its construction.

Under the north end of the warehouse was a deep circular

pit. At one time the mechanism for a large, buried, movable stage had been in that pit; a stage set beside the original, smaller warehouse. Then the stage had been discarded, the warehouse had needed enlarging, and workmen had floored the unused pit and built the warehouse out over it.

Dark, secret, forgotten, it had yawned beneath the cement floor untouched for years. But it was untouched and forgotten no longer.

Less than four hundred yards from the conference room in which eight executives sat in pallid fear, the pit teemed now with activity.

In the center was a big electric motor, once the power source of the movable stage mechanism; then left to rust, outmoded; now cleaned and repaired again. It was running, sending out a low hum that filled the round pit with a murmuring noise.

Beside it were three men—one normal and average, the other two like gargoyles out of a nightmare.

The one was a workman in coveralls with rubber-insulated pliers in his hand. He shrank from the other two as he stood there. And no wonder.

One of these two was a giant of a man with no legs, who moved about between his swinging arms with an astonishing speed and agility. The other was a small fellow with matted hair over his face through which pale, cruel eyes peered like those of a sadistic monkey. The legless giant was Bostiff, servant of Doctor Satan. The smaller man was Girse, another henchman.

"I tell you this old motor won't hold together much longer," chattered the man in coveralls. "I didn't think I'd ever get it in working order in the first place."

"You got it in working order," rumbled Bostiff, "because you'd have been killed if you hadn't. You'll keep it in working order for the same reason."

"What are you using it for, anyhow?" babbled the workman. "And how long are you going to hold me here?"

A sinister smile appeared on Bostiff's stupid, savage face. "We'll hold you here as long as we need an electrician," he growled. "As for what the motor is used for—it's to make things happen to women like Joan Harwell and men like that damn rich man, Stang!"

"But how in the name of—"

"Shut up," snapped Bostiff, cracking the flat of his huge hand against the electrician's mouth.

The electrician staggered back, with blood flowing from his lips. And as he did so, a red light near the roughly cut entrance of the circular pit snapped on and off.

"It's *him!*" said Girse, hopping monkey-like toward the entrance.

Bostiff drew his gigantic body up on the backs of his hands as though standing to attention. Girse opened the door.

A figure came through that was as bizarre and extraordinary as something cut from a book of ancient illustrations; a figure that looked as though made up for the part of Lucifer in some ghastly masquerade.

A red robe sheathed its gauntness as a red scabbard might sheathe a lean blade. Red rubber gloves covered the hands; a red mask concealed the face save for burning black eyes; over the hair was a red skull-cap with two small knobs like sardonic devil's horns.

"Doctor Satan," murmured Bostiff hoarsely.

The electrician whimpered and drew back from the sinister form in red. Doctor Satan's jet-black eyes flicked over the unfortunate man, noting the blood oozing from his cut lips. "He has been trying to get away?" he asked Bostiff.

The legless giant shook his head. "Not that. Feared he could not keep this old equipment running."

The red mask over Doctor Satan's face moved a bit, as though to a smile. "He will keep it running," came the voice. "He loves life." Doctor Satan turned toward Girse. The little man's pale eyes wavered under the impact of the coal-black ones glaring from the eye-holes in the mask.

"Girse, there is more for you to do. Take the fine wire and run it from this pit to the R-G-R conference room. Attach it there to the light socket over the third chair on the left-hand side of the big table. The third chair, Girse! Make no mistake! It is in that chair that Bertrand Phillips sits."

A chuckle came from the masked lips. "Because that light gives diffused illumination instead of a beam of it like a spotlight, we shall be unable to control the rays quite so thoroughly. It will be amusing to see the result—if Phillips defies me. He might become a partial skeleton from the waist up, instead of merely exchanging a normal head for a skull."

"The wire is to be laid from this pit to the third light on the left side of the conference table," muttered Girse, parrot-like. "It shall be done, Master. And it is to be attached at this end?"

"To the transformer," nodded Doctor Satan. He paused an instant, then said gently, "This man has not been allowed to examine that transformer?"

Bostiff stared with dull ferocity at the electrician. "He has not."

Doctor Satan walked to one wall of the pit, near the humming old motor. A cable led from the motor to a black box leaning against this wall. Doctor Satan raised the lid of the box. Over his red-robed shoulder could have been observed a maze of cobweb wires in the box, with vacuum tubes studding the maze and glass terminals at the wire's ends. From the opposite end of the box came a small length of the fine wire that had led to the baby spot in the sound stage. To this would be spliced the wire leading to the conference room.

Doctor Satan's Luciferian head moved in a gesture of satisfaction. "All is ready. Prepare the wiring, Girse. And—if by the luck of the devil, my master, you should see Ascott Keane, you know what to do. If you can!"

Bostiff started. His dull eyes swung toward the red mask. "Keane?" he croaked.

"Yes. He is here. In Hollywood. He is to be killed at sight."

THE EIGHT MEN who headed the motion picture industry of the nation were in the R-G-R conference room at eleven-fifty next night. They faced Ascott Keane, who sat at the head of the board.

Bertrand Phillips' face was dewed with sweat. He kept staring at the clock, and running his tongue over his dry lips.

"In ten minutes," he said huskily, "if the payment is not made I am to become as Stang became! Keane, I must make that payment!"

Keane shook his head. His face was pale, tense. "Payment would only put off your fate. You would pay—and pay again. There would come a time when you could pay no longer, and then Doctor Satan would strike. For he must keep terror alive in the hearts of others, and to do that he must give a horrible object lesson at regular intervals."

"But what can we do? You have found out nothing. You admit it."

"No, I have not admitted it. I have found out a little. I have found out how Doctor Satan creates his ghastly illusion, for one thing. The man has devised a ray that changes the molecular arrangement of flesh. The ray, playing on flesh, so lines up the atoms of which that flesh is composed, that they fade from the range of vision of the average eye. It is as if a cloud of dust particles were so shaken as to line the particles up one behind the other. The cloud would become a thing of straight lines, seen end on, and hence not seen at all."

"But how is the ray controlled? From what place can it come?"

"I don't know," said Keane.

"And where does this Doctor Satan hide? Such a ray would mean equipment of some sort. Perhaps bulky equipment. Where is it concealed?"

"I don't know."

Phillips sprang from the chair he habitually used and paced up and down the room, with the eyes of the others following him.

"I can't stand the strain any longer! I want to pay!" He mopped at his forehead. "Fancy going through the rest of my life as Stang is doomed to do! Unless he kills himself...."

HE STOPPED ABRUPTLY, and a look of terror froze his face. "Do you hear it?" he whispered, after a moment.

Ascott Keane stared at him. "Hear what?"

"A voice." His whisper shivered in the conference room. "A voice! I heard it distinctly. It said: 'Remember—at midnight! Pay, or doom overtakes you at midnight!'"

Frozen silence chained the room for an instant. Then the eyes of all swung back to Keane.

"Telepathy," said Keane quietly. "There was no voice. The words grew in your brain, Phillips. But I think it means that Doctor Satan is very near us."

"I'm afraid!" panted Phillips. "Keane—what are you going to do?"

"I've told you. We will wait here till midnight. Satan will strike then, or attempt to. And the nature of the attack—and its source—will determine my next move."

"But he strikes at me!" sobbed Phillips. "At *me!* If you can't act quickly enough...."

He stopped and stared at the clock. Two minutes of twelve. With a groan he sank into his chair again and buried his face in his hands.

Keane stared at him with pity in his steely eyes, though inexorable purpose shaped his countenance. Then his eyes, too, sought the clock. A minute and a half to twelve. A minute....

How did Doctor Satan project his diabolical ray? How could he control the invisible current that made flesh transparent so that the bony structure beneath, whose mineral content no doubt made it impervious to the ray, could be made so hideously plain?

Forty seconds to twelve o'clock.

Phillips' breathing rasped through the silence. The little fat man choked out a curse. The rest of the picture executives held their breaths.

Thirty seconds. There was a slight flicker of the lights....

"Out of that chair!" yelled Ascott Keane, springing up so swiftly that his own chair was overturned. "That's how he does it! The lights! *Out of that chair!*"

Phillips stared at him in dazed lack of comprehension, with a kind of bleating noise coming from his lips, Keane bounded toward him.

"*Move, man!* Damn it—then—"

Keane's arm shot out. His hand clutched Phillips' coat collar and he pulled backward with all his strength. Phillips shot back against the wall, crying aloud, and Keane, with a leap and a smash of his hand, broke the light bulb in the ceiling over the spot where the man had been sitting.

Then, in the pandemonium of men unused to action and made into terrified animals by the nearness of peril, Keane looked grimly at his hand.

The fingers of that hand looked as if they had suddenly been turned to frosted glass. They were not quite opaque. In them could faintly be seen the outline of finger and knuckle bones. Doctor Satan's ray had accomplished a fraction of its deadly purpose before the bulb had been smashed.

"*Touché,*" he whispered. "A slight, partial victory for you, Doctor Satan. But also, I think, the beginning of the end."

He stared at the light socket.

"Of course! It came from the lights! I should have thought of it instantly. Joan Harwell's flesh became invisible when the spotlights were played on her. Stang's head changed under the ceiling light above his desk. The lights! With Satan's ray traveling along their beams!" He placed a chair beneath the shattered fixture, and examined it closely.

A fine bare wire came into view, soldered deftly to the socket, and threading up through the plaster of the ceiling with the main light wire. Disregarding the men who babbled and clutched at his arm, and who stared with horrified eyes at the milky fingers of his right hand, he walked to the window and leaned out.

The rays of a small flashlight showed him more of the fine wire stretched unobtrusively down the outside wall of the building. Down the wall, to the ground. And at the other end of that wire....

"Gentlemen," Keane's vibrant voice cut across the din, "I shall see you soon. And I think I will have conclusive news!"

He went down and out of the building, and around beneath the window. Off into the night the fine wire ran, so inconspicuously that it would never have been seen by eyes not searching specially for it.

Off into the night—toward the great dark building which was R-G-R's property warehouse!

Drawing a deep breath, Keane started tracing the wire—to the source of the ray and, he prayed, the man who had devised it.

4.

IN THE PIT beneath the property warehouse, Doctor Satan stood with his head bowed a little as though listening. He stood near the secret door, with Girse and Bostiff near him.

Behind the big electric motor, the electrician lay with eyes closed as though asleep. But under the fringe of his lashes he was watching the three near the door. And now and then, at long intervals, he moved a little. His movements were always in one direction—toward the mysterious black box to which a cable ran from the motor and from which a fine bare wire trailed on the opposite end from the cable.

Girse and Bostiff hardly breathed as they watched their master. The red-masked face lowered a bit more. They stared in silent respect, careful not to distract him.

They knew what Doctor Satan was doing. They had seen him do it often before.

Somewhere in the night outside, there was a person in whom Doctor Satan was vitally interested. He was reading that person's mind, through his marvelously advanced telepathic powers.

Suddenly the red-robed form stiffened. The red mask moved with words.

"Phillips will pay," the quiet voice stated." He has escaped the doom of the ray. Someone suspected the source, and broke the light bulb. Ascott Keane, probably." The red-gloved hands clenched. "But Phillips will pay. He has just telephoned his home to deliver to whatever messenger calls for it the package of currency he made up before Keane persuaded him to hold off. Girse, you will call for that package. First, as you go out, remove the wire from this pit to the conference room before it is traced. Then go to Phillips' home."

A malevolent chuckle sounded from the covered lips. "Half a million dollars! And it is only a beginning—"

THE WORDS STOPPED with awful suddenness, and coal-black eyes glaring from the mask's eye-holes began to gleam like fire opals.

Doctor Satan turned suddenly, and stared at the black box from which the fine wire ran. He stared also at the figure beside it.

The electrician had edged his way from the motor to the box. Leaning on one elbow, with his terrified gaze going constantly to the ominous red form by the door, he had raised the lid, and was peering in at the maze of wires and tubes the box housed.

The man cried out, a low, choked exclamation. There was no chance for him to pretend sleep as he had done before. Satan had whirled and caught him as though he'd had eyes in the back of his head and had watched all along.

No chance to conceal his fatal curiosity! The man could only stare, panting, into the awful black eyes, with his hand still holding open the lid of the box.

Doctor Satan walked slowly toward him. On either side, Girse and Bostiff moved with him. The terrible three advanced soundlessly, save for the slight rasp of Bostiff's calloused knuckles on the floor as he propelled his great body forward.

The man screamed, and cowered away from the box. He got to his feet, wildly, and tried to run. But there was no place to run to.

Girse got him on one side, and Bostiff on the other. They dragged him to confront Doctor Satan. The eyes behind the eye-holes in the mask were like small black windows into hell.

"So," murmured Doctor Satan, "you were curious to see what was in the box."

His red-sheathed arms folded themselves across his chest. His voice was as soft as satin—and as deadly as a snake's hiss.

"Scientific curiosity," he purred. "The inquisitiveness of the trained man. It is an odd thing. You are a prisoner here, afraid for your life—and rightly. But in the same room with you there is a bit of electrical equipment such as you have never seen before. Mysterious equipment. A new invention. And you must look. With death staring you in the face, you can still be moved by that professional inquisitiveness! The human animal is an odd object."

The man held by Girse and Bostiff said nothing. It was doubtful if he heard the words, or, hearing, understood them. He stood there, half fainting in the grasp of the sinister two, staring at the death in the coal-black eyes.

"So you would have read the secret of my ray," the calm voice went on, "and perhaps have exploited it for your own profit when you got out of here! Fool, you will never leave here. I could not have let you live, in any case, to bear witness as to what happened here. Now I am doubly forced to remove you."

The red-clad form seemed to grow, to tower taller in the low, cement-covered pit. "Girse! Bostiff! Stand aside!"

The two released the man and moved away from him. The electrician sank to his knees, unable to support his weight on his trembling legs.

"I saw nothing!" he chattered. "I learned nothing! I swear—"

He stopped. His lips continued to move for a moment, but no more words came. His eyes were like those of a bird paralyzed by a serpent as he kneeled there.

"You wanted the secret of the box?" purred Doctor Satan. "Well, you shall have it. But it will be a different secret from the one you already have an inkling of. That transformer of mine has two functions. The primary ray it can produce realigns molecules to make them invisible. The secondary ray causes atoms to collapse."

The coal-black eyes beneath the mask burned more fiercely yet.

"Have you ever speculated on what would happen if atoms collapsed? Matter is nothing but a few atoms moving within certain confines. The rest is space. Your body, for example, is not a solid at all, really. It would be interesting to see what would happen if the atoms of your body were compacted to their limits."

Gasping, the man stared at him. Doctor Satan moved to the box, with his eyes constantly impaling his victim. He reached within. A tiny light glowed in the side of the box. Doctor Satan trained its rays on the electrician.

The man began to scream. The agony of hell was in those

screams. But he did not move. His body twitched and jerked, but seemed incapable of muscular action.

On and on the screams continued, but gradually they changed tone. They grew higher, shriller in pitch, keeping time in their change of pitch with a phenomenal change in the man's body.

It was growing steadily smaller!

With poorly concealed terror in their eyes, Girse and Bostiff watched the fate of Doctor Satan's latest victim. They watched him shrivel from a man to a figure the size of a child. It was like peering down a telescope so adjusted as to reduce an adult form to a statuette the size of a doll.

On and on the unfortunate man screamed. But now the screams were like the shrilling of an insect, piercing the eardrums in the upper reaches of sound, but still scarcely audible.

"My God!" whispered Bostiff at last.

The man was a thing two inches high, that peered up and up at the towering giants in the mile-high room. Girse and Bostiff bent far down to see, keeping carefully out of the ray's beam. And they saw that the feebly shrilling, tiny thing that had been a human being was sinking into the packed earth that made the floor of the pit.

"Small as he is," the voice of Doctor Satan whispered, "he weighs as much as ever. And a thing two inches tall and weighing a hundred and sixty or seventy pounds will sink through pretty solid substance."

Now the ear could no longer hear the tiny shrilling of the man's screams. And the eye could no longer see him save as a blot, a pinpoint. The pinpoint remained the same in size....

Doctor Satan turned off the deadly little light. Girse and Bostiff bent till their eyes were within six inches of the pinpoint....

It was a hole in the hard-packed earth. A hole that might have been made by a fine needle. Down that hole the man had sunk. To where? God knew! Such concentrated weight might stop with the first rock layer of the earth's crust—or it might sink and sink till earth's center was reached! Either way, a slight threat to Doctor Satan's peace of mind had been removed.

The pit was very quiet as, sweating, Bostiff looked up at Doctor Satan again. The red-robed figure was moving convulsively. And with horror in even his savage heart, Bostiff read the meaning of the movement. Doctor Satan was laughing!

"At least he will see things, if he lives, that no human eyes have ever seen before—" Doctor Satan began.

But the sentence was never finished.

Another voice rang out in the pit, the voice of neither Girse nor Bostiff nor their hellish master. "Perhaps he will sink far enough to pay his respects to the demon you emulate, if there is a devil and a deep-buried hell."

A monkey-like cry came from Girse's lips, and a rasping exclamation from the thick lips of Bostiff. Doctor Satan whirled toward the door with his hands clenched so hard over the rim of the black box that it seemed as if the red gloves must split.

"Ascott Keane! By heaven—"

Keane walked slowly forward from the door to which he had trailed the wire. He was empty-handed. He needed no weapons for defense from such as Bostiff and Girse; and he knew that no ordinary weapons could injure Doctor Satan. But it was eerie to see him walk, without apparent defense, into the lair of the cold-blooded monster in red.

"YOU TRAILED THE wire," breathed Doctor Satan. "You found me—and you came alone. It is more than I could have hoped for."

Suddenly his body moved convulsively again. And Bostiff and Girse saw that again he was laughing, but with a laughter now more terrible than that with which he had watched the disappearance of the electrician.

"More than I could have hoped for, Ascott Keane. You came—but you shall not leave as you entered!"

"That's what you said when I found you beneath the graveyard in New York," said Keane. "But I left—and you very nearly stayed behind, dead!"

Doctor Satan's laughter stopped. His eyes glowed with cold triumph. "That time I did not have the black box. This time I have. *And you shall receive its emanations as the other did!*"

With the words his red-gloved hand flashed down. The tiny light glowed again—with its rays leveled straight at Keane.

Keane shouted once, a yell of agony, then was silent. But he was not silent because the agony had ceased. The torture of that beam of light was a thing that tripled by the second, a thing that knocked the breath from his body and seemed to sear him in flame.

With legs wide apart, he stood there like a figure of stone, unable to move a muscle. And as he stood there, he became smaller.

From Doctor Satan's masked lips came a grating cry more eloquent of triumph than the waving pennants of a victorious army. "I've got you!"

Ascott Keane's once tall frame had dwindled till his head was almost on a level with the head of the legless Bostiff. And still he stood there, braced on widespread legs, glaring at the figure in red.

"Success, and your doom, Ascott Keane!"

Doctor Satan moved closer to his victim, along the side of the clear-cut path of the beam. He thrust his red-covered face down close to Keane's face, which was a mask of agony.

"*Watch out!*" screamed Girse.

But the words came too late. Already, Keane had moved. His right hand shot out and clutched Doctor Satan's red-robed shoulder. His left gripped the fabric of the robe at his throat.

Indescribable amazement and almost superstitious fear glinted in the black eyes of the man who had roused such awe and such superstitious fear in others.

"My God!" he gasped. "My God! You moved! But you can't move! No one can move with the paralysis of the beam on him! It's… impossible… but you did …"

The hoarse, astounded words ended in a scream that was a faint echo of the shriek of the electrician. For Keane had pulled the red-cloaked figure before him so that the light from the black box caught it directly.

"See—how—you—like—it," whispered Keane, between gasps of agony.

Bostiff and Girse leaped forward. They clutched at Doctor Satan's robe and tried to tear him from Keane's grasp. But though his hands were so small that they looked like the hands of a child, they held their grip. His body was shrunken, but all its weight and all its muscle texture was left. He held the man with an unbreakable clutch.

"The light!" screamed Doctor Satan thinly. "Turn it—off!"

Both Girse and Bostiff leaped toward the black box, Girse bounded monkey-like over the earth floor. Bostiff swinging in great loops on his thick arms.

"*Quick!*"

Girse fumbled in the box and apparently found no switch, for the deadly light continued to shine, and the red-robed form continued to shrink in size. He looked at Bostiff.

The legless giant growled something impotently, and caught up a hammer. He raised it over the box.

"*No, no!*" Doctor Satan shrieked. "The ray must be reversed! Don't wreck the transformer!"

Bostiff dropped the hammer. Girse continued to fumble. The red-clad body was now less than four feet tall, scarcely an inch taller than Keane's grim, compacted frame.

"Behind the light!" choked Doctor Satan. "Girse—"

His cry stopped, as the light did. Girse had found the switch. Agony rolled from Keane. He could breathe again. But he kept his clutch on Doctor Satan.

Keane spoke, his voice piping because of his shortened vocal cords. But there was no lack of relentlessness in it. "Make me as I was before, or you die!"

"YOU CAN'T KILL me!" Doctor Satan, trying fruitlessly to break Keane's grip. "No man can kill me!"

"You thought it was impossible for any mortal to move while in the path of the atom-compacting beam," said Keane. "But I moved. You have occult as well as scientific methods of fighting—but so have I. I've come to close grips with you at last. You'll go to the devil, your maker, at once, if you don't do as I say."

"Bostiff! Girse!" panted Doctor Satan.

The two swung in on Keane. But, with their arms reaching for him, they stopped. His steely eyes were drilling into theirs, now Bostiff's, now Girse's. Under that hypnotic gaze they seemed to congeal.

"The switch, Girse," snapped Keane, moving Doctor Satan as he spoke, till he was in the path of the light instead of the red-robed body. "Move it backward—and we'll see what happens."

"Girse—don't move!" panted Doctor Satan. "You hear me—"

Girse moved like a sleepwalker toward the box.

"Girse—" It was a cry of rage from the red-masked lips.

But the monkey-like man went on, with Keane's power in the ascendency even over Satan's. His hand found the switch. The light in the box snapped on.

In no particular did the light seem to differ from that which had flashed like a baleful eye to collapse the atoms in a man's body and shrink him in stature. Yet, now, under what seemed the same beam, Keane's stature increased.

To five feet he grew, to six. His face was a stony mask of triumph—tempered by the fact that Doctor Satan grew as he did. The rays filtered through his body, apparently, to affect the red-robed body he had tried to block from the light.

"Enough," he snapped.

Moving mechanically, Girse turned the switch. Once more the light went out. And now Keane saw a curious thing. His half-transparent right hand, affected in the conference room, had become opaque again! In the beam, that had been altered back to normal along with his stature.

At every point in this encounter with Doctor Satan, he had won! Now he had only to destroy that black box by the wall, and then destroy its master....

With all the tiger strength in his big body, he thrust the red-robed figure suddenly from him and leaped toward the box. Doctor Satan staggered back against the wall. But his jet-black eyes suddenly flamed savage hope instead of impotent rage.

Keane did not see the change in expression. He was too intent on catching up the hammer Bostiff had dropped, too sure he had won completely.

He raised the hammer over the box, with Girse and Bostiff making no move to stop him. Doctor Satan's eyes flared like the live coals....

"And now, damn you, you're next!" grated Keane, bringing down the hammer on all the intricate and delicate apparatus in the box as if it were the red-covered skull he struck.

There was a soft explosion. Rays of blue flame leaped from the black box, bathing Keane in malevolent fire.

He choked, cried out, and staggered back. Still a third secret the box had yielded: almost certain destruction to him who wrecked it!

Doctor Satan stared at his two men, and, stirring as though waking from sleep, they moved toward him with Keane's occult chains broken. The blue flame licked at Keane's body.

"And so you die," came the voice of Doctor Satan, gentle now. "You have stopped me again. But this is the last time you'll interfere in my plans."

With Girse and Bostiff following him, Satan left the pit.

And behind them, as the door closed, Ascott Keane lay with death playing through his body from the wrecked black box....

The hum of the motor beside him grew to a wail, a scream, and then with a grinding roar subsided into silence. With no constantly tending hand to keep it running, the motor had at last burned out.

But Doctor Satan did not know that; he was not, after all, infallible.

THE CONSUMING FLAME

THE SERVICE TELEPHONE rang. The chauffeur, in whipcord pants and shirt sleeves, picked it up. The crisp voice of Besson, president and majority stockholder of Besson Motors, sounded out. "Carlisle, is the sedan in running order?"

The chauffeur stared at the phone with bulging eyes. His gasp sounded out. Then he collected his wits, and said: "Of course, sir."

"Bring it around to the side entrance, then," Besson ordered. "Full tank, check everything. I'm going to drive down to Cleveland. I'll drive it myself."

Carlisle kept staring at the phone in that unbelieving way. He opened his lips several times as it to express the amazement showing on his face. But no words came.

"Well? Do you hear me?" snapped Besson.

"Yes, sir," responded the chauffeur. "Certainly, sir. The sedan will be at the side entrance at once, sir."

He hung up, swore in profound perplexity, then shrugged into his whipcord coat and went downstairs to the garage.

He got into the sedan, an immense, gleaming thing built specially in the shops of the Besson Motors Company, and sent it out of the wide doors and down the graveled lane to the portico of the Besson mansion.

He got out of the car and waited respectfully for the master to appear. But while he waited, with a bemused scowl, he felt the radiator.

It was quite warm. The car *had* been used recently.

Besson came out of the door, followed by a footman who carried a small bag and a briefcase. Besson was a short man, heavy-set, inclined to rather loud checked suits which would have looked humorous on his squat frame had it not been for the quiet, tremendous power lying obviously in eye and jaw. No one laughed after looking into the motor magnate's face!

"Everything ready?" said Besson.

"Yes, sir," nodded the chauffeur.

Once more he seemed to be on the verge of saying something further, but once more he repressed himself.

BESSON GOT INTO the car. The footman put the bag and case in the rear. Besson nodded bruskly to the two servants, and sent the great machine out of the drive and swirling onto the street with the practiced rapidity that was still his after his early years as a race-track driver before he made his money. The sedan hummed out of sight in an incredibly short time.

Carlisle turned to the footman. In the chauffeur's eyes was something like fear, and small beads of perspiration stood out on his forehead. "Well, I'll be damned!" he said.

"What's up?" asked the footman.

"The boss! Either he's going crazy—or I am."

"Why?"

"An hour ago," explained Carlisle, "the chief came out to the garage. I was washing down the town car. He called to me to ask if the sedan was checked, and I said it was. He got into it and drove out of the garage with it. He had a bag, and I thought he was starting his Cleveland trip then. It seemed kind of funny that he came out to the garage himself for the car instead of having me bring it around, but I didn't pay too much attention to it."

"He started out an hour ago, with a bag?" said the footman, staring. "That's funny."

It isn't as funny as what happened next," Carlisle said. "In twenty-five minutes I heard a car roll into the garage—I was upstairs in my rooms. I came down, and there was the sedan". So I figured the boss had changed his mind and wasn't going to Cleveland after all.

"I went back upstairs, and three minutes ago, I'll be damned if he didn't phone out, ask if the sedan was checked, and tell me to bring it around to the side door here—just as if he hadn't been out in the thing himself a little while ago and *knew* it was checked and ready for the trip."

"First the boss came out and drove away himself?" repeated the footman. "Then, just now, he called for the car to be sent around, just as though he hadn't been in it the first time? That is funny! In fact—it's impossible."

Carlisle stared at him, forehead wrinkled.

"For the last hour," said the footman, "Mr. Besson has been in his rooms. I overheard him dictating a few letters to his private secretary, and I helped his man pack his bag. So he couldn't have driven out of the garage and then back again!"

The chauffeur bit his lip. He was silent for a long time as the meaning of the statement came home to him.

"He didn't drive out of the garage an hour ago and come back again twenty-five minutes later? Then who did? And why?"

The footman shook his head.

"Did you see the boss's face?"

"No," admitted the chauffeur. "As I said, I was washing down the town car. I heard his voice, and saw his body as he climbed in behind the wheel. But it was his voice! I'll swear to that."

"Well," said the footman slowly, "somebody besides Besson took that car out for half an hour. I wonder—if they did something to it?"

The chauffeur wiped sweat from his forehead. "It—it felt all right as I drove it out of the garage. But if a steering-rod was sawed half in two, or something...."

He stopped. Besson was a notoriously fast driver. He burned the roads at ninety miles an hour in his frequent trips to cities near Detroit.

"Maybe nothing was done to the car," said the footman through lips inclined to be a little pale. "Better not say anything, anyhow, about this. It might get you into trouble."

Carlisle nodded. He went back to the garage. But on his face a look of foreboding grew.

With all his heart he hoped the sedan hadn't been tampered with. But common sense told him it must have been. A man wouldn't take risk and trouble to get it off the Besson property for half an hour without some reason behind the act.

"Who took that car out?" he whispered to himself as he went up to his quarters again. *"And what did they do to it?"*

OUT ALONG THE road to Cleveland, Besson sent the great sedan leaping like a live thing, unaware of the short trip it had made before he stepped into it. It was only eight in the evening. The road was fairly crowded with traffic, so Besson did not hit his highest road speed. The speedometer needle quivered at seventy.

Besson frowned a little in a puzzled way. And he was puzzled. He squirmed uneasily behind the wheel of the car.

His nerves felt as though each tiny end were being filed. And his hair was acting queerly. It had a tendency to rise on his scalp, prickling and itching as if it had turned to fine wires.

He took his hands off the wheel for an instant to see if there were a short circuit somewhere in the ignition system that was sending a little current up the steering-column and into the wheel. His sensation was vaguely of the kind induced by a slight electric shock. But lifting his hands from the wheel did not lessen the sensation. And glancing down at the seat beside him he saw that a bit of paper from a torn cigarette package clung to the velous as tissue paper clings to a comb that has just been drawn through hair.

Traffic cleared. Frowning, Besson pressed harder on the accelerator. The car leaped up to ninety-four miles an hour, roaring down the road with a sonorous, low-pitched scream.

No man saw what happened after that. A dozen pairs of eyes were drawn to the spot a second later; but none observed the entire proceeding.

At one moment the special-built car was racing along the concrete. At the next there was an enormous flare of violet-colored light—and there was no car there. Furthermore, there was no trace anywhere on the road or along the road that such a car had existed.

Besson, the sedan and everything else, had utterly disappeared.

A woman behind the counter of a roadside stand was the first of the dozen witnesses to break the awful silence following the blinding violet flare in which a man and a car had vanished utterly from the earth.

"Oh, my God!" she screamed.

It snapped the spell. Truck drivers, pleasure car owners, proprietors and patrons of the roadside stands near by, raced to the spot.

"My God!" the woman screamed again, shrill and high.

The men did not cry out, nor did they say anything. They simply looked first at each other and then at the road.

A long black streak of charred concrete was all the evidence left of the speeding sedan.

2.

IN THE EXPERIMENTAL room of the Dryer Automobile Corporation, three men stood looking at a roadster.

Outside, in the great shop, all was thunder and clangor. The big machines that turned out the production stream of Detroit's third largest motor factory were so expensive that they had to be run day and night; so that now, at ten in the evening, the uproar was as great as at ten in the morning.

But here in the corner laboratory the roar penetrated only as a murmur, and in critical silence the three men examined the roadster.

It was a tremendous thing. The wheelbase was nearly a hundred and sixty inches. The hood sloped off and away from the windshield as if the power of a locomotive were under it—which was almost the truth. It gleamed with the finest and latest of enamels; a toy to delight the heart of a rajah.

"Everything is all right?" said the chief engineer to a mechanic in dungarees near by.

"Listen for yourself," said the mechanic, switching on the motor.

Standing right next to the hood, you could scarcely hear the engine. The engineer nodded. A sour look was on his face. "Twenty-eight thousand, that thing cost to build. Well, it's some car. It'll do about a hundred and forty, won't it?"

"A hundred and forty-eight," said the mechanic.

The engineer grinned bleakly. "And Dryer's pampered son will use the speed, too. This is certainly a birthday present! When is it to be delivered?"

"First thing in the morning," replied the assistant. "I got orders two hours ago. I'm to drive it up in front of the Dryer house and leave it to 'surprise' Tom Dryer. Though he knows all about it, of course."

The head engineer turned to the mechanic. "Stick a canvas over it," he ordered. "It would be a shame to get a scratch on papa's darling's plaything. I'll lock up."

The mechanic draped a great canvas, such as painters use, over the enormous roadster. The men went to the door of the experimental room, and stepped out into the clangor of the shop. The engineer locked it.

But behind that closed door was not emptiness.

As the lock clicked on the room and the roadster, a shadow stirred in a far corner near a work-bench. The shadow was that of a man who had been lurking in there for over an hour.

The man, a shapeless outline in the darkness, went toward the roadster. He lifted the canvas from over the hood and raised the hood catch. From his pocket he took what appeared to be an aluminum box, a third as big as a cigarbox. He attached it to the reverse side of the dashboard.

From the box trailed four fine wires. One went to each wheel of the roadster. Then the man worked with the wheels. To each spoke was attached an almost invisible, flexible fin of colorless material. The fine trailing wires were adjusted so that the ends would almost touch the fins on the spokes as the wheels whirled.

The shadowy figure fastened the hood down and replaced the canvas. It glided toward the door. Over the penetrating roar of the busy shop outside sounded a faint laugh. It was an icy, blood-chilling sound, twice repeated. Then the door opened as if it had never been locked—closed again, this time on a room containing no human thing, but in which was a roadster that was far indeed from being the same mechanism as that which had been hand-built in the shop.

It was hardly fifteen minutes later when the door was opened once more and the lights switched on.

THE CHIEF ENGINEER and another man were in the doorway. The other man was young, barely twenty-four. He was blond, dressed in a tuxedo, with no hat on and with his hair rumpled a little. His blue eyes were too bright, and he swayed a bit on his feet.

"I'm going to take her out, I tell you," he was insisting to the engineer. "It's my car, isn't it? Why should I wait till tomorrow?"

"Your father will be very disappointed if you don't wait till tomorrow and use it then, on your birthday, for the first time," urged the engineer.

But the man, young Tom Dryer, only shrugged. "I want it

tonight. And what I say goes around here. Wheel it out."

"But...."

"Wheel it out, I tell you!"

The engineer shrugged. He got into the roadster, after taking off the shrouding canvas. A side door of the laboratory opened. He drove the roadster out and onto the cinder driveway leading from the fenced factory grounds.

"Boy, that's a job!" said Tom Dryer, his too bright eyes taking in the lines and power of the machine. He got in behind the wheel. The motor boomed.

"So long."

The young man waved his hand to the engineer, and drove off. The watchman at the yard gate barely had time to open the portals for the flying thing. Then young Dryer was out and off.

The engineer shook his head. His face was pale.

"*So long,*" the boy had said. And it seemed to the older man that the words, and the parting wave of the hand, were prophetic. The farewell given for a long trip. A long, long one, perhaps.

"Drunk, and at the wheel of a thing that will go nearly a hundred and fifty miles an hour," the engineer whispered to himself. "I certainly hope...."

He turned back, into the experimental laboratory without finishing the sentence.

AN HOUR LATER, at a little after midnight, the great new roadster fled like a silent, tremendous night bird over the open highway. Swaying a little behind the wheel was young Dryer. Beside him sat a girl with unnatural-looking red hair, and predatory gray eyes set in a face as flawlessly regular—and as uninspiring-looking—as a beauty on a magazine cover.

"Seventy," said Tom Dryer. "And you don't feel it any more than if you were going twenty. Wait till we hit an open stretch! I'll show you speed, baby!"

"Let's be satisfied with seventy," urged the girl. She was a little pale under her rouge as she glanced from the speedometer to his face.

"Don't be like that," laughed the boy. That's an old maid's speed. I want to show you what this buggy can *do!*"

The girl was silent for a moment. She moved restlessly in the seat. "Say," she exclaimed finally, "do you feel funny?"

"How do you mean?" said Dryer.

"Kind of itchy and nervous," said the girl.

"Nope."

"Well, I do. And my hair feels like—like it was being pulled by someone. I don't like it. And I don't like going so fast on a road where you're apt to go round a corner and meet a car piling toward you."

"Like this?" laughed Dryer, steering around a curve on the wrong side of the road with screaming tires. "Hang on, kid! This is a straight stretch ten miles long. Bet we can make it in five minutes.

The needle went to eighty-five.

"Tommy," shrilled the girl. "Don't, please! I—I feel…."

"Hang on!" Dryer repeated, shouting over the rush of wind. "You'll never have another ride like this!"

The needle went to a hundred.

"Tommy!" shrieked the girl. "I—oh, *God*…."

The night was split by a violet flare that could be seen for miles. Like concentrated lightning it burst forth, shattering the darkness along the road.

It blazed into being with no warning, persisted for about a half-second, and died as suddenly.

And on the road, where the great roadster had been, with a man and girl in it, was nothing. A charred black streak showed. That was all.

THE CONSUMING FLAME

3.

IN A TOWER of the Book Hotel next noon, two men sat talking.

One, thin, of average height, with thin gray hair and eyes lidded by colorless flaps, that looked like the membranes veiling the eyes of a bird of prey, was president of the Universal Motors Corporation. Detroit's biggest automobile combine. The other was Ascott Keane, criminologist.

Keane got up from his chair and paced slowly back and forth across the room, his wide-shouldered, athletic body moving with the perfect muscular coordination of a trained athlete. His gray eyes were like chips of ice in his lean face. His black brows were drawn low.

"There is only one person on earth who could possibly be responsible for this," he said.

Corey, president of Universal, stared up at him. His veiled eyes looked more than ever like the eyes of a bird of prey—but of a very frightened bird, now. But even in his fright, he preserved his business caution. So many men, these days, claimed knowledge to which they had no right—and tried to extort money from you on that claim!

Who is that?" he asked, warily.

"Doctor Satan," said Keane.

Corey sighed and leaned back in his chair. "You are right. I guess you know the answer behind the—the disappearances, as you claim to do. The voice that spoke to me ended by insisting that its owner was somebody with the bizarre name, Doctor Satan."

Keane stared at the man. On Keane's face was a trace of impatience. He had read the man's thoughts, and didn't like them. But Corey, wealthy and powerful as he was, was only a pawn in this game. And one doesn't become annoyed with pawns. "Tell me about the voice," he said.

COREY SWALLOWED WITH difficulty. His face went greenish. "I was in my office. The office is sound-proofed, so that no voice could have come from outside. I was alone—even my secretary had been sent out—and the door was locked. I sit alone like that often when I want to think out a problem. And while I was sitting there—a voice came to my ears.

"'You have heard the news,' the voice said. "'You have heard how Charles Besson, and Thomas Dryer, son of Dryer the motor magnate, were consumed in a mysterious violet flame.'"

Corey looked at Keane like a terrified child. "It was almost like the voice of a second self speaking! It came so unobtrusively and—and naturally—that for a minute I wasn't startled at all. But then—I was. I realized that there wasn't a soul but myself in that locked, soundproof room. A voice—save mine—*couldn't* sound in there! But this one did; a soft, almost gentle voice, but it gave me chills. It went on:

"'You are thinking of that news now. You are planning how best to take advantage, in a business way, of the fact that Besson has died suddenly, and that Dryer is stunned and helpless from the blow of his son's death.'

"That—that was true," Corey blurted out. "It was as if someone was reading my mind...."

Someone was," Keane murmured. "Go on."

"Well, I *was* thinking about the business advantages that might accrue to Universal by the tragedies. Any man would. Corey shivered. "The voice said:

"'You have more important things to think about now. One is—your own life. Another is, how you can arrange your financial affairs so that you can take ten million dollars in cash from your fortune. For that is the price of your life. Ten million dollars. You will deliver it to my servant within the next few days, or you will die as Besson and Dryer died. I swear that, and Doctor Satan has never broken a vow.'"

Corey gnawed at the back of his bony, prehensile hand. "Those aren't the exact words, but that's the message given by the voice. And that was the name: Doctor Satan. I'd have said the whole thing was some clever trick, played by a master at hypnotism or ventriloquism to cheat me out of money. I'd have defied the orders of the voice, of course—if it hadn't been for the awful way in which Besson and Dryer's son died. My God, can anyone really do that—consume people in violet flame—at will?"

Keane shrugged. "According to the newspaper and many witnesses, someone can. What do you intend to do?"

"I don't know. That's what I came here to ask. I had about decided to pay, when you phoned. How did you happen to get in touch with me, anyway, at such a crucial moment? A bit of the old wariness and business suspicion came back to Corey's face.

Keane smiled. "The moment I read, in New York, of the inexplicable tragedies that had happened here, I flew to Detroit. Both victims had been prominent in motor manufacturing circles, so I looked for the next one. Your name is first on the list of prominence here, so I began with you, intending to run down the list of executives till I found one who had been threatened. I knew who was behind the crimes, and I know something of how he works, so my course of action was outlined for me. You told me you had been threatened; I asked you to see me—and that's the answer."

Corey sighed. "Shall I pay this Doctor Satan? Ten million dollars! It's colossal! But life is more important than money...."

"Even if the price asked was only ten cents," snapped Keane, "you shouldn't pay it."

But he'll kill me! The flame...."

Keane's long jaw squared. His firm mouth became firmer, grimmer. "I've fought this man more than once," he said. "I've beaten him before. I'll do it again. Don't pay. Your life will be saved—if you take one precaution."

"And that?" said Corey eagerly.

"Don't ride in a car. In fact, don't ride in anything capable of high speed: bus, train, anything." He glanced toward the door, indicating that the interview was over. "If you refrain from that, you'll be all right."

Corey went out. The door opened after his exit, and Keane's secretary came into the room. Tall, lithe, beautiful, with dark blue eyes and hair more red than brown, she stared at her employer with a look in her eyes that would have revealed much to him had he been gazing at her at the moment instead of looking unseeingly out the window at the roof-tops of the automobile city.

Beatrice sighed and came up to him.

"You have found out how the deaths were caused?" she asked, professionally, with the glow hidden in her eyes.

Keane nodded absently. "I have found out several things. Not exactly, in detail, but closely enough to map out my plans.

"Doctor Satan is up to his old methods of harnessing the forces of nature to do his crimes for him. It was nature that killed Besson and Dryer's son. Static electricity.

"Both Besson and young Dryer were notoriously fast drivers. Very well, Doctor Satan contrived a method of generating and storing static electricity in enormous amounts. Probably the generating was done by the wheels themselves, turning at fast speeds. The electricity was stored in some small device that wouldn't be noticed if examination was made of the car before it was taken out. When a voltage was built up that would be far beyond any amount that could be registered on any recording instruments yet devised, it exploded the storage device—and utterly consumed car and occupants and everything else. That is the only thing that would explain the violet light told of by the witnesses. In a way, a natural death. But a gruesome, fearful, spectacular death—which would so horrify and cow other motor manufacturers that they would give Doctor Satan anything he asked rather than risk the same fate themselves."

"Horrifying and fearful enough," breathed Beatrice with a shiver. "Ascott—you have escaped the other deaths this fiend has invented. Can you escape this? For of course he'll turn the new weapon on you, too. More than anything else on earth, he wants to get rid of you. He'll try to kill you as soon as he learns you are here."

Keane laughed a little, without humor. "As soon as he knows I'm here? My dear, you underestimate him. As surely as we live and breathe—he knows that now!"

At twenty minutes past noon a man in the dungarees of the Union Airlines mechanics turned off a sidewalk into the yard of a factory. It was a small factory, two stories high, less than an eighth of a block square. Its windows were boarded up. The yard was grown with weeds.

A man sat in the open doorway of the deserted-looking building. He was an elderly man, poorly dressed. His faded blue eyes stared straight ahead with curious blankness. His face was stubbled with three days growth of grayish beard.

The man in dungarees came up to the doorway. A small, monkeylike fellow with a mat of hair over his face through which peered small, cruel eyes, he hopped as he walked in an oddly animal way.

"Is anyone in?" he asked the watchman.

The watchman's faded blue eyes did not move. They continued to look straight ahead as he sat there like a statue. "Yes, sir," he said.

"How many?" asked the man in dungarees.

"Two, sir."

The watchman's lips moved like mechanical things. He looked and acted like something actuated with springs and wires.

The little man in dungarees shivered a bit. His pale eyes narrowed with an emotion that might have been fear. He walked past the watchman, who did not move a muscle, and into the factory building.

It was dark in here in spite of the noon daylight outside. The reason was that the entire inside of the first floor was draped closely in heavy black fabric, which also stretched from a frame crossing in front of the door, so that the door could be open innocently and yet outside eyes could not see in and detect the black drapes.

The little man passed under the door drape. He entered the dark interior, which was dimly lit by red electric bulbs so that it resembled a corner of some weird inferno.

Over a bench on which was a glistening small receptacle about a third the size of a cigar-box, a figure bent which was like something seen in a fanciful illustration of hell: a tall, gaunt figure draped from head to heels in a red robe, with red gloves shielding the hands, and a red mask of the figure, a skull-cap, from which protruded two Luciferian horns in imitation of the horns of the Devil.

Next to this eerie figure was the body of a legless man—gigantic torso supported by calloused, powerful hands.

"Girse," said the imperious, red-draped figure, without turning its head.

The little man in dungarees drew a quick breath. The red figure had its back toward him. It could not have heard his soft entrance. Yet, as though it had been facing him, that entry had been noted.

"Yes, Doctor Satan," he said.

"Report, please."

Girse hopped closer in his monkey-like fashion, and stood next to Bostiff, the legless giant. From under the voluminous dungarees he drew a flat leather case.

"Miller, the truck manufacturer, did as you ordered," he said docilely to Doctor Satan. "Here are thirty checks, of one hundred thousand dollars apiece."

Doctor Satan's coal-black eyes glowed from the eyeholes of the red mask. In them was glacial triumph.

"It is well. You got into the Union Airlines hangar?"

"I did," said Girse, his pale eyes glinting.

"You attached the storage cube?"

"I did, with the wire leading to the propeller, and with fins attached to the propeller blades."

Unholy satisfaction glittered in the coal-black eyes. Then it was dimmed, and the light of rage glowed there.

"It will be as we wish it—unless Keane discovers it in time."

"Keane—is here?" quavered Girse.

Bostiff spat out an oath, his dull eyes red with fury.

"He is here," replied Doctor Satan. "I gleaned that from the mind of Corey. He is here, in Detroit. And Corey has seen him and was advised not to meet my demands. That was foreseen—which is why you attached the storage cube to the propeller. He is in a tower suite at the Book Hotel, with his secretary Beatrice Dale. And he is daring to match his wits against mine once more."

Icy murder flared in the coal-black eyes. The red-gloved hands closed slowly, quiveringly.

"This time, Ascott Keane dies! This time I will get rid of the one obstacle between me and unlimited power, through fear, over the minds of men."

He turned back to the bench, with his red-gloved fingers delicately adjusting tiny, fine plates of some substance like mica which packed the interior of the small metal container on which he was working—a container like that which had been attached to the sedan of Besson and the roadster of young Tom Dryer.

"With Keane out of the way," he said, "I could be supreme on earth—and I will be!"

4.

THE LATE EVENING papers gave the news of Doctor Satan's latest blow against the ancient law: Thou shalt not kill. Beatrice Dale brought the paper in to Keane, who was about to go out, and handed it to him without a word.

> *This afternoon at four o'clock Mr. H.C. Corey, president of Universal Motors, was killed in an airplane accident twenty miles out from the Detroit landing-field.*
> *Mr. Corey, called on urgent business to New York City, chartered the plane for himself alone and took off at three-forty. The plane circled the field once, then headed east. Twenty miles from the field it exploded.*
> *Union Airline officials have no explanation to make. The explosion, according to eye-witnesses, was accompanied by a violet flame, which is not the type of flame resulting from gasoline explosions...*

Keane read the account, then crumpled the paper in a grim hand. "*Corey dies in unique plane accident,*" the item was headed. And across half the front page was spread the account

Keane drew a deep breath. "'Called on urgent business to New York City,'" he quoted. "The fool! He committed suicide. Doctor Satan gave that call, of course. And Corey, fearing financial loss, disobeyed my orders. I told him not to ride in anything capable of speed."

He went toward the door. "I'm going to Besson's home," he said to Beatrice. "I want a talk with Besson's chauffeur about the sedan the man was killed in. I'll be back in an hour."

CARLISLE, BESSON'S CHAUFFEUR, bit his lips as he faced Keane in the cool dimness of the great garage.

"I suppose I should have gone to the police about it," he said unsteadily. "But I couldn't see what good that would do them, and I knew I'd get in a lot of trouble over it."

"Tell me more exactly what happened," Keane urged.

"Well, at a little before seven o'clock, I was in here washing down the town car. Mr. Besson came out and asked if the sedan was ready. I said yes, and he got into it...."

"You're sure it was Besson?"

"No, later I realized I couldn't be sure," Carlisle admitted. "I heard his voice, and I'll swear it *was* his voice. And I saw his back, and he was wearing a checked suit as he usually does. But I'll have to confess I didn't see his face."

"Girse," murmured Keane. "Made up as Besson—with Satan himself speaking in Besson's voice from a distance...."

"What?" said Carlisle.

"Nothing. Go on."

"That's about all. The man I thought was Mr. Besson went out, with a bag and everything as if on the Cleveland trip, and then came back in about half an hour. I didn't see him return—I only heard the car drive in and went down and found the sedan. The first I knew something was wrong was when Besson called, half an hour later, asking if the sedan was ready for his trip! I thought he'd gone crazy, then."

"You have no idea where the sedan was driven in that half-hour?" said Keane.

"None at all," said Carlisle. "And now, of course, no one will ever know. Because there isn't any sedan to look over any more."

Keane's lips compressed. "There's no sedan, but I think we can find out where it went in that fatal half-hour. Have you cleaned out in here recently?"

Carlisle looked at the floor of the garage and shook his head. "We haven't kept up quite the schedule we usually do since the boss—died. The garage floor hasn't been swept...."

"Good," said Keane. "Where did the sedan stand in here?"

Carlisle indicated the space nearest the end wall. Keane went there, bending low, critically examining the concrete. "The man drove it back into this spot before Besson took it out?"

Carlisle nodded. Keane got to his knees. There were slight flakes of dust and dirt from a car's tires on the floor. Keane took up some of these and put them carefully in an envelope. He turned to go.

"Shall I tell the cops about this?" said Carlisle, white-faced.

Keane shook his head. "It would get you in a lot of trouble, as you said. And I don't think it would do any good. You can't be blamed for being fooled by the man who killed your employer."

He went out, with the chauffeur's thankful and admiring gaze following him.

At the curb before the Besson home was the coupe Keane had hired to get about the city in. He got in behind the wheel and headed for the near-downtown section.

He was on his way to the laboratory of a friend of his. In New York he had his own laboratory, vastly better than the one owned by his friend; but he hadn't time to send to New York and he thought the friend's equipment would be sufficient enough to perform the task he wanted.

As a man will do sometimes, Keane broke his own strict rule—disregarded the very warning he had given Corey: not to ride in anything capable of speed.

In a hurry to get the scrapings of the sedan's tires analyzed, he drove-like a black comet along the boulevards; drove that way till suddenly his hair began to feel as though it were standing on end and every nerve in his body tingled and rasped with exasperating sensitivity.

His face paled a little then. With his lips drawn back to show his set teeth, he jammed down the brakes of the car.

"Static electricity!" he whispered to himself. "The devil! Does he think he can get *me* that way?"

He opened the hood of the car. Attached to the underside of the dash was a metal container. From it led a fine wire. The wire went to the fan whirling at the front of the motor. And to the fan-blades fine fins of some flexible, colorless stuff had been attached.

With a savage jerk, Keane ripped the wire loose from the metal box. But the box itself he detached carefully to take home for futher study. He knew that the secret of the violet explosions lay in that box; a secret consisting in what possible manner of substance could act as a storage battery for static electricity and store the stuff till an explosion point was reached.

With Doctor Satan frustrated and his life no longer in danger, Keane went on to his friend's laboratory and presented the tire scrapings for analysis.

"Mixed in with the normal dirt of the streets," the friend reported a little later, "there are two substances which might tell you where the car has been. One is a trace of cinders, such as is to be found in many factory yards. The other is a powdered chemical which turns out to be a special kind of lime fertilizer."

"So?" said Keane.

"So this," replied the man. There is only one plant in Detroit which manufactures that particular type of lime fertilizer. That is a plant out on Jefferson Avenue." He gave the address. "It is at least possible that Besson's sedan was driven near the plant during its half-hour absence and picked up a little of the fertilizer, spilled on the street from trucking."

"And the trace of cinders?"

The man shrugged.

That particular company does not have cinder surfaces in its yards. I telephoned to find out. They must have come from somewhere else."

Keane thanked him and went out. His light gray eyes were glittering, his firm mouth was a bleak slit in his face. Cinders, and dust of a fertilizer made only in one spot in the city! He thought that should provide a trail to the spot in Detroit where Doctor Satan lurked like a human spider spinning new and ever more ghastly webs.

He went to the Book Hotel, to study the shining metal container he'd got from his dash, and try to penetrate its secret, before making the next and last move that should bring him face-to-face with Doctor Satan himself.

AT THE HOTEL desk he told the clerk to ring Miss Dale's room and ask her to come to his suite with notebook and pencil. His phone was ringing when he opened his door.

"Miss Dale is not in her room, sir," the clerk reported.

Keane's eyebrows went up. Then they drew down into heavy, straight black lines over his light gray eyes as apprehension began to gnaw at his brain.

He went to the room in the tower suite which he had set aside to use as office and workroom. "Beatrice," he called, looking around for the quietly beautiful girl who was more right hand to him than mere secretary.

The room was empty. So were the other rooms. With the apprehension mounting to chill certainty in his mind, Keane looked around. He found his hands clenching and sweat standing out on them as his quick imagination grasped the significance of her absence.

An exclamation burst from his lips. Half under the desk in his temporary office he saw a glove. It was a tan glove of the type he had seen Beatrice wear last. Just the one glove.

Near the door, now, he saw the other....

"My God!" he whispered.

Beatrice had gone out of the hotel. That was a certainty. But—she never went out ungloved. It was one of her fastidious habits. Yet there were the gloves she wore with the brown street costume she'd had on when Keane left her....

His head bent swiftly, and a terrible fear leaped into his eyes. A voice had sounded.

"Ascott Keane," it said—and it was hard to tell whether it

was an actual voice or a thought making itself articulate in his own brain. "You escaped the death waiting for you under the hood of your coupe. You shall face death later at my hands, in spite of that. But before death comes for you, you shall have the pleasure of imagining, as you are doubtless doing now, the lingering fate that shall be dealt out to your able assistant, Beatrice Dale. I have her, Keane. And when you next see her, if you ever do, I'm afraid you'll be unable to recognize her."

There was a low, icy laugh, and the voice ceased.

"My God!" breathed Keane again.

And then he was racing from the room, with agony in his heart but keeping the agony carefully walled off from the cold and rapid efficiency with which his keen mind could work in times of great emergency.

There is only one plant in Detroit which manufactures that particular type of lime fertilizer," his laboratory friend had said. "That is a plant out on Jefferson Avenue...."

Keane got into the coupe, wrenched the wheel around, and pressed the accelerator to the floorboard as he sped out to Jefferson Avenue.

5.

KEANE WENT STRAIGHT to the plant from near which the tires of Besson's sedan had picked up the significant trace of fertilizer. There he paused a moment outside the high wire fence enclosing the company's grounds. But he hesitated only a moment. There were no cinders in that yard, as the laboratory man had said. And the sedan had been some place where cinders had paved a space. Also the company grounds were swarming with workmen. No one could drive a car in, tamper with it, and drive away again unnoticed.

He started on away from the plant, and father away from

the center of town. There was only the one direction to go in. The sedan, to have picked up the cinder trace, would have had to go beyond this point.

He drove very slowly, examining intently the properties on each side of the street. But it was only with an effort that he kept himself from driving like mad, senselessly, aimlessly, so long as he covered a lot of ground in a hurry.

Beatrice....

Never had he had such urge for speed—but speed did no good when he didn't know where he was going.

Beatrice....

"I have her, Keane. And when next you see her, if you ever do, I'm afraid you'll be unable to recognize her."

That was what Doctor Satan had said. Where in God's name was she? And what was Satan planning to do to her?

He bit his lips, and kept the coupe down to a speed at which he could scan the buildings he passed. And then he started a little, and lowered his head rapidly and drove by the place that had attracted his attention. The place was perfectly innocent-looking. It was a small factory less than fifty yards from the sidewalk on the left-hand side. But two things had riveted his attention.

The first was that the grounds around the factory were cinder-paved. The second was that the place was abandoned, with boarded-up windows and an air of desolation.

An abandoned factory, in a not-too populous part of the city....

Keane got out of the coupe and walked back a half-block. He saw that an elderly man, patently a watchman, sat in the open side-doorway of the factory.

He hesitated an instant, then walked openly toward the man. He couldn't have hidden his approach anyhow, and thought he could overpower the watchman if his suspicions of the place were verified and the man tried to give an alarm to others inside.

His eyes fastened to the watchman with increasing curiosity as he approached. He saw that the man was cheaply dressed, with faded blue eyes and a stubble of grayish beard on his face. And he saw that the eyes stared oft and away in the oddest, most unseeing way imaginable. Also he noticed how unmoving the old man was. He sat in the doorway like a statue, not shifting his position in any way. Even when Keane had come quite close, he did not move.

KEANE STARED DOWN at him with growing grimness. He could see the man's pulse beat in the vein in his throat; but it seemed to him that the pulse-beat was incredibly slow. He could see the hair of his stubble of beard closer; and it appeared that the flesh of the man's face had receded from hair-roots, more than that the hair itself had grown.

Keane felt a chill touch his spine. Realization, like a spike of ice, began to sink into his brain. But he still could not quite believe.

"Hello," he said to the man, in a low voice. "Hello," the man replied.

He said the word with his lips hardly moving, and with his eyes staring blindly straight ahead.

Keeping his voice almost in a whisper, so that it could not be heard through the open doorway in which the man sat, he said: "Are you alone here?"

"There are—four inside," the watchman replied, creakily.

Keane moistened his lips.

"What is your name?" he asked.

"It is…."

The man stopped, like a run-down machine. His faded, unblinking eyes stared straight ahead.

Keane stopped, then. He touched the watchman's wrist, and shuddered.

Perceptibly he could feel a pulse, beating perhaps twenty to the minute. He could see the man's chest rise and fall with immensely decelerated breathing.

Pulse, and breathing. And the man could speak and, up to a point, answer questions. But that man was dead!

Keane dropped the wrist, icy as something long immersed in water. His lips were a thin line in his face. A dead man on guard! A watchman whose presence here would be missed, and who therefore had been left in his accustomed place so that passers-by would have no suspicion that anything unusual was taking place inside!

He had found Doctor Satan. The presence of a living dead man where a live and vital human being should be, proclaimed the fact like a shout.

Keane drew a long breath. Then he stepped past the dead man, who sat on with faded blue eyes staring into space. He entered the doorway. His eyes, accustoming themselves to the darkness, detected the presence of the black drapes swathing the interior and making of it a smaller room-within-a-room. At the same time his ears caught a soft, gentle voice—a voice that made the hair on his neck crawl with remembrance and primeval fear. The voice of Doctor Satan.

Edging his way along between the drapes and the wall, careful to touch neither, Keane moved to a spot where the soft but imperious voice sounded farthest away. Then he took out a knife, slit the black fabric, and looked through.

The first thing his eyes rested on—was Beatrice Dale.

She sat on the floor of the abandoned factory with her slim arms down by her sides, and her silk-sheathed legs out in front of her. Arms and legs were bound; and a gag was around her lips. Over the gag her eyes stared out, wide and frightened, yet, in the last analysis, composed. Keane felt a hard thrill of admiration for her fortitude go through him as he looked into her eyes.

Over her bent the figure he had seen before several times in the flesh—and many times in nightmares. A tall, gaunt body sheathed in a red robe, with a red mask covering the face and a red skull-cap over the hair.

Keane bit his lips as he noted the knobs, like horns, that protruded from the Luciferian skull-cap. Those mocking small projections were the keynote of the character motivating Doctor Satan. A man who took pride in his fiendishness! A man who robbed and killed, and broke the laws of man and God, not for gain, because he already had more than any one person could spend, but solely for thrills! A being jaded with the standard pleasures of the world, and turning to monstrous, sadistic acts to justify his existence and give him the sense of power he craved!

Next to the red-robed figure, Keane saw Doctor Satan's two malevolent henchmen, Girse and Bostiff.

Girse, small and monkey-like, was gazing at the girl's form with his pale eyes like cruel beads in the hair covering his face. Bostiff, supporting his giant's torso on his calloused hands, swayed back and forth in a sort of full ecstasy.

AGAIN DOCTOR SATAN'S voice came to Keane's ears. "I have not yet decided what I shall do with you," the soft voice pronounced. "You are beautiful. I am alone in the world—and it is not inappropriate that Lucifer take a consort. But that consort should not be a mere living woman such as lesser beings have. You noticed the watchman as you were borne into this place?

Keane saw a spasm twitch Beatrice's face, saw her eyes wince with terror.

"I see you did," Doctor Satan said. "And I see you sensed his state. A dead man, my dear—yet a man who will breathe and move in a sort of suspended animation as long as I shall will it. A man whose automatic reflexes can still dimly function, so that the dead brain may direct the muscles of throat and lips to answer verbally any questions not too complex, and so that the body may move to orders not too difficult."

Doctor Satan's grating, inhuman laugh sounded out. "It comes to my mind," he said, "that Lucifer might here find a fitting mate. The devil's consort—death. A beautiful woman who must answer as required, and who must move without question to fulfill her master's least demand. That would be unique—and amusing. Think how Ascott Keane would react to that."

Keane, motionless behind the drape, with his eye to the slit in the fabric, felt perspiration trickle down his cheeks. The man was diabolical. He was beyond madmen in the aims he pursued and goals he achieved. Yet he was not mad. That was perhaps the most hideous part of it. He was sane. Icily, brilliantly sane!

And now Doctor Satan went on with that in his voice which made Keane suddenly tense in every muscle as instinctive small warnings prickled in his brain.

"The reactions of Ascott Keane to that spectacle… Very interesting. I must see them. In fact—*I will see them!*"

Like a flash of light the red-robed body whirled. The coal-black eyes of the man glared through the eyeholes of the red mask—glared straight into the eyes of Keane, pressed to the slit in the black fabric.

Impossible that he should see Keane's eyes in the dim red light of the black-shaded room! Impossible that he should have heard Keane breathe or move! Yet he knew the criminologist was there!

For a moment that seemed an age, Doctor Satan's glittering black eyes stared into Keane's steely gray ones. Then the red mask moved with words. "You will come here, Ascott Keane."

Keane's legs moved. Savagely he fought the muscles of his own body, which were like relentless rebels in the way they disobeyed the dictates of his will. But the muscles won.

His legs moved. And they bore him forward, like an automaton, so that the black drapes moved forward with him, slithered over his head, and sank back into place behind him.

He walked up to where Doctor Satan and Girse and Bostiff ringed the bound, helpless girl. There he stood before the man in red, eyes like steel chips as they glinted with savage but impotent fury.

"Will you never learn, Keane, that my will towers over yours, and my power goes beyond yours?" Doctor Satan crooned.

Keane said nothing. He looked at Beatrice, and saw that into her eyes had crept a horror that went beyond the fright that had entered them at mention of the living dead man who guarded this red-lit inferno.

He could feel his body responding sluggishly to the commands of his brain, now. But the recovery was feeble. He could not have moved toward Doctor Satan to save his life, though with every fiber of him he craved to throw himself on the man and rip the red mask from his face and batter that face into a thing as unhuman in appearance as its owner's soul was in reality.

"Girse," said Doctor Satan.

That was all. The little man hopped in obedience. He came close to Keane with his right hand hidden behind his back.

Keane gasped and tried to throw his arms up as he read in the little man's mind the command Satan had wordlessly given him. But his arms moved too slowly to prevent the next act.

Girse lashed forward with his own arm. Something glittering in his right hand pressed into Keane's flesh. He felt a sharp sting, then complete physical numbness.

He sank to the floor. But though his body was a dead thing, his mind continued to function with all its normal perception.

Doctor Satan's glacial laugh rang out.

"The great Ascott Keane," he said. "We shall see how he meets his own fate—and that of his efficient secretary, toward whom his secret emotions are not quite as platonic as his conscious mind believes."

He turned to the little man. "Girse," he said again. That was all. The rest of the command was unspoken. But all too clearly, with the telepathic powers that were his, Keane caught that too. He fought in an agony of helplessness to make his body move, as Girse hopped toward Beatrice. But he was as immobile as though paralyzed.

Again Girse held a hypodermic needle, but this was a larger one than the one had plunged into Keane's body.

WITH HIS PALE eyes shining, the monkey-like little man pressed the needle into Beatrice Dales's bound left arm. The girl closed her eyes. A strangled moan came through the gag that bound her lips. Keane croaked out an oath and struggled again with a body as limp and moveless as a dead thing.

"The drug in that hypodermic is quick-acting," Doctor Satan said. "Observe, Keane."

With starting eyes, Keane saw how true the words were.

Into the girl's eyes already had crept the terrible, unseeing look that characterized the faded eyes of the thing outside in the doorway. He could see the pulse in her throat slow down. Slower... slower....

"She's dead, Keane," said Doctor Satan emotionlessly. "Though, dead, she will obey better than alive. Girse.

Once more the monkey-like small man approached the girl. In his hand was a knife. He slit the bonds that held her, and removed her gag. "Come to me, Beatrice Dale," commanded Doctor Satan.

Through a red haze, Keane saw the girl get to her feet, slowly, unsteadily. She walked toward the figure in red, moving like one asleep. "You are mine, Beatrice Dale," Doctor Satan said softly.

There was a perceptible hesitation. Was the girl's brain, even in death, struggling against the monstrous statement? Then her lips moved, as the lips of the thing in the doorway had moved, like the lips of a mechanical doll. "I am yours."

Keane panted on the floor. He could not even cry out. His

vocal cords were numbed by the drug, as was the rest of his body.

Doctor Satan stared down at Keane. "And so, my friend, we see the end. Your aide has become—as you see. You yourself shall presently die as Besson and Dryer and Corey died. The end... Bostiff."

The legless giant hitched his way forward on his long arms.

"The flywheel, Bostiff, Doctor Satan said. "Girse, attach the cube of death to Keane."

AND NOW KEANE glanced at a thing he had seen only perfunctorily, and noticed not at all, until now: On a length of rusty shafting in the rear of the factory room was a big flywheel, which had performed some power service when the factory was busy. To this was belted an electric-motor.

Bostiff hitched his way to the flywheel. As he went, he trailed behind him a fine wire only too familiar to Keane; the kind of wire that had led to the metal box Keane had detached from his coupe before death should strike him. To the spokes of the flywheel, Keane knew, were fastened the colorless, unobtrusive fins which generated the static death that had struck down the motor millionaires.

Girse fastened to Keane's chest a metal cube which had been resting on a low bench near by. Bostiff fastened the other end of the wire leading from it, to a point near the flywheel. Then he started the motor.

The big flywheel started turning over. Doctor Satan's eyes burned down at Keane.

"In five minutes, approximately," he said, "there will be a violet flare. In that flare, you will be consumed. Just before it occurs, the drug that holds you will begin to disappear, so that you shall be the more keenly aware of your fate. We shall, naturally, wait outside till the bursting into flame of the building announces that you are no longer alive to annoy me.

He turned toward the dead girl. "Come, my dear."

Beatrice walked toward the draped door, her body swaying a little from the impairment of her sense of balance, her eyes staring unblinkingly ahead. Doctor Satan followed. Behind came Girse and Bostiff.

Doctor Satan raised the drape. The three passed through ahead of him. He stared at Keane. Four minutes now," he said. And then he followed the others.

6.

KEANE WAS LYING so that he could see the watch at his wrist. He watched the little second hand fly around its circle three times. He listened to the whirling of the great flywheel, gathering static electricity through its fins; such a colossal store of it as even the lightning could not rival—to be held in the mysterious metal cube on his chest till it had gathered beyond the cube's power to contain it any longer. Then the cube would be consumed, and consume everything around it like a tremendous blown fuse….

Keane stared at the watch. He had a hundred seconds of life left. One hundred seconds….

But his counting of the seconds was not actuated solely by the fear of death. His mind had never been keener, colder than it was now. Ascott Keane was waiting for the first sign of returning movement in his muscles. When that occurred he had a plan to try. It was a plan the success of which hinged on facts unknown to him. But its steps seemed logical.

He felt burning pain in his finger ends, then in his hands. Grimly he moved his fingers, searing with returning life. He flexed his hands. He had forty seconds—perhaps a little longer, perhaps a little less, for Doctor Satan could not foretell to the second when the static force stored in the metal cube should burst its bonds in the terrific violet flare.

Now he could move his right arm feebly from the elbow. He dragged it up by sheer will till it went to his coat pocket. In that coat pocket was a factor—which Doctor Satan had not reckoned with: the metal cube with its broken end of wire, which Keane had taken from his coupe for analysis which he had not had time to make.

He got the cube from his pocket. His watch told him he had twenty seconds, a third of a minute, to live.

With maddening slowness, his hand moved. It found the wire from the box in his pocket. With numbed fingers it pressed the broken bit of wire to the other cube....

The fifteen seconds that passed then were an age.

Keane's idea was that with two of the storage cubes hooked together, it would take twice as long for the spinning flywheel to generate the static force that was presently to consume him. As simple as that! And, even though he knew nothing of the substance in the cubes capable of storing the force, he thought its action must be as logical as it was simple.

If it took minutes longer for the building, with Keane in it, to go up in violet flames, Doctor Satan might come back to see what was wrong....

The zero second approached, passed. Keane held his breath. Ten seconds passed, and still death did not strike. The flywheel turned, the gathering static electricity rasped his nerves and stood his hair on end, but the violet flare did not dart toward the heavens.

Twenty seconds went by, and Keane breathed again—and watched the draped door. He could move arms and legs now, and a bath of flaming agony told that all his body would be soon released from the grip of the paralyzing drug.

Two minutes had gone by before he saw the drapes at the door move. And then—Girse came in. Girse! Not his master! But Girse, Keane thought, would do.

The monkey-like little man came into the red-lit room, and

to his merited end. Keane's steely eyes were on him. Through them, as through shining little gates, his iron will leaped at the man.

Girse stiffened in the doorway. Then, in obedience to Keane's unspoken command, he walked to Keane's side.

"You came to see why the violet flame has not burst out?" Keane said.

"Yes," said Girse, his wide, helpless eyes riveted on Keane's.

"Doctor Satan is outside with Bostiff and the girl?"

"Yes," said Girse. A spasm passed over his hairy face, as though apprehension struggled with the deep hypnosis in which he was held.

"Answer this," snapped Keane, "and answer it truly. The girl, Beatrice Dale, is now dead. Do you know of a way to make her live again?"

God, the agony that went into Keane's waiting for that answer! And then Girse's lips moved. "Yes."

Keane drew a deep breath. He was standing now, tottering a little, but almost entirely recovered. "What is the method? Tell me quickly—and truly."

"The drug that killed her is its own antidote. More of it will bring back to life any who have been dead for not more than half an hour."

"Thank God!" said Keane.

And then he acted. And as he did so, before his mind ran the list of crimes this man, with Doctor Satan as his leader and the unspeakable Bostiff as his comrade had committed. The list took all pity from his face.

He fastened the two metal cubes to the man whose body was held in his mental thrall. Then he went to the door, backing toward it with his commanding eyes ever on Girse.

The flywheel turned with a monotonous whirring. The fins attached to its spokes sent down the fine wire the accumulation of current. Millions, billions of volts, filling the mysterious storage capacity of the first cube, reaching toward the capacity of the second.

Keane looked at his watch. In thirty seconds, if Doctor Satan were right, the two cubes should explode with double the violence planned on....

There was a violet flare that seemed to fill the world. Keane was knocked backward out of a doorway that an instant later became nonexistent.

A glimpse he had of a man who sprawled over and over with the force of the shock and then relaxed to lie at last in the actual death hitherto denied him. The dead watchman! Then he was staring into coal-black eyes that glinted with a fear that never before had touched their arrogant depths.

Keane!" whispered Doctor Satan, as the criminologist faced him. You weren't... then it was Girse...."

"It was Girse who died," said Keane—and sprang. With a pleasure that sent a savage thrill to his finger-tips, he got his hands around the red-swathed throat.

"The drug that made that girl as she is," he grated. "I want it."

Doctor Satan's voice gurgled behind the red mask. His hand went under his robe. The fear of death—that exaggerated fear felt by all killers when they themselves feel death approach—gleamed in his eyes. He drew out the big hypodermic.

"How much is the reviving amount?" grated Keane.

"Two... calibrated marks... on the... plunger," gasped Doctor Satan as Keane's fingers relaxed. "The same as... the lethal dose...."

"Death, or renewed life, the same," whispered Keane.

Then a bleak smile shaped his firm lips. He took the hypodermic.

With the swiftness of a leaping serpent his hand moved. And death poured into Doctor Satan's veins!

Keane slowly got up. The coal-black eyes faded. They became

dull splotches through the mask's eyeholes.

Keane shot the stated amount into Beatrice's white arm. There was barely enough. With his heart in his throat he watched her reactions.

"Thank God!" he whispered.

Color was slowly seeping into her cheeks. Her eyes blinked, then began to lose that deathly dullness. The pulse increased toward normal in the throat vein.

Keane turned toward Doctor Satan and his face wore the same grim look it had worn when he left Girse to his merited destruction.

"Get up," he said.

Slowly, stiffly, Doctor Satan rose. His dead eyes peered straight ahead.

The factory building was a solid blaze. Shouts and sounds of running feet announced the beginning gathering of a crowd in the street.

"Walk straight ahead—and keep walking," Keane snapped.

The red-clad figure, like a dread automaton, walked straight ahead—toward the roaring flames. Keane waited, with bleak victory in his tired eyes, till the figure was on the brink of the flames. Then he turned to Beatrice.

"What?" she faltered

He helped her up. "Don't talk. Just come with me," he soothed. And, in answer to the look in her eyes: "Doctor Satan? He's dead at last. In the flames. It's triumph for us."

He helped her to the curb and through the milling crowd to his coupe....

It was the one of the few major mistakes of Keane's life.

"Two calibrated marks on the plunger," Doctor Satan had said was the reviving dose of the drug. "The same as the lethal dose...."

The revival amount had been correct; Beatrice was alive again to prove it. It did not occur to Keane that Satan might have lied about the other.

So he did not see the red-clad figure draw back from the flames as soon as he had turned and started leading the girl from the cinder yard. He did not see Doctor Satan crawl behind a rusted pile of metal tanks, nor see, a moment later a figure clad in conventional dark clothes emerge, leaving behind it a red, Luciferian costume that would have been too conspicuous to wear where many could observe.

"Victory," Keane said again, with shining eyes, as he drove toward the hotel.

But not far from the blazing factory behind him and Beatrice, a tall figure had drawn itself up with clenched fists, and the soft voice quivered with fury as Dr. Satan whispered:

"Ascot Keane thinks he has killed two of us, you, my faithful servant, Girse, and myself. He shall learn his mistake. I shall bring you back, Girse, and together we shall have proper and fitting revenge for the humiliation we have suffered at his hands. This I swear by the Devil, my master!"

HORROR INSURED

IT WAS NOON. The enormous National State Building hummed like a beehive with the activity of its tenants. Every office spewed forth men and women on their way to lunch. The express elevators dropped like plummets from the seventy-ninth floor, while the locals handled the crowds from the fortieth floor down.

At the top floor an express elevator tarried beyond its usual schedule. The operator paid no attention to the red flash from the starter downstairs signaling the Up cages to start down as soon as possible. He acted as though he was beyond schedules, as indeed he was.

This elevator, though not entirely private, was at the disposal of Martial Varley, owner of the building, whose offices took up the top floor. Others could ride in it, but they did so with the understanding that at morning, noon and evening the elevator waited to carry Varley, whose appearances at his office occurred with time-clock regularity. Hence, if the cage waited inactively those in it knew why and did not exhibit signs of impatience.

There were half a dozen people in the elevator that paused for Varley to ride down. There was an elderly woman, Varley's office manager and two secretaries; and there were two big business men who had been conferring with Varley and were now waiting to go to lunch with him.

The six chatted in pairs to one another. The cage waited, with the operator humming a tune. Around them, in the big building, the prosaic business of prosaic people was being done. The glass-paneled doors to Varley's office opened. The operator snapped to attention and those in the cage stopped talking and stared respectfully at the man who came to the cage doors.

Varley was a man of sixty, gray-haired, with a coarse but kindly face dominated by a large nose which his enemies called bulbous. He wore the hat that had made him famous—a blue-gray fedora which he ordered in quantity lots and wore exclusive of all other colors, fabrics or fashions.

"Sorry to keep you waiting, Ed," Varley boomed to one of the two business men in the cage. "Phone call. Held me up for a few minutes."

He stepped into the elevator, nodding to the others. "Let's go," he said to the operator.

The cage started down.

The express elevators were supposed to fall like a plummet. They made the long drop to the ground in a matter of seconds, normally. And this one started like a plummet.

"Damn funny, that phone call I got just before I came out of my office," Varley boomed to the two men he was lunching with. "Some joker calling himself Doctor Satan—" He stopped, and frowned. "What's wrong with the elevator?" he snapped to the operator.

"I don't know, sir," the boy said.

He was jerking at the lever. Ordinarily, so automatic was the cage, he did not touch the controls from the time the top floor doors mechanically closed themselves till the time the lobby was reached. Now he was twitching the control switch back and forth, from Off to On.

And the elevator was slowing down.

The swift start had slowed to a smooth crawl downward. And the crawl was becoming a creep. The floor numbers, that had flashed on the little frosted glass panel inside the cage as fast as you could count, were now forming themselves with exasperating slowness. Sixty-one, sixty, fifty-nine....

"Can't you make it go faster?" said Varley. "I never saw these cages go so slow. Is the power low?"

"I don't think so, sir," said the operator. He jammed the control against the fast-speed peg. And the cage slowed down still more.

"Something's wrong," whispered one of the girl secretaries to the other. "This slow speed... And it's getting warm in here!"

Evidently Varley thought so too. He unbuttoned his vest and took his fedora off and fanned himself.

"I don't know what the hell's the matter," he growled to the two men with him. "Certainly have to have the engineer look into this. There's supposed to be decent ventilation in these shafts. And if they call this express service... Gad, I'm hot!"

Perspiration was bursting out on his forehead now. He began to look ghastly pale.

Fifty-two, fifty-one, fifty... the little red numbers appeared on the frosted glass indicator over more slowly. The elevator would take five minutes to descend, at this pace.

"Something's the matter with me," gasped Varley. "I've never felt like this before." One of the secretaries was standing near him. She looked at him suddenly, with wide eyes in which fear of something beyond normal comprehension was beginning to show. She shrank back from him.

"Get this cage down," Varley panted. "I'm—sick."

The rest looked at each other. All were beginning to feel what the girl, who had been nearest him, had felt. Heat was beginning to radiate from Varley's corpulent body as if he were a stove!

"Good heavens, man!" said one of the two business men. He laid his hand on Varley's arm, took it away quickly. "Why—you're burning up with fever. What's wrong?"

Varley tried to answer, but couldn't. He staggered back against the wall of the cage, leaned there with arms hanging down and lips hanging slack. There was no longer perspiration on his face. It was dry, feverishly dry; and the skin was cracking on his taut, puffed cheeks.

"Burning!" he gasped. "Burning up!"

The girl secretary screamed, then. And the man who had put his hand on Varley's arm jerked at the operator's shoulder.

"For heaven's sake get this cage down! Mr. Varley's ill!"

"I—I can't," gasped the boy. "Something's the matter—it never acted like this before—"

He jerked at the controls, and the elevator did not respond. Slowly, monotonously, it continued its deliberate descent.

And abruptly a scream tore from Varley's cracking lips. "*Burning!* Help me, somebody—"

The slowly dropping cage became a thing of horror, a six-foot square of hell from which there was no escape because there were no doors opening onto the shaft at the upper levels, and which could not be speeded up because it did not respond to the controls.

Screaming with every breath he drew, Varley sank to the floor. And those who might otherwise have tried to help him cowered away from him as far as they could get. For from his body now was radiating heat that made a tiny inferno of the elevator.

"God!" whispered one of the men. "Look at him—he really is burning up!"

THE HEAT FROM Varley's body had become so intense that the others in the cage could hardly stand it. But far worse than their bodily torment was the mental agony of watching the thing that for a week had New York City in a chaos.

Varley had stopped screaming now. He lay staring up at the gilded roof of the elevator with frightful, glazing eyes. His chest heaved with efforts to draw breath. Heaved, then was still.

"*He's dead!*" shrieked one of the secretaries. "Dead—"

Her body fell to the floor of the cage near Varley's. The elderly woman quietly sagged to her knees, then in a huddled heap in the corner as her senses fled under the impact of a shock too great to be endured.

But the horror that had gripped Varley went on. *"Look! Look! Look!"* panted the office manager.

But he had no need to pant out the word. The rest were looking all right. They'd have turned their eyes away if they could, but there is a fascination to extremes of horror that makes the will powerless. In every detail they were forced to see the thing that happened.

Varley's dead body was beginning to disappear. The corpulent form of the man who a moment ago had been one of the biggest figures in the nation seemed to have been turned to wax, which was melting and vaporizing.

His face was a shapeless mass now; and the flesh of his body seemed to be melting and running together. As it did so, his limbs writhed and twitched as if still imbued with life. Writhed, and shriveled.

"Burning up!" whispered the office manager, his eyes bulging with horror behind their thick lenses. *"Melting away... burning up...."*

It was so incredible, so unreal that it was dream-like.

The cage descended slowly, slowly, like the march of time itself which no man could hasten. The operator stood like a wooden image at the controls, staring with starting eyes at the heap on the floor which had been Varley. The two business men shrank together, hands to their mouths, gnawing the backs of their hands. The office manager was panting, "Look...look... look..." with every breath, like a sobbing groan. And Varley was a diminishing, shapeless mass on the floor.

"Oh, God, let me out of here!" screamed one of the business men.

But there was no way out. No doors opened onto the shaft

here. All in the cage were doomed to stay and watch the spectacle that would haunt them till they died.

On the cage floor there was a blue-gray fedora hat, and a mound of blackened substance that was almost small enough to have been contained in it.

Twenty-nine, twenty-eight, twenty-seven... The cage descended with its horrible, unchangeable slowness.

Twenty-five, twenty-four...

On the floor was Varley's hat. That was all.

The operator was last to go. Eleven, ten, the red numerals on the frosted glass panel read. Then his inert body joined the senseless forms of the others on the floor.

The cage hit the lobby level. Smoothly, marvelous mechanisms' devised by man's ingenuity, the doors opened by themselves; opened, and revealed seven fainting figures—around a gray-blue fedora hat.

THREE O'CLOCK. ON the stage of the city's leading theater, the show, *Burn Me Down*, was in the middle of the first act of its matinee performance.

The show was a musical comedy, built around a famous comedian. His songs and dances and patter carried it. To see him, and him alone, the crowds came. Worth millions, shrewd, and at the same time as common as the least who saw him from the galleries, he was the idol of the stage.

He sat on a stool in the wings now, chin on fist, moodily watching the revue dance of twenty bare-legged girls billed as the world's most beautiful. His heavy black eyebrows were down in a straight line over eyes like ink-spots behind comedy horn-rimmed glasses. His slight, lithe body was tense.

"Your cue in a minute, Mr. Croy," warned the manager.

"Hell, don't you suppose I know it?" snapped the comedian. Then his scowl disappeared for a moment. "Sorry."

The manager stared. Croy's good humor and even temper

were proverbial in the theater. No one had ever seen him act like this before.

"Anything wrong?" he asked.

"Yeah, I don't feel so hot," said Croy, scowling again. "Rather, I feel *too* hot! Like I was burning up with a fever or something."

He passed a handkerchief over his forehead. "And I feel like trouble's coming," he added. He took a rabbit's foot from his vest pocket and squeezed it. "Heavy trouble,"

The manager bit his lip. Croy was the hit of the show—was the show. "Knock off for the afternoon if you feel bad," he advised. "We'll have Charley do your stuff. We can get away with it at a matinee—"

"And have the mob on your neck," interrupted Croy, without false modesty. "It's me they come to see. I'll go on with it, and have a rest afterward...."

THE TWENTY GIRLS swept forward in a last pirouette and danced toward the wings. Croy stood up.

"It must be a fever," he muttered, mopping at his face again. "Never felt like this before, though."

The stage door attendant burst into the wings and ran toward the manager. The manager started to reprimand him for leaving his post, then saw the afternoon newspaper he was waving.

He took it from the man's hand, glanced at the headlines.

"What!" he gasped. "A man burn up? They're crazy! How could a... Varley—biggest man in the city!..."

He started toward the comedian.

"My God, could it be the same thing happening here?... *Croy! Croy—wait!*"

But the famous comedian was already on the stage, catapulting to the center of it in the ludicrous stumble, barely escaping a fall, that was his specialty.

The manager, clutching the newspaper, stood in the wings with death-white face, and watched. Croy went into a dance to the rhythm of the theme song of the show. He was terribly pale, and the manager saw him stagger over a difficult step. Then his voice rose with the words of the song:

"Burn me down, baby. Don't say maybe. Put your lips against my lips—*and burn me down!*"

The audience half rose. Croy had fallen to his knees on a dance turn. The manager saw that the perspiration that had dewed his forehead no longer showed. His skin looked dry, cracked.

Croy got up. The audience settled back again, wondering if the fall had been part of his act. Croy resumed his steps and his singing. But his voice was barely audible beyond the fifth row:

"Burn me down, Sadie. Oh-h-h, lady! Look into my eyes and *burn me*—"

Croy stopped. His words ended in a wild high note. Then he screamed almost like a woman and his hands went to his throat. They tore at his collar and tie.

"Burning!" he screamed. *Burning*—"

The manager leaned, shaking against a pillar. The newspaper, with the account in it of what had happened to Varley, rattled to the floor.

It was the same! The same awful thing was happening to Croy! "Curtain!" he croaked. "Ring down the curtain!"

Now the audience was standing up, some of them indeed climbing to their seats to see what was happening on the stage. Croy was prone on the boards, writhing, shrieking. The canvas backdrop billowed a little with the heat coming from his body.

"Curtain!" roared the manager, "For God's sake—are you deaf?"

The curtain dropped. Croy's convulsed body was hidden from the sight of the audience. With the curtain's fall, he stopped screaming. It was as though the thing had sliced through the sound like a great descending guillotine. But it was not the curtain that had killed the sound.

Croy was dead. His limbs still jerked and writhed. But it was not the movement of life. It was the movement of a twisted roll of paper that writhes and jerks as it is consumed in flame.

The manager drew a deep breath. Then, with his knees trembling, he walked out onto the stage.

"Ladies and gentlemen," he announced, trying to make his voice sound out over the pandemonium that ruled over the theater. "Mr. Croy has had a heart attack. The show will not go on. You may get your money at the box-office on the way out."

He fairly ran from the stage and back of the curtain, where terrified girls and men were clumped around Croy's body—or what was left of it. Heart attack! The manager's mouth distorted over that description.

Croy's body had shrunk—or, rather, *melted*—to half its normal size. His features were indistinguishable, like the features of a wax head with a fire under it. His clothes were smoldering. The heat was such that it was hard to stand within a yard of him. The big, horn-rimmed glasses slid from his face. His body diminished, diminished....

A stage hand came racing back. Behind him trotted a plump man in black with rimless spectacles over his eyes.

"I got a doctor," the stage hand gasped. "From the audience."

He stopped. And the doctor stared at the place where Croy had lain, and then gazed around at the faces of the others.

"Well?" he said. "Where is Croy? I was told he was dangerously ill."

No one answered. One after another stared back into his face with the eyes of maniacs. "Where is he, I say?" snapped the doctor. "I was told—"

He stopped, aware at last that something far worse than ordinary illness was afoot back here.

The manager's lips moved. Words finally came. "Croy is— *was*—there."

His pointing finger leveled tremulously at a spot on the stage. Then he fell, pitching forward on his face like a dead man.

And the point on the stage he had designated was empty. Only a blackened patch was there, with a little smoke drifting up from it. A blackened patch—with a pair of comedy horn-rimmed glasses beside it.

2.

IN THE ELEVATOR control room of the Northern State Building, a man in the coveralls of an electrician bent over the great switchboard. He was examining the automatic control switch of the elevator in which Varley had ridden down from his top-floor office for the last time in life; had ridden down—but never reached the bottom!

Grease smeared the man's face and hands. But an especially keen observer would have noted several things about the seeming electrician that did not match his profession.

He would have noticed that the man's body was as lithe and muscular as that of a dancer; that his hands were only superficially smeared with grease, and were without calluses; that his fingers were the long, steely strong ones of a great surgeon or musician. Then, if he were one of the very few in New York capable of the identification, he might have gone further and glanced into the man's steely eyes under coal-black eyebrows, and stared at his patrician nose and strong chin and firm, large mouth—and have named him as Ascott Keane.

The building manager stood beside Keane. He had treated Keane as an ordinary electrician while the building engineer was near by. Now he gave him the deference due one of the greatest criminal investigators of all time. "Well, Mr. Keane?" he said.

"It's about as I thought," Keane said." A device on the order of a big rheostat was placed on the switch circuit. In that way the descent of the elevator could be slowed as much as the person manipulating the switch desired."

"But why was the elevator Mr. Varley rode down in made to go slower? Did the slowness have anything to do with his death?"

"No, it had to do only with the spectacle of his death!" Keane's face was very grim. His jaw was a hard square. "The man who killed Varley wanted to be sure that his death, and dissolution, were witnessed lingeringly and unmistakably, so that the full terror of it could be brought out."

He straightened up, walked toward the door. "You've set an office aside for me?"

"Yes. It's next to my own on the sixtieth floor. But you aren't going to it yet, are you?"

"Yes. Why not?"

"Well, there might be fingerprints. Whoever tampered with the control board might not have been careful about clues."

A mirthless smile appeared on Keane's firm lips. "Fingerprints! My dear sir! You don't know Doctor Satan, I'm afraid."

"Doctor Sat—"

The building manager clenched his hands excitedly. "Then you already know about the phone call to Mr. Varley just before he died."

"No," said Keane, "I don't."

"But you named the man who called—"

"Only because I know who did this—have known since I first heard of it. Not from any proofs I've found or will ever find. Tell me about the phone call."

"There isn't much. I'd hardly thought of it till you spoke of a Doctor Satan… Varley was leaving his office for lunch when his telephone rang. I was in his office about a lease and I couldn't help hearing a little of it—his words, that is. I gathered that somebody calling himself Doctor Satan was talking to Varley about insurance."

"Insurance!"

"Yes. Though what a physician should be doing selling insurance, I couldn't say—"

"Doctor Satan is not exactly a physician," Keane interrupted dryly. "Go on."

"That's all there is to tell. The man at the other end of the wire calling himself Doctor Satan seemed to want to insist that Varley take out some sort of insurance, till finally Varley just hung up on him. He turned to me and said something about being called by cranks and nuts, and went out to the elevator."

Keane walked from the control room, with the building manager beside him. He went to the elevator shafts.

"Sixty," he said to the operator.

In the elevator, he became the humble workman again. The manager treated him as such. "When you're through with the faulty wiring in sixty, come to my office," he said.

Keane nodded respectfully, then got out at the sixtieth floor.

A suite of two large offices had been set aside for him. There was a door through a regular anteroom, and a smaller, private entrance leading directly into the rear of the two offices.

Keane went through the private entrance. A girl, seated beside a flat-topped desk, got up. She was tall, quietly-lovely, with dark blue eyes and copper-brown hair. This was Beatrice Dale, Keane's more-than-secretary.

"Visitors?" said Keane, as she handed a calling-card to him.

She nodded. "Walter P. Kessler, one of the six you listed as most likely to receive Doctor Satan's first attentions in this new scheme of his."

Keane was running a towel over his face, taking off the grease—which was not grease but dark-colored soap. He took off the electrician's coveralls, emerging in a perfectly tailored blue serge suit complete save for his coat. The coat he took from a closet, shrugging into it as he approached the desk and sat down.

"What did you find out, Ascott?" said Beatrice.

Her face was pale, but her voice was calm, controlled. She had worked with Keane long enough to know how to face the horrors devised by Doctor Satan calmly, if not fearlessly.

"From the control room?" said Keane. "Nothing. The elevator was slowed simply to make the tragic end of Varley more spectacular. And there is Doctor Satan's autograph! The spectacular! All of his plans are marked by it."

"But you found out nothing of the nature of his plans?"

"I got a hint. It's an insurance project."

"Insurance!"

Keane smiled. There was no humor in the smile. There had been no humor in his smiles—or in his soul—since he had first met Doctor Satan, and there would be none till finally, somehow, he overcame the diabolical person who, already wealthy beyond the hopes of the average men, was amusing himself by gathering more wealth in a series of crimes as weird as they were inhuman.

"Yes, insurance. Send in Kessler, Beatrice."

The girl bit her lip. Keane had told her nothing. And the fact that she was burning to know what scraps of information he had picked up showed in her face. But she turned obediently and went to the door leading into the front office.

She came back in a moment with a man who was so anxious to get in that he almost trod on her heels. The man, Walter P. Kessler, was twisting a felt hat to ruins in his desperate fingers; and his brown eyes were like the eyes of a horrified animal as he strode toward Keane's desk.

"Keane!" He paused, looked at the girl, gazed around the office. "I still can't quite understand this. I've known you for years as a rich man's son who never worked in his life and knew nothing but polo and first editions. Now they tell me you are the only man in the world who can help me in my trouble."

"If your trouble has to do with Doctor Satan—and of course

it has—I may be able to help," said Keane. "As for the polo and first editions—it is helpful in my hobby of criminology to be known as an idler. You will be asked to keep my real activities hidden."

"Of course," gasped Kessler. "And if ever I can do anything for you in return for your help now—"

Keane waved his hand, "Tell me about the insurance proposition," he said.

"Are you a mind-reader?" exclaimed Kessler.

"No. There's no time to explain. Go ahead."

Kessler dug into his inside coat pocket.

"It's about insurance, all right. And it's sponsored by a man who calls himself Doctor Satan. Though how you knew?"

He handed a long envelop to Keane. "This came in this morning's mail," he said. "Of course I paid no attention to it. Not *then!* In fact, I threw it in my waste basket. I only fished it out again after reading the early afternoon papers—and finding out what happened to poor old Varley—"

He choked, and stopped. Keane read the folded paper in the long business envelope:

Mr. Kessler: You are privileged, among a few others in New York City, to be among the first to be invited to participate in a new type of insurance plan recently organized by me. The insurance will be taken out against an emotion, instead of a tangible menace. That emotion is horror. In a word, I propose to insure you against feeling horror. The premium for this benevolent insurance is seven hundred and fifty thousand dollars. If the premium is not paid, you will be subjected to a rather unpleasant feeling of horror concerning something that may happen to you. That something is death, but death in a new form: If you do not choose to take out my horror insurance, you shall burn in slow fire till you are utterly consumed. It may be next month or next year. It may be tomorrow. It may be in the privacy of your room, or among crowds. Read in this afternoon's paper of what will shortly happen to two of the town's leading citizens. Then decide whether or not the premium payment

asked is not a small price to pay for allaying the horror the reading of their fates will inspire in you.
Signed, DOCTOR SATAN.

Keane tapped the letter against his palm. "Horror insurance," he murmured. "I can see Doctor Satan's devilish smile as he coined that phrase. I can hear his chuckle as he 'invites' you to take out a 'policy'. Well, are you going to pay it?"

Kessler's shudder rattled the chair he sat in. "Certainly! Am I mad, that I should refuse to pay—after reading what happened to Varley and Croy? Burned alive! Reduced to a shapeless little residue of consumed flesh—and then to nothingness! Certainly I'll pay!"

"Then why did you come to me?"

"To see if we couldn't outwit this Doctor Satan in future moves. What's to keep him from demanding a sum like that every year as the price of my safety? Or every month, for that matter?"

"Nothing," said Keane.

Kessler's hand clenched the chair-arm. "That's it. I'll have to pay this one, because I daren't defy the man till some sort of scheme is set in motion against him. But I want you to track him down before another demand is presented. I'll give you a million dollars if you succeed. Two million...."

The look on Keane's face stopped him. "My friend," said Keane, "I'd double your two million, personally, if I could step out and destroy this man, now, before he does more horrible things."

He stood up. "How were you instructed to pay the 'premium'?"

For a moment Kessler looked less panic stricken. A flash of the grim will that had enabled him to build up his great fortune showed in his face.

"I was instructed to pay it in a way that may trip our Doctor Satan up," he said. "I am to write ten checks of seventy-five thousand dollars each, payable to the Lucifex Insurance

Company. These checks I am to bring to this building tonight. From the north side of the building I will find a silver skull dangling from a wire leading down the building wall. I am to put the checks in the skull. It will be drawn up and the checks taken by someone in some room up in the building."

His jaw squared. "That ought to be our chance, Keane! We can have men scattered throughout the National State Building—"

Keane shook his head. "In the first place, you'd have to have an army here. There are seventy-nine floors, Kessler. Satan's man may be in any room on any of the seventy-nine floors on the north side of the building. Or he may be on the roof. In the second place, expecting to catch a criminal like Doctor Satan in so obvious a manner is like expecting to catch a fox in a butterfly net. He probably won't be within miles of this building tonight. And you can depend on it that his man, who is to draw up the skull with the checks in it, won't be in any position where he can be caught by the police or private detectives."

Kessler's panic returned in full force. He clawed at Keane's arm. "What can we do, then?" he babbled. "What can we do?"

"I don't know, yet," admitted Keane. "But we've got till tonight to figure out a plan. You come to the building as instructed, with the checks to put in the skull. By then I'll have weapons with which to fight"—his lips twisted—"the Lucifex Insurance Company."

3.

THE NATIONAL STATE BUILDING is situated on a slanting plot in New York City. The first floor on the lower side is like a cavern—dark, with practically no light coming in the windows from the canyon of a street.

Near the center of that side was an unobtrusive small shop

with "Lucian Photographic Supplies" lettered on it. The window was clean-looking, yet it was strangely opaque. Had a person looked at it observantly he would have noticed, with some bewilderment, that while nothing seemed to obstruct vision, he still could not see what was going on behind it. But there are few really observant eyes; and in any event there was nothing about the obscure place to attract attention.

At the back of the shop there was a large room completely sealed against light. On the door was the sign, "Developing Room."

Inside the light-proof room the only illumination came from two red light bulbs, like and yet strangely unlike the lights used in developing-rooms. But the activities in the room had nothing to do with developing pictures!

In one corner were two figures that seemed to have stepped out of a nightmare. One was a monkey-like little man with a hair-covered face from which glinted bright, cruel eyes. The other was a legless giant who swung his great torso, when he moved, on arms as thick as most men's thighs. Both were watching a third figure in the room, more bizarre than either of them.

The third figure bent over a bench. It was tall, spare, and draped from throat to ankles in a blood-red robe. Red rubber gloves were drawn over its hands. The face was covered by a red mask which concealed every feature save the eyes—which were like black, live coals peering through the eye-holes. A skullcap fitted tightly over the head; and from this, in sardonic imitation of the fiend he pretended to be, were two projections like horns.

Doctor Satan stared broodingly at the things on the bench which were engaging his attention. These, innocent enough in appearance, still had in them somehow a suggestion of something weird and grotesque.

They were little dolls, about eight inches high. The sheen of their astonishingly life-like faces suggested that they were made of wax. And they were so amazingly well sculptured that a glimpse revealed their likeness to living persons.

There were four of the little figures clad like men. And any reporter or other person acquainted with the city's outstanding personalities would have recognized them as four of the nation's business titans. One of them was Walter P. Kessler.

Doctor Satan's red-gloved hand pulled a drawer open in the top of the bench. The supple fingers reached into the drawer, took from it two objects, and placed them on the bench.

And now there were six dolls on the bench, the last two being a man and a woman.

The male doll was clad in a tiny blue serge suit. Its face was long-jawed, with gray chips for eyes, over which were heavy black brows. An image of Ascott Keane.

The female doll was a likeness of a beautiful girl with coppery brown hair and deep blue eyes. Beatrice Dale.

"Girse." Doctor Satan's voice was soft, almost gentle.

The monkey-like small man with the hairy face hopped forward.

"The plate," said Doctor Satan.

Girse brought him a thick iron plate, which Doctor Satan set upon the bench.

On the plate were two small, dark patches; discolorations obviously made by the heat of something being burned there. The two little discolorations were all that was left of two little dolls that had been molded in the image of Martial Varley, and the comedian, Croy.

Doctor Satan placed the two dolls on the plate that he had taken from the drawer; the likeness of Beatrice Dale and Ascott Keane.

"Kessler went to Keane," Doctor Satan said, the red mask over his face stirring angrily. "We shall tend to Kessler—after he has paid tonight. We shall not wait that long to care for Keane and the girl."

Two wires trailed over the bench from a wall socket. His

red-gloved fingers twisted the wires to terminals set into the iron plate. The plate began to heat up.

"Keane has proved himself an unexpectedly competent adversary," Satan's voice continued, "with knowledge I thought no man on earth save myself possessed. We'll see if he can escape *this* fate—and avoid becoming, with his precious secretary, as Varley and Croy became."

Small waves of heat began to shimmer up from the iron plate. It stirred the garments clothing the two little dolls. Doctor Satan's glittering eyes burned down on the mannikins. Girse and the legless giant, Bostiff, watched as he did….

FIFTY-NINE STORIES ABOVE the pseudo-developing shop, Keane smiled soberly at Beatrice Dale. "I ought to fire you," he said.

"Why on earth—" she gasped.

"Because you're such a valuable right-hand man, and because you're such a fine person."

"Oh," Beatrice murmured. "I see. More fears for my safety?"

"More fears for your safety," nodded Keane. "Doctor Satan is out for your life as well as mine, my dear. And—"

"We've had this out many times before," Beatrice interrupted. "And the answer is still; No. I refuse to be fired, Ascott. Sorry."

There was a glint in Keane's steel-gray eyes that had nothing to do with business. But he didn't express his emotions. Beatrice watched his lips part with a breathless stirring in her heart. She had been waiting for some such expression for a long time.

But Keane only said: "So be it. You're a brave person. I oughtn't to allow you to risk your life in this private, deadly war that no one knows about but us. But I can't seem to make you desert, so—"

"So that's that," said Beatrice crisply. "Have you decided how you'll move against Doctor Satan tonight?"

Keane nodded. "I made my plans when I first located him."

"You know where he is?" said Beatrice in amazement.

"I do."

"How did you find it out?"

"I didn't. I thought it out. Doctor Satan seems to have ways of knowing where I am. He must know I've located here in the National State Building. The obvious thing for him to do would be to conceal himself on the other side of town. So, that being the expected thing, what would a person as clever as he is, do?"

Beatrice nodded. "I see. Of course! He'd be—"

"Right here in this building."

"But you told Kessler he was probably miles away!" said Beatrice.

"I did. Because I knew Kessler's character. If he knew the man who threatened him was in the building, he'd try to do something like organizing a raid. Fancy a police raid against Doctor Satan! So I lied and said he was probably a long distance off." Keane sighed. "I'm afraid the lie was valueless. I can foretell pretty precisely what Kessler will do. He will have an army of men scattered through the building tonight, in spite of what I said. He will attempt to trace Doctor Satan through collection of the checks—and he will die."

Beatrice shuddered. "By burning? What a horrible way to—" She stopped.

"What is it?" said Keane urgently, at the strained expression that suddenly molded her face.

"Nothing, I guess," replied Beatrice slowly. "Power of suggestion, I suppose. When I said 'burning' I seemed to feel hot all over, myself."

Keane sprang from his chair. "My God—why didn't you tell me at once! I—"

He stopped too, and his eyes narrowed to steely slits in his rugged face. Perspiration was studding his own forehead now.

"It's come!" he said. "The attack on us by Satan. But it wasn't wholly unexpected. The suitcase in the corner—get it and open it! Quickly!"

Beatrice started toward the suitcase but stopped and pressed her hands to her cheeks. "Ascott—I'm... burning up... I—"

"Get that suitcase!"

Keane sprang to the desk and opened the wide lower drawer. He took a paper-wrapped parcel from it, ripped it open. An odd array was disclosed; two pairs of things like cloth slippers, two pairs of badly proportioned gloves, two small rounded sacks.

Beatrice was struggling with the snaps on the suitcase. Both were breathing heavily now, dragging their arms as if they weighed tons.

"Ascott—I can't stand it—I'm burning—" panted the girl.

"You've got to stand it! Is the case open? Put on the smaller of the two garments there. Toss me the other."

The garments in question were two suits of unguessable material that were designed to fit tightly over a human body—an unclothed human body.

Beatrice tossed the larger of the two to Keane, who was divesting himself of his outer garments with rapid fingers.

"Ascott—I can't change into *this*—here before—"

"Damn modesty!" grated Keane. "Get into those things! You hear! Quickly!"

Both were no longer perspiring. Their faces were dry, feverish. Heat was radiating from their bodies in a stifling stream.

Beatrice stood before Keane in the tight single garment that covered body and arms and legs.

"These gloves on your hands!" snapped Keane. "The sack over your head. The shoes on your feet!"

"Oh, God!" panted Beatrice.

Then she had done as Keane commanded. From soles to hair she was covered by the curious fabric Keane had devised. And the awful burning sensation was allayed.

There were eye-slits in the sacks each wore. They stared at

each other with eyes that were wide with a close view of death. Then Beatrice sighed shudderingly.

"The same thing Varley and Croy went through?" she said.

"The same," said Keane. "Poor fellows! Doctor Satan thought he could deal us the same doom. And he almost did! If we'd been a little farther away from these fabric shields of ours—"

"How do they stop Doctor Satan's weapon?" said Beatrice. "And how can he strike—as he does—from a distance?"

"His weapon, and this fabric I made," said Keane, "go back a long way beyond history, to the priesthood serving the ancestors of the Cretans. They forged the weapon in wizardry, and at the same time devised the fabric to wear as protection against their enemies who must inevitably learn the secret of the weapon too. It is the father of the modern voodoo practice of making a crude image of an enemy and sticking pins into it."

He drew a long breath.

"A small image is made in the likeness of the person to be destroyed. The image is made of substance pervious to fire. In the cases of Croy and Varley, I should say after descriptions of how they perished, of wax. The image is then burned, and the person in whose likeness it is cast burns to nothingness as the image does—*if* the manipulator knows the secret incantations of the Cretans, as Doctor Satan does. But I'll give you more than an explanation; I'll give you a demonstration! For we are going to strike back at Doctor Satan in a manner I think he will be utterly unprepared for!"

HE WENT TO the opened suitcase, looking like a being from another planet in the ill-fitting garments he had thrown together after analyzing Varley's death. He took from the suitcase a thing that looked like a little doll. It was an image of a monkey-like man with a hairy face and long, simian arms.

"How hideous!" exclaimed Beatrice. "But isn't that Doctor Satan's assistant Girse?"

Ascott Keane nodded. "Yes. I wish it were the image of Satan himself, but that would be useless. Satan, using the ancient death, would too obviously be prepared for it just as I was."

Beatrice stared at the image for a moment, perplexity in her eyes. "But—Ascott! Didn't you tell me that Girse was dead? Wasn't he—consumed instead of you when…?"

Keane nodded. "Yes, he was—and I was foolish enough for a while to believe what I saw as final. But Doctor Satan knows as much about the ancient evil arts as I do—at least as much—and I know of a way to bring a dead person back, even if the body is destroyed, so long as I had the foresight to preserve some parts like hair or nail-clippings. I forgot that any close associate of Doctor Satan must be killed twice, so long as Satan is free to work his magic. That is why I made this image of Girse as soon as I realized what Doctor Satan is doing. There's just a chance that he hasn't prepared any protection for Girse, on the assumption that I already considered Girse out of the picture forever."

"It's made of wax?" said Beatrice, understanding and awe beginning to glint in her eyes.

"Made of wax," Keane nodded.

He looked around the office, saw no metal tray to put the little doll on, and flipped back a corner of the rug. The floor of the office was of smooth cement. He set the image on the cement. With her hand to her breast, Beatrice watched. The proceeding, seeming inconsequential in itself, had an air of deadliness about it that stopped the breath in her throat.

Keane looked around the office again, then strode to the clothes he and Beatrice had flung to the floor in their haste a moment ago.

"Sorry," he said, taking her garments with his own and piling them on the cement. "We'll have to send down to Fifth Avenue for more clothes to be brought here. I need these now."

On the pile of cloth he placed the image of Girse. Then he touched a match to the fabric….

HORROR INSURED

IN THE DEVELOPING room, Doctor Satan fairly spat his rage as he stared at the two wax dolls on the red-hot iron plate. The dolls were not burning! Defying all the laws of physics and, as far as Satan knew, of wizardry, the waxen images were standing unharmed on the metal that should have consumed them utterly.

"Damn him!" Doctor Satan whispered, gloved hands clenching. "Damn him! He has escaped again! Though how—"

He heard breathing begin to sound stertorously beside him. His eyes suddenly widened with incredulity behind the eye-holes in his mask. He whirled.

Girse was staring at him with frenzy and horror in his eyes. The breath was tearing from his corded throat, as though each would be his last.

"Master!" he gasped imploringly. "Doctor Satan! Stop—"

The skin on his face and hands, dry and feverish-looking, suddenly began to crack. *"Stop the burning!"* he pleaded in a shrill scream.

But Doctor Satan could only clench his hands and curse softly, whispering to himself, "I did not foresee it, Girse. I brought you back with the essential salts, one of the most guarded of all occult secrets, and I was sure that Ascott Keane would never suspect. But he did, damn him, and he was ready for me...."

Girse shrieked again, and fell to the floor. Then his screams stopped; he was dead, and this time there would be no return; the essential salts could be used to restore a man only once. Girse's body moved on, jerking and twisting as a tight-rolled bit of paper twists and jerks in a consuming fire.

"Keane!" whispered Doctor Satan, staring at the floor where a discolored spot was all that remained of his follower. His eyes were frightful. "By the devil, my master, he'll pay for that a thousand times over!"

4.

AT HALF-PAST TWELVE that night a solitary figure walked along the north side of the National State Building. The north side was the one the Lucian Photographic Supplies shop faced on; the side street. It was deserted save for the lone man.

The man slowed his pace as he saw a shining object hanging from the building wall about waist-high, a few yards ahead of him. He clenched his hands, then took out his handkerchief and wiped his forehead.

The man was Walter B. Kessler. And the flourish of the white handkerchief in the dimness of the street was a signal.

Across the street, four floors up in a warehouse, a man with a private detective's badge in his pocket a pair of binoculars to his eyes. He watched Kessler, saw the shining object he was approaching, and nodded.

Kessler drew from his pocket an unaddressed envelope. In it were ten checks made out to the Lucifex Insurance Company. He grasped the receptacle for the checks in his left hand.

The receptacle was a cleverly molded skull, of silver, about two-thirds life size. There was a hole in the top of it. Kessler thrust the envelope securely into the hole.

The skull began to rise up the building wall, toward some unguessable spot in the tremendous cliff formed by seventy-nine stories of cut stone. Across the street the man with the binoculars managed at last to spot the thin wire from which the silver skull was suspended. He followed it up with his gaze.

It came from a window almost at the top of the building. The man grasped a phone at his elbow.

He did not dial operator. The phone had a direct line to the building across the way. He simply picked up the receiver and said softly: "Seventy-second floor, eighteenth window from the east wall. *Hop it!*"

In the National State Building a man at an improvised switchboard on the ground floor turned to another. "Seventy-second floor, eighteenth window from the east. Get everybody."

The second man ran toward the night elevator. He went from floor to floor. At each floor he opened the door and signaled. And on each floor two men, who had been watching the corridors along the north side, ran silently toward the other local elevators, which had shaft doors on every floor all the way up to the top. At the same time a third man, at the stairs, drew his gun as he prepared to guard more carefully yet the staircase, rarely used, threading up beside the shafts.

And on the ground floor within fifty yards of the man at the switchboard, a chuckle came from the masked lips of a red-robed figure who stood straight and tall in a red-lit room.

Across the street the man with the binoculars suddenly picked up the phone again.

"Damn it they tricked us. Somebody took the money in on the sixty-third floor!"

Changed orders vibrated through the great building. And the red-robed figure in the room at the heart of the maze chuckled again—and moved toward the bench.

Doctor Satan picked up one of the dolls remaining there. It was the image of Kessler. He placed it on the iron plate, which was already heated by the wires trailing from the socket. He watched the little doll broodingly.

It writhed and twisted as the heat melted its wax feet. It fell to the plate. And from the street, far away, sounded a horrible scream.

Doctor Satan's head jerked back as if the shriek were music to his ears. Then, once more, his hissing chuckle sounded out.

"For disobeying commands, my friend," he muttered. "But I knew you'd be obstinate enough to try it—"

He stopped. For a second he stood as rigid as a statue swathed in red. Then, slowly, he turned; and in his coal-black, blazing eyes was fury—and fear.

There was an inner door to the developing-room, but the door was locked, and it still stood locked. It had not been touched. Neither had the outer door. Yet in that room with the red-robed figure was another figure now. That of Ascott Keane.

He stood as rigid as Doctor Satan himself, and stared at his adversary out of steel-gray, level eyes.

"It seems we are alone," Keane said slowly. "Bostiff, I suppose, is retrieving the money from Kessler. And Girse? Where is he?"

Doctor Satan's snarl was the only answer. He moved toward Keane, red-swathed hands clenching as he came. Keane stood his ground. Satan stopped.

"How—" he asked.

"Surely *you* do not need to ask that," said Keane. "You must have penetrated the secret of transferring substance, including your own, from one place to another by sheer power of thought."

"I have not!" rasped Doctor Satan. "Nor have you!"

Keane shrugged. "I am here."

"You discovered my hiding-place and hid here while I was out, a short time ago!"

Keane's smile was a deadly thing. "Perhaps I did. Perhaps not. You can provide your own answer. The only thing of importance is that I *am* here—"

"And shall stay here!" Doctor Satan's soft voice lifted. The fear was fading from his eyes and leaving only fury there. "You have interfered in my plans once too often, Keane!"

As he spoke he raised his right hand with the thumb and forefinger forming an odd, eerie angle.

"'Out of the everywhere into the here,'" he quoted softly. "I have servants more powerful than Girse, whom you destroyed, Ascott Keane. One comes now—*to your own destruction!*"

As he spoke, a strange tensity seized the air of the dim room.

Keane paled a little at the blaze in the coal-black eyes. Then he stared suddenly at a spot in thin air to Doctor Satan's right.

Something was happening there. The air was shimmering as though it danced over an open fire. It wavered, grew misty, swayed in a sinuous column.

"'Out of the everywhere into the here,'" Doctor Satan's voice was raised in final triumph. "The old legends had a basis, Keane. The tales of dragons… There was such a thing, is such a thing. Only the creations the ancients called dragons do not ordinarily roam Earth in visible form."

The sinuous misty column at the right of the red-robed form was materializing into a thing to stagger a man's reason.

Keane found himself gazing at a shimmering figure that looked like a great lizard, save that it was larger than any lizard, and had smaller legs. It was almost like a snake with legs, but it was a snake two feet through at its thickest part, and only about fourteen feet long, which is not typical serpentine proportion. There were vestigial stubs of wings spreading from its trunk about a yard back of its great, triangular head; and it had eyes such as no true lizard ever had—eight inches across and glittering like evil gems.

"A dragon, Keane," Doctor Satan purred. "You have seen old pictures of some such thing, painted by artists who had caught a glimpse of these things that can only visit earth when some necromancer conjures them to. A 'mythical' creature, Keane. But you shall feel how 'mythical' it is when it attacks you."

A hiss sounded in the dim room. The serpentine form was so solidly materialized now that it would scarcely be seen through. And in a few more seconds it was opaque. And weighty! The floor quivered a little as it moved—toward Keane.

Its great, gem-like eyes glinted like colored glass as it advanced, foot by foot, on the man who had pitted himself against Doctor Satan till the death of one of them should end the bitter war. But, Keane did not move. He stood with shoulders squared and arms at his sides, facing the red-robed form.

"'Out of the everywhere into the here,'" he murmured. His lips were pale but his voice was calm. "There is another saying, Doctor Satan. It is a little different.... 'Out of the *hereafter* into the here!'"

The unbelievable thing Doctor Satan had called into being in the midst of a city that would have scoffed at the idea of its existence, suddenly halted its slow, deadly approach toward Keane. Its hiss sounded again, and it raised a taloned foot and clawed the thin air in a direction to Keane's left.

It retreated a step, slinking low to the floor, its talons and scales rattling on the smooth cement. It seemed to see something beyond the reach of mortal eyes. But in a moment the things it saw were perceptible to the eyes of the two men, too. And as Doctor Satan saw them an imprecation came from his masked lips.

Three figures, distorted, horrible, yet familiar! Three things like statues of mist that became less misty and more solid-seeming by the second!

Three men who writhed as though in mortal torment, and whose lips jerked with soundless shrieks—which gradually became not entirely soundless but came to the ears of Satan and Keane like far-off cries dimly heard.

And the three were Varley and Croy and Kessler.

A gasp came from Doctor Satan's concealed lips. He shrank back, even as the monstrosity he had called into earthly being shrank back.

"'Out of the hereafter into the here,'" Keane said. "These three you killed, Doctor Satan. They will now kill you!"

VARLEY AND CROY and Kessler advanced on the red-robed form. As they came they screamed with the pain of burning, and their blackened hands advanced, with fingers flexed, toward Satan. Such hatred was in their dead, glazed eyes, that waves of it seemed to surge about the room like a river in flood.

"They're shades," panted Doctor Satan. "They're not real, they can't actually do harm—"

"You will see how real they are when they attack you," Keane paraphrased Satan's words.

The three screaming figures converged on Doctor Satan. From death they had come, and before them was the man who had sent them to death. Their eyes were wells of fury and despair.

"My God!" whispered Doctor Satan, cowering. And the words, though far from lightly uttered, seemed doubly blasphemous coming from the lips under the diabolical red mask.

The hissing of the dragon-thing he had called into existence was inaudible. Its form was hardly to be seen. It was fleeing back into whatever realm it had come from. But the screaming three were advancing ever farther into our earthly plane as they crept toward the cowering body of Doctor Satan.

"My God!" Satan cried. "Not that! Not deliverance into the hands of those I—"

The three leaped. And Keane, with his face white as death at the horror he was witnessing, knew that the fight between him and the incarnate evil known as Doctor Satan was to end in this room.

The three leaped, and the red-robed figure went down....

There was a thunderous battering at the door, and the bellow of men outside: "Open up, in the name of the law!"

Keane cried out, as though knife-blades had been thrust under his nails. Doctor Satan screamed, and thrust away from the three furies, while the three themselves mouthed and swayed like birds of prey in indecision over a field in which hunters bristle suddenly.

"Open this door!" the voice thundered again. "We know there's somebody in here—"

The shock of the change from the occult and unreal back to prosaic living was like the shock of being rudely waked from sound sleep when one has walked to the brink of a cliff and opens dazed eyes to stare at destruction. The introduction of such a thing as police, detectives, into a scene where two men were evoking powers beyond the ability of the average mortal even to comprehend, was like the insertion of an iron club into the intricate and fragile mechanism of a radio transmitting-station.

Keane literally staggered. Then he shouted: "For God's sake—get away from that door—"

"Open up, or we'll break in," the bellowing voice overrode his own.

Keane cursed, and turned. The three revengeful forces he had evoked for the destruction of Doctor Satan were gone, shattered into non-existence again with the advance of the prosaic. And Doctor Satan—

Keane got one glimpse of a torn red robe, with dots of deeper crimson on its arm, as the man slid through the inner door of the room and out to—God knew where. Some retreat he had prepared in advance, no doubt.

And then the door crashed down and the men Kessler had stubbornly and ruinously retained in his fight with Doctor Satan burst in.

They charged toward Keane. "You're under arrest for extortion," the leader, a bull-necked man with a gun in his hand, roared out. "We traced the guy that took the dough from the skull here before we lost him."

Keane only looked at him. And at something in his stare, though the detective did not know him from Adam, he wilted a little. "Stick out your hands while I handcuff you," he tried to bluster.

Then the manager of the building ran in. "Did you get him?" he called to the detective. "Was he in here?" He saw the man the detective proposed to handcuff. "*Keane!* What has happened?"

"Doctor Satan has escaped," said Keane. "That's what has

happened. I had him"—he held his hand out and slowly closed it—"like that! Then these well-intentioned blunderers broke in and—"

His voice broke. His shoulders sagged. He stared at the door through which the red-robed figure had gone. Then his body straightened and his eyes grew calm again—though they were bleak with a weariness going far beyond physical fatigue.

"Gone," he said, more to himself than to anyone in the red-lit room. "But I'll find him again. And *next* time I'll fight him in some place where no outside interference can save him."

BEYOND DEATH'S GATEWAY

THE SEA WAS as calm as a pond. Over it the great ship floated like a ghost vessel, dipping a little to long, slow swells but otherwise as motionless as a thing on a backdrop. The white moon poured down its peaceful flood, but somehow the peace was an eerie thing and not reassuring.

In a large cabin on deck A, two men sat behind a locked door and talked in whispers too low to be recorded if there were a dictograph receiver concealed anywhere. One of the two had the often-photographed face of Assistant Secretary of War Harley. The other was Jules Marxman, inventor and manufacturer.

Harley, a slim, precise, elderly man who looked more like a high school principal than an important Government official, shook his head a little.

"Then, as the invention now stands, it is useless," he summed up.

Marxman, the inventor, nodded his bushy gray head. His heavy grizzled brows drew into a straight line.

"Useless," he conceded. "I have the formula for the poison gas completed. It is perfect—a gas so volatile that it spreads at a rate of a hundred feet a second in all directions, and wipes out all living things, including vegetable matter. But its very speed makes it impossible to use it as other war gases are used. It would wipe out the men releasing it as well as the enemy."

"Special masks to protect our own men?" suggested the Assistant Secretary of War.

Marxman shook his head.

"I though of that, of course. I worked along that angle for a long time. But no mask can be devised to protect a man from the gas. So the answer lies in another direction. That is, an antidote of some sort for it that will permit the men releasing it to feel no ill effects from it."

"That sounds difficult. Look here, couldn't the stuff be shot from guns to explode and radiate at a distance?"

No. It is so highly explosive itself that no shell can be designed to keep it from exploding when the gun charge bursts, when its high volatility spreads it all around the gun. Again, our own men would die from it. No, the only answer is the antidote that will make the corps releasing it immune to its deadly effects."

Harley stroked his long, spare chin.

"You've worked along that line, Marxman?"

"Yes, I have been working on an antidote for eighteen months. The final solution is not yet worked out. But I'm getting close."

Marxman looked at the locked cabin door, and lowered his voice still more.

"I have an antidote at present that will counteract the effects of the gas. But its own effects are almost as serious: The man who takes it literally dies for a short space of time. His heart and breathing stop. Blood circulation ceases. He's a dead man—for about twelve hours. Most curious."

"And, most unfortunate," Harley said dryly. "In twelve hours the enemy from beyond the radius of the spreading gas could gun and bomb the helpless crew out of existence. But tell me, how can men 'die' for twelve hours, with the blood stream stilled and liable to coagulate, and then come to life again?"

"Or—do they?"

"Yes, they do, I don't yet know how. The blood should coagulate, but it doesn't. Perhaps some life force beyond power of detection still functions enough to keep the body in shape to be reanimated when the effect of the antidote wears off. Anyhow, that's what happens to a man who takes it in its present state. He literally dies for half a day, then comes slowly back to life again."

"Have you tried it on anyone?"

Marxman nooded. His face was a little paler than normal.

"What happens to the subject of experiment?"

MARXMAN LOOKED AT Harley for a moment before replying.

"I tried it on a dock laborer, several times. He wasn't a clever or educated man. He didn't manage to express very well the things that happened to him. But as far as I could gather, he was in the land of the dead during the coma induced by the drug."

"Land of the dead!" Harley exclaimed. Then he smiled. "And where is that?"

"I don't know."

"What's it like?"

"I don't know that, either, My man hadn't the vocabulary to describe such things in the first place. In the second, he didn't want to talk! And, though he was fearless in a blunt, animal way, he refused to take the stuff more than twice."

"Probably it has some sort of harsh effect," said Harley shrugging. "Land of the dead! That's a little thick! But regardless of that angle of it—the poison gas invention is not yet ready to turn over to the war department. Is that it?"

"That's it," said Marxman. "The gas is perfected, but the antidote is not. And until it is, the whole thing remains only a novelty, a dream of empire that can't be crystalized till I have finished work."

Harley fingered his lean chin.

"Don't overlook the fact that, even as matters stand, you have a very valuable secret," he warned. "Any power on earth would pay millions for the uncompleted formulae, on the chance that they could work out the conclusion in their laboratory. You have the formulae written out?"

Marxman nodded.

"They're too complicated to carry in my head."

"You keep the papers in a safe place?"

Marxman smiled a little. He drew from his vest pocket a small capsule, like a quinine capsule. It looked like some sort of dyspepsia medicine he carried for use after meals.

"The formulae are on onion-skin paper, in this capsule. If ever I am threatened for them, I swallow them. The capsule dissolves in my stomach—and so do the formulae! I hope the necessity for swallowing them doesn't arise, for it would take me six wasted months to rediscover a few of the obscure chemical combinations in the formulae. But it can be done if necessary."

Harley nodded. "As safe a way as any, I think. Well, goodnight, Marxman. Take care of yourself, and for God's sake give the United States first chance at your gas and antidote when it's worked out."

"I am American," was Marxman's simple answer. "I have worked in France because a colleague there has just the laboratory equipment I needed. That's all. My own country gets the invention when it is completed, as a matter of course."

The two men shook hands. Harley left Marxman's cabin.

Marxman stared at the little capsule in his hand, which contained the nucleus of the mightiest war weapon ever devised. Then he slipped it into his vest pocket again.

The night was warm, almost stuffy. He lit a cigar, put on a plaid cap, and went up on deck....

At that moment, in the salon at the opposite end of the ship, from which he had not stirred all evening, a man who looked like a high school principal but was really Assistant Secretary of War Harley, was talking in low tones with his secretary, a good-looking young fellow of twenty-eight.

"I hear Marxman is on board with an interesting invention," the secretary was saying. "Are you going to see him?"

"By all means," said Harley. "I think a little later in the evening."

Marxman passed the windows of the salon without looking in. Assistant Secretary of War Harley had already seen him, he thought. It never occurred to him that a man could make up like Harley so exactly as to fool him—he was well acquainted with the man—and then proceed to pump him dry of details concerning his latest invention.

He walked to the rail, fingers touching the capsule in his vest pocket.

Sea calm as a pond. Great ship like a ghost vessel floating over it. Moon pouring down a peaceful but somehow eerie white flood.

From the stern came strains of music as the ship's orchestra played for those in evening dress who cared to dance. From the salon nearest to where Marxman stood by the rail came a burst of laughter as members of a salesmen's convention to Europe laughed over a joke.

Right behind Marxman there was an iron staircase leading up to the boat deck. From that deserted upper deck a figure appeared. It blotted out the faint light at the head of the stairs. It began to descend, slowly, without a sound, like a great snake slithering down on its prey.

Once Marxman turned for a moment. The black figure became a motionless blot on the staircase. Marxman looked out over the sea again. Then the figure recommenced its crawling descent. A faint streak of light from the drawn shutters of a near-by cabin flicked over it.

It revealed a form in a black cloak with a black hat pulled low. That was all. The face could not be seen. Yet evil radiated from the form as heat radiates from black-hot iron.

The black figure reached the deck and took two rapid strides toward the inventor....

Gay laughter from the salon—casual music from the dance floor—and on the deck, death!

Marxman tried to cry out. A steely arm hooked around his throat prevented a whisper from coming from his lips. His hand darted for his vest pocket and he raised the capsule to his lips and took it into his mouth.

The arm around his throat was replaced by steely hands. He couldn't swallow. His face grew blue, purple, with eyes starting from their sockets as he fought for breath. Then his writhing body became still. It hung from the iron grip of the hands around his throat.

One of the hands shifted. Fingers, gloved, pried open Marxman's jaws. They took the melting capsule from his mouth. Then the dark figure heaved upright.

A thing like a badly tied bundle of rugs went over the ship's rail. There was a faint splash, almost inaudible in the plashing of the ship's progress.

The dark figure watched Marxman's body float astern like a drift log in the white wake of the moonlight. Then it turned, and melted into the darkness of the nearest companionway. And with it went the formulae of the new gas—and its partly perfected antidote.

2.

ON A HILL fronting the shore of the bay among great estates forming the cream of the big houses in the wealthy resort town of Red Bank, New Jersey, was the home of Linton R. Yates. A thirty-room mansion, it crowned the hill like a coronet of gray, cut stone.

At the moment it was dark. No lights showed from any

window, even the windows in the servants' quarters. It looked empty. But it wasn't. In the darkness of the side driveway a roadster stood. The roadster had been driven there, alone, by Linton Yates himself. And Linton Yates was at present in the basement of the house.

Down there, with none of the electric light showing from any barred and steel-shuttered basement window, he stood beside the square furnace at the end wall. His withered old hand went out. He touched a small, discolored patch in the wall next to the back of the furnace. A section of the wall hinged out.

Gray bearded, wizened, crafty-looking, the rich man stared furtively around him before he stepped into the hidden basement room revealed by the swinging back of the concealed door. As he entered the room he touched another discolored patch in the stone wall, and the door closed after him.

There was a great safe door in the floor of the ten-by-ten cube. So large was it that it almost formed the floor of the room. Rubbing his hands together with a dry, rasping sound, Yates walked over the safe door to a big knob in its center. He twirled that to the required combination, walked off the door, and threw a small switch.

There was a hum as a half-horsepower electric motor spun gears that slowly raised the ponderous door. Yates went down two steps into the safe. Here was a great heap of small, dirty yellow bars, and a square steel box. The yellow bars were gold; tons of the stuff, hoarded here by Yates against the day when the country would return to the gold standard—at a new and high dollar-value that should give him two dollars for every one he had spent for the precious metal. The steel box….

Yates chuckled aloud as he passed the bars of gold and went to the box. It weighed perhaps a hundred pounds. It was with a panting effort that the wizened old man managed to open the lid. With the lid opened, he crooned aloud, as a man might talk to an adorned pet.

A coruscating, varicolored fire came from within the box. It was cold fire. Yates plunged his hands in and lifted them. The fire trickled back down between his fingers and into the box again. The fire of diamonds, hundreds of them, unset but perfectly cut.

Diamonds and gold! The two commodities, particularly gold, that always have at least some solid worth, no matter to what low price other commodities sink.

"With these," whispered Yates, eyes gleaming, "I am secure. No man or form of government can harm me—make me poor."

He let diamonds trickle through his claw-like fingers again, then stiffened suddenly.

But his stiffening was not that of alarm, nor was it that of listening. He stared straight ahead of him, at the steel and copper wall of the sunken safe. But he did not see that wall. His filmed eyes were glazing rapidly, as the eyes of a man glazing in death. His body was as stiff, suddenly, and for no apparent reason, as a thing of wood.

For perhaps a full minute he stood there, bent over the box a little, with the last of the diamonds trickling from his cupped hands to the strong-box. Then slowly, he began to sag toward the floor. He sank to his knees, his rigid stare still centered on the safe wall. He fell, like a falling log, prone beside the treasure box.

He was dead. A glance could reveal that fact. But in a moment it was revealed that his death was not the most horrible part of the unseen drama to be played in the sunken safe.

The dead body abruptly began to lose its solidarity of outline. Its demarcations became blurred, as the surface of hot stone is blurred when heat waves shimmer up from it. And as the outlines became more and more blurred, they commenced to dwindle.

The dead body shrank, like wool in hot water. It got smaller till it was like the form of a doll dressed in doll's clothes to resemble an old man. And then—there was nothing in the safe but the dirty bars of gold and the small box of gems. At least, a glance would have intimated that there was nothing. Only a careful look would have shown, on the floor beside the box, a tiny thing like a watch-charm shaped in human form.

That was at eleven-thirty at night. At twelve, a big closed car drew up behind Yates' roadster under the side portico. The closed car had come thirty miles in thirty minutes. From it descended a figure cloaked in black, with a black hat on its head, the brim of which hid all trace of its features.

The figure worked an instant with the lock of the side door, opened it, and walked in darkness to the basement stairs. Beside the furnace a gloved hand—gloved in red instead of in more conventional hue—went out and touched the discolored patch.

Leisurely the figure went into the hidden basement room. It lifted the box of gems first. The box was borne to the big closed car. Then, bar by bar, the gold followed, carried by the dark figure as though the two hundred and fifty pounds each weighed were scarcely more than a normal load.

With plenty of time between trips, the big car was loaded till it sagged drunkenly low on its springs. Then it was backed out of the drive under the red-gloved hands of the dark form at the wheel.

It slid soundlessly into the main road, turned, and took the wide pike toward New York City....

IT WAS AT three in the morning when the Red Bank chief of police, a dark-faced, slow-moving man named Carlisle who was high in New York's detective bureau, and a man with black hair and steel-gray eyes, entered the sunken safe in the hidden basement room.

"See?" said the Red Bank chief. "It's all like I phoned you, Carlisle. Yates' roadster is at the side door, lights out and motor cold. The cook next door reported seeing the old man drive in, and after he'd been in the place two hours, with no lights on, she had sense enough to think something funny was going on. So she phoned me. But I get here and find this safe open and empty, and no sign of Yates! Now where the hell is he? He ain't in the house, and he ain't on the grounds. He couldn't have gone far without his roadster. And anyhow, his safe's cleaned. It must have had something pretty valuable in it. He certainly didn't clean it out himself and then just walk away somewhere leaving it wide open!"

The tall man with the coal-black hair and the gray eyes stopped suddenly. He picked up something from the floor, near a square in the dust that looked as though a box had rested there recently.

"What'd you find, Keane?" Carlisle asked.

Ascott Keane, probably the most competent detective alive, though few knew him as anything but a polo-playing rich man's son, faced Lieutenant Detective Carlisle.

"Nothing but a burnt match," he said, holding out a paper match with a charred end. "I don't think it will tell us much."

He gave the charred match to Carlisle.

But into his coat pocket went another small object, hardly bigger than the match, which he had picked up from the floor at the same time and palmed.

Carlisle grunted at the match, then looked expectantly at Ascott Keane.

"Well," he said, "you once told me to get in touch with you any time an especially mysterious crime was done. This is crime, sure enough. And, damned if it isn't mysterious enough. Think your pal, Doctor Satan, did it?"

Keane shrugged.

"There undoubtedly was something of great value in this carefully concealed strong-room. There must have been a great deal of it. Probably hoarded gold. Certainly Yates wasn't able to carry it away; he was an old man, rather feeble. Somebody got rid of him, somehow, when he was down here counting over his buried treasure. And, from the complete absence of all clues, I'd say the person clever enough to do that might have been—Doctor Satan."

Carlisle stared curiously at Keane. Keane's face was as calm as a poker-player's. But it was to be noted that fine beads of perspiration were on his face, and that his cheeks were not quite as calm as his expression. Hard marks ridged them.

"That all you got to tell me?" he said.

"That's all for the moment. I think I'll run along—"

"But you just came!" Carlisle said, disappointed and a little suspicious. "You haven't looked around at all.

"Looking around won't get you anywhere—if this is the work of Doctor Satan. And I'm sure it is. A lot of quiet study in a secluded spot is more to the point. I'm off the indulge myself in that now."

He nodded to the two men, and left the basement.

Behind Yates' car was the police car the Chief and Carlisle had come in. Behind that was Keane's long-low-hooded sedan with its streamlines and its hundred and thirty miles an hour of speed under its hood.

Beside the driver's seat was a girl, waiting for him. She was tall and lithe. Her dark blue eyes, in the light from the dash, softened as they turned on him. Her hair, escaping in a few tendrils from under a smart, small hat, was coppery brown. This was Beatrice Dale, Keane's secretary. No, more than secretary! She was his able assistant, his right-hand man. More than once in his pursuit of the monster of crime who called himself Doctor Satan, Keane had reached the point where he could hardly have carried on without her aid.

"What did you find?" she said eagerly, as he took the seat beside her and started the motor. "Was it— Doctor Satan's work?"

Wordlessly, in answer, Keane handed her the small thing he'd picked up from the floor in the rifled strong-room. Then he slid into reverse gear as she looked at it.

"Ascott, what is it?" Beatrice said. "It looks like a tiny doll. Yet it gives me the creeps somehow. It seems to be made of rubber or some such stuff. A little doll, hardly more than, half an inch long. What is it?"

Keane tooled the car onto the highway and started along the New York pike. He glanced somberly at her.

"What is it? Well, it isn't a doll. Here, give it back to me before I tell you."

He took it from her fingers and put it back into his pocket.

"That," he said, "is a man. Not a doll. A dead man!"

"What—" Beatrice faltered.

"It's the remains of Linton R. Yates. Now, you're not going to faint! I wouldn't have told you if I'd though you were apt to do anything silly."

Beatrice Dale straightened her swaying body into the seat. She drew a deep breath, and her voice was measurably calm as she said:

"You flatter my nerves, I'm afraid. My God! A dead man! And I held it!"

It was notable that she didn't question for an instant the statement that a thing like a tiny doll, which could be held in the palm of her hand, was, impossibly, a dead body. She had worked with Keane long enough to know that his statements were apt to be infallible. And the feel of the little thing that "had given her the creeps" bore out his fantastic declaration.

"Yes," he said as the car leaped toward eighty miles an hour, "that little thing is Linton Yates, retired oil magnate. Can you imagine his loving family gathered around that, during a burial ceremony" Like burying a watch-charm with all due pomp and surroundings!"

"Then it was Doctor Satan!" Nobody else on earth could have done so hideous and bizarre a thing! But how—"

She stared at him, still pale, eyes wide.

Keane frowned at the night, into which they were boring at express train speed.

"I think I know how. I'll make sure when we've got to my library at home."

THAT WAS AT a little after three. At four, they stood in Keane's book-lined library beside the great ebony desk at which he had sat studying so many problems arising from the ghastly genius of Doctor Satan.

Keane was reading a two-year-old scientific paper entitled "The Possibilities of a Death, or Disintegrating, Ray," by someone named Barnard Hallowell:

> "The death ray, so-called from popular speculations of a disintegrating device by the public press, is not at all an impossible dream. I am working on some such device now. I have come close to its solution several times. As none of the features of my invention has yet been perfected to the point where they can be patented, I will naturally not reveal particulars to you. But I can describe the result of the machine when—and *if*—it is completed,
>
> "My apparatus could be pointed and aimed as accurately as any gun, so that the ray it emits can kill one person, and one person, alone, at a distance up to forty miles. Or the ray could be so diffused that all things within a forty-degree arc of its muzzle (at a lesser distance, however) would die. The ray strikes instantly dead the thing it is loosed upon. Then it further disintegrates the flesh of the carcass by causing the molecules to split apart and stream away, through solid objects around it, and eventually, into empty space. How can I know this, when I never yet quite completed a machine? My only answer unfortunately, not provable since I cannot let anyone see the fruits of my experiments to date, is that I have come near enough to the solution to what the problem is in effect, similar to what I describe, to begin on bodies of animals in my laboratory...."

Keane closed the paper, and looked at Beatrice.

Her blue eyes were level with concentration. She stared at the paper in his hand, then at his face.

"Doctor Satan got to the man who wrote that paper, Bernard Hallowell," she said. "Since he wrote it, he has completed the death-ray machine. Doctor Satan forced the secret of it from him. That is what the little figure you picked up in Yates' safe means."

Keane slowly shook his head. On his forehead again appeared fine drops of sweat. And again, hard muscle ridged out on his lean cheeks.

"No, Beatrice, it means more than that—much more. You see, Bernard Hallowell is dead. He died two years ago, just after reading this paper before a meeting of the American Scientific Institute."

Beatrice stared at him, color slowly draining from her face as she vaguely sensed something of what was in his mind.

"Bernard Hallowell, the one man on earth capable of doing to a human body what was done to Yates, is dead. Yet Doctor Satan got from him the secret of the death ray—which was not quite completed when he died. That can mean only one thing:

"Doctor Satan has found out how really to do that which charlatans and self-deluded investigators have often claimed baselessly they could do—communicate with the dead."

3.

THE DISAPPEARANCE ON shipboard of the great inventor, Jules Marxman, stirred police circles as a stick stirs muddy water. The vanishing of Linton Yates was distinctly secondary: Yates, though far richer, was not as internationally known.

At the hotel suite booked by Marxman for himself and his assistant, swarms of detectives and newspaper reporters filed in and out interviewing, or trying to interview, Slycher, the assistant.

But there was one man who had no trouble closing himself with Slycher, known to police and news hawks if not the public, he was treated with amazing deference. That was Ascott Keane. He sat in the tower suite now with Slycher.

"You say you thought Assistant Secretary of War Harley talked to Marxman just before Marxman disappeared?" Keane repeated.

Slycher nodded, white-faced, more than a little frightened. He was himself a murder suspect, of course.

"But Harley denies seeing Marxman?" Keane went on.

"Yes," said Slycher. "Most of the police think I'm making up the story. But I swear I saw Mr. Harley go into Mr. Marxman's cabin. Also, I saw him come out again, and shortly afterward, Mr. Marxman went on deck—and was never seen again."

Keane looked at the man. He was obviously telling the truth, as he saw it.

"Harley is above suspicion," Keane mused. "If he denies he was with Marxman, it's quite likely he wasn't there, in spite of appearances. That means someone must have impersonated Harley. Marxman was bringing home a nearly completed war formula, wasn't he?"

Slycher nodded and told him about the poison gas, which was perfected, and the antidote which was not.

"The gas was useless as a weapon till the antidote could be worked out better," he concluded. So, anyone stealing the gas formula couldn't use it anyhow: if he tried, he'd be knocked out himself."

Keane's eyes were intent, and were glinting a little as they always did when he was uncovering a warm scent.

"This formula of the antidote," he said slowly. "As it stood, it figuratively killed anyone who took it—"

Not figuratively—actually!" the inventor's assistant interrupted. "Anyone taking it dies, as far as medical examination can show, for twelve hours."

"And Doctor Satan can communicate with the dead!" Keane breathed.

"What?"

"Nothing, I think I'm beginning to see light, that's all. And now for a very important question. And you'll have to judge for yourself, from recommendations given you concerning me, whether you dare answer truly. Did Marxman, by any chance, have a sample of the antidote among his effects?"

Slycher hesitated a long time before he answered that. Then slowly he nodded.

He did. He dared to do it because the formula was so complicated that he doubted if any laboratory could fully analyze the sample and duplicate it."

"Let me have it, will you?" said Keane.

Again the assistant studied his face for a long time. But Keane's sincerity and authority were unquestionable. Slycher got up and went to the next room of the suite. He came back with a heavily sealed envelope in his hand. The envelope was padded out as though it contained a handkerchief or some other small but bulky thing.

"Here it is, do want all of it?"

"No," said Keane softly. "Just enough for one dose."

Slycher opened the envelope. Onto a sheet of writing-paper he shook a minute quantity of purplish powder. It was coarse powder. It was small crystals, really and looked like powdered amethyst.

"This is one dose of the antidote," he said. "May I ask what you intend to do with it?"

Keane looked at, and through, the man. His voice, when he answered, was a little hushed.

"I'm going to take it—and die. I'm going to find out where a man goes when he's dead. And I hope to meet another person in that place—and perhaps leave him there!"

Beatrice Dale, to whom he announced the same intention, when he returned home, was horrified.

"My God, Ascott! Meet Doctor Satan in death? You can't! The risk—"

"The risk is a little thing compared to what may happen if I don't," Keane said quietly. "Have you thought at all what this means? Doctor Satan, with the aid of Marxman's uncompleted formula, can visit the dead. From them he can obtain the secrets they died without revealing to any other mortal. Why, the world is his if he can't be stopped! Think of being able to discover the last, and perhaps greatest of the inventions Edison was working on when he died. Or the chance of learning from Captain Kidd's own lips where his treasure is hidden! Or of finding out the true political machinations of European diplomacy from any of the great statesmen who have recently passed on! Satan can be emperor of earth with that knowledge!"

He looked at the pinch of purplish crystals.

"The gateway to death. Bring me a glass of water, will you? Even if nothing is accomplished beyond that gateway, even if I never come back from beyond it, it will be interesting to pass through it."

MIDWAY BETWEEN NEW YORK and Red Bank, in New Jersey, on a flat-topped knoll near the sea, there stands a rather hideous replica of a Rhenish castle built by an eccentric rich man long dead. The people living near there call it Furlowe's Folly, and know that it has been untenanted and in bad repair for many years. What they did not know was that it had been purchased recently by a man who never made a personal appearance during the transaction. What they also did not know was that in a steel-lined room in the basement of the house, the purchaser, and his ugly assistant, often engaged at night in occupations that could have blanched their faces would they have looked on.

The two were there tonight.

One, the secret purchaser of Furlowe's Folly, was Doctor Satan, dressed in the masquerade it amused him to wear; red cloak covering his lean, powerful body from heels to throat; red mask over his face; red gloves on his hand; and on his head, the skullcap of red with the little projections, like horns, that completed his costume of Lucifer.

The other was Bostiff, who was a figure out of an illustration of Dante's Inferno. He had no legs. He hitched his gigantic, formidably muscled torso about by using his arms as legs and resting his weight on the calloused backs of his hands. His eyes, dull, dog-like stupidly brutal, followed the red-clad figure of his master constantly.

Doctor Satan was bending over a long, plain table which was littered with laboratory instruments. He was manipulating a small glass beaker in which a purplish, heavy liquid was rapidly drying into fine purplish crystals. From time to time, he consulted a wrinkled small bit of onion skin paper that had formerly been rolled up in a capsule.

He shook the dried crystals from the beaker onto the table.

"Ready, Bostiff," his harsh voice droned out.

Bostiff went to a corner of the steel-lined room. There was a low divan there. He wheeled it toward Doctor Satan, who lay down on it.

"For twelve hours, Bostiff," Doctor Satan Said, "My body is helpless, a dead thing. Remember that. And don't let anyone force a way in here!"

"Yes, Master," Bostiff rumbled, gazing at the purplish crystals with dull fear in his eyes.

On my first trip to the land of the dead," Satan said harshly, "I got from Hallowell the secret of the death ray. Now I can kill from a distance, and loot the possessions of the victim at leisure. This trip I expect to get from the recently assassinated dictator of Texas, Kelly Strong, full details of his plan to become dictator of the United States, and names of men he placed in key positions to carry out the scheme. He was ready to start up his plan in motion when he was killed. I shall carry on for him, and become dictator in his place. How would you like to be Secretary of State of the United States, Bostiff, with countless men—and women—dancing to your whims to avoid being killed or thrown into jail?"

Bostiff licked his thick lips, and his dull eyes gleamed. Doctor Satan laughed arrogantly, and poured the purplish crystals into a glass of wine.

"Then guard my helpless body with your life, oh good and faithful servant," he said mockingly. "And—don't be so misguided as to attempt to remove my mask and see my face. No man may do that and live!"

Doctor Satan raised the glass of wine, in which was the little death of Marxman's antidote, and drank.

4.

TWO PEOPLE HAD taken Marxman's drug and died the little death. The dock laborer on whom Marxman had experimented, and Doctor Satan. Now, with Ascott Keane's taking of the purplish crystals, there were three.

His first sensation after swallowing the stuff was—pain.

His body ached as though every bone in it had been broken. He felt as though each nerve were being slowly rasped with red-hot files.

It hurts to die, was his last conscious thought. And after that, he seemed to fall into a deep and dreamless sleep that might have lasted a moment or two, or a thousand years, so that his next thought was the gateway of death is no black river, or cavern mouth guarded by the many-headed watchdog, it is sleep.

But that was a dim thought, quickly lost in a fog of blind horror as his senses slowly struggled back to him. What was it that horrified him? For a long time, he did not know, could not define it.

He had been sitting at his ebony desk when he drank the antidote. When he regained conscious thought, he did not know whether he was sitting or standing; for he seemed to have no body, no weight. And that was odd, for when he opened his eyes he could see a body. He seemed as solid and weighty as when he had swallowed the drug; and was clothed as he had been then—in most prosaic blue serge.

Yet, the inability to tell whether he was standing or lying persisted. He simply was; he existed in—

In what?

It was the answer to that which finally brought his blind feeling of horror to a head. For he seemed to exist, now in nothingness!

Beneath him he could see nothing. No ground, as we know it, or surface of any kind. Around him was—nothing. Over him was nothing. It was as though he had been transported, with the drinking of the purplish liquid, into the immensities of space—and then had been seeing the stars wink out till none remained.

Yet, this vast nothingness in which he found himself, was not a thing of darkness. Vague gray light was diffused everywhere; like dim moonlight, which is not strong enough to outline things tangibly, yet gives an impression of so doing.

A nothingness of gray space, with Ascott Keane existing in it, but not knowing whether he lay or stood because around him was no single thing by which to orient himself! Where was he? In the land of the dead! And the land of the dead, it seemed, was nowhere!

Yet, he existed, saw himself as he had been last in life. He had, at least to his own perceptions, body and individuality.

But that may be simply the materialization of my thoughts of myself, he thought. If that is so, then I have the answer to the question; does living intelligence die? It does not. The body does, but not the intelligence directing it.

Now, as he existed in the spaceless, dimensionless, objectless gray nothingness, Keane became aware of sensation of other thoughts and feelings all around near him. Countless forces had their source near him. He felt as one feels when surrounded by a great host of people. Yet, he could see nothing, though the feel of being hemmed in by countless others grew stronger with each passing minute. (Minute? That was a figurative term. For along with a loss of dimension and space and outline as the living know them, Keane had lost all time-sense).

Maybe, thought Keane, I am invisible to them too. Perhaps only the thinking of myself makes me perceptible, and that only to me.

The corollary notion came at once:

But if that is so, then I should be able to see others if I think of them! Then it is directed thought which makes outline here in this gray place; which makes tangible outline.

Well, there was a way to test that. If he thought of someone he had known, now dead, that person might appear....

The most obvious person was his father, who had died when Keane was twelve, and whom he had admired as much as he loved. He thought of his father—heavyset, with keen gray eyes under bristling gray brows, and with stubby, powerful hands thrust always in his pockets.

And his father appeared before him!

Keane thought he cried aloud. But there was no sound in this land of the dead. He felt his throat swell with the impulse for sound, and that was all.

"Dad!"

"Ascott."

But there was no sound. Vibration, thought-waves—the

means of communication were as intangible and cloaked in luminous gray mystery as everything else here. Keane only knew that he looked at his father, dead for twenty years, and felt him name him.

"So you have died, my son," emanated from the figure seemingly of solidified mist, that had appeared with Keane's thought of it. "Your mother will be anxious to see you—"

"My mother! Then everyone we knew—all people—have a life after death! They exist as they did on earth?"

Keane thought his father smiled. But he could not be sure, because he could not be sure if the face and form of his father were appearing before him, in actual sight—or behind his eyelids, formed by imagination.

"Not quite as on earth," his father said—or, rather radiated. "Here nothing has actual form. You and I, as well as all other living things, are bits of the great central plant of Life Force, which actuates everything that breathes. When we 'die', we are re-absorbed by the great life stream, though we know no more about it than a drop of water knows the meaning of the river that re-collects it after it has been drawn to the sky by the sun and released again in rain."

"But I see you! I see myself—"

"You see your thought of me, of yourself, not substance. There is no substance here. You will find out, now that you have died."

KEANE THOUGHT: QUEER he doesn't know that I haven't really died; that I will return from this gray land. Then he realized that secret thoughts were as evident to his father as specially directed ones were.

For again he seemed to smile, and he said: "I know nothing of what goes on on earth. None of us do, which is contrary to the idea that I, at least, used to have: that the dead know all. Sometimes I would like to know, but I can't find out. The veil of death keeps us from communicating with the living as well as preventing them from communicating with us."

"But now there is communication between dead and living," Keane replied. "And that is why I'm here. On earth a man invented a war weapon which is useless without an antidote that makes it harmless to the men who use the weapon. The antidote, falling in its intended purpose, gives death for half a day to whoever swallows it. Another man, a person without conscience as well as without fear, stole his secret. He has used it to 'die' and while 'dead' to speak to those actually dead and get from them important information; though how he can do that when they must know his purpose is evil, and must try not to give it to him—"

"Here where all thought either takes physical expression or can be interpreted as clearly as audible speech in life, no thought can remain hidden," his father informed him. "The man you describe has but to think his question, and whoever the thought is directed at will necessarily think the answer. For thought is involuntary. It cannot be controlled, and there is nothing physical here."

Thought involuntary? Keane repeated to himself. He did not believe that. It had always been his contention that thought could be controlled by a strong-willed man. But now he was to have immediate proof of his father's correctness.

It was miraculous to converse with him! It was miraculous, and appealing, to think of conversing with his dead mother too. But there was a thought more insistent than either of these; that was the thought (recalled strongly to him by speaking of Doctor Satan to his father) of the diabolical being he had come here to thwart.

And so, converse with his mother, and further converse with his father, were not to be. For with his thought of Doctor Satan—the vague outlines of his father faded, and other outlines began taking their place.

"Satan!" he thought. "Now—I will see his face!"

But he had forgotten his own prosaic blue serge, the fabric that seemed to clothe him now as it had when he "died".

More and more plainly, the outlines of the figure driving his father from his mind appeared to him. And they were still as secretive as they had been on earth!

He saw a lean, red-cloaked shape, tall, with a red mask, and red-gloved hands. He saw no revealed feature save arrogant, glittering black eyes through the red mask's eye-holes.

Doctor Satan—still masked against disclosure of identity!

But with the detestably familiar red form another was appearing. And, with the ability here to guess at all thought, even when that thought tries to conceal itself, he realized why.

He was seeing the man Doctor Satan had taken the little death to find! His thought of Satan had brought him into materialization and, as one object roped to a second will lift the second when it itself is lifted, with Satan had come the person he had been conversing with when Keane visioned him.

Keane saw a face that was a little hazy and yet very familiar, topped by wavy, iron-gray hair; a face in which a large mouth was mobile over a long, cleft chin; a face often pictured, in life, in the papers. It was the face of Kelly Strong, in life political dictator of the state of Texas, presumed to have been designing the presidency—and not quite the same presidency as that in the minds of the nation's founders!—before he died.

At the same time, Keane perceived with horror the significance of the meeting of these two. The strange but inevitable phenomenon of thought-transference, which was the rule here, instantly spelled it out for him.

Doctor Satan meant to get the whole of Strong's plans of dictatorship, almost completed before he died, and become dictator himself! And the idea of Satan as dictator was one to stagger the mind!

"My God!" thought Keane. And: "I wonder if I've come in time to stop it...."

WITH HIS FIRST materialization, Doctor Satan, as aware of Keane as Keane was of him, had turned snarling soundlessly from Strong. His black eyes bored into Keane's gray ones, insane with thwarted purpose. And as both he and Keane concentrated only on each other, the materialization of Kelly Strong slowly disappeared.

And in that instant Keane had his answer, given him as helplessly by Satan's involuntary thoughts as Satan's dead informants gave up their secrets to him.

Doctor Satan had not yet sucked the information he wanted from Strong! Keane had got to him in time!

"Keane!" was Satan's enraged thought. And, though the following words were born in Keane's brain, rather than actually heard, he yet thought to hear the man's harsh, arrogant voice. "In the devil's name—how do you manage to cross me here?"

But in Keane's mind, he read the answer, as the question called up in Keane's brain the memory of his talk with Marxman's secretary-assistant, and the obtaining of a dose of the antidote.

"So Marxman's man made it possible!" Satan raged. "And you guessed what I was doing by the results of the death ray on Linton Yates! Yes, I read it all! I tried to find you with the death ray first. But your damned ability, in life if not here, of shielding your thoughts from me, made you an unlocatable target where ordinary men were not! And so you're here—"

"And so I'm here," was Keane's response. "And of the two of us, one is going to stay. And I intend that that one shall be you!"

ALONE IN THE great nothingness of gray, misty light, there two were. Alone in the place of the dead. For here nothing existed that was not thought of. And the two had no slightest thought of anything but each other.

Doctor Satan's red-clad outline shimmered toward Keane, only a projected shadow of the red-clad body that lay in the steel-lined basement room the Furlowe's Folly, but a shadow as sinister and real-appearing as the body itself.

"There is a hell in this place, my friend," he stated. "I have been here once before, and I have found that out. It is like its denizens, only to be perceived when it is thought of. In that hell you shall remain—while I go back to life, a dictator, and freed from your bungling interference forever."

His black eyes gleamed more brightly.

"A hell, Ascott Keane! It's singularly fitting that I, Doctor Satan, should be the one to cast you into it!"

Keane made no reply. He couldn't have if he had wanted to. For now his eyes began to see strange things in the gray mist. Things conjured up by Satan's thought of them.

Slowly, the empty space around him was being defined in the shape of a hollow globe, of which he and Satan were the center. And slowly the walls of the globe were narrowing down on them and were becoming more definite.

And Keane tried to cry aloud again as he saw of what the globe was composed, but he could not, since there was no such thing as sound there.

The walls of the globe were a solid, or seemingly solid, mass of bodies. But they were bodies such as had never before been seen outside a nightmare.

Some had no heads. Some seemed all face and mouth, with tiny puny limbs attached. Some were legless or armless or both. And all were blind.

Pallid gray shapes in the pallid grayness, they writhed and reached toward Keane and Satan; yet Keane knew intuitively that it was not Doctor Satan who engaged their attention, but solely himself. And he shuddered as he thought of being engulfed by the crippled, maimed, writhing things.

"This is just what shall happen," he perceived Satan speaking to him. "They shall take your soul here, Keane. These things were men and women on earth. They were "crippled morally," as society chose to express it—just as you believe I am morally crippled when, really… but we won't go into that."

The black eyes glittered satanically.

"Here, after death, they are warped and deformed as they were in life. Creatures of hell, Keane. And as destructive and murderous here as when they had actuality. But it is seldom they have the chance to try their talent for destructiveness now. They shall try it on you."

The hollow globe was very small now; Keane had the impression that he could almost reach out and touch the hideous shapes composing the wall—had there been anything there really to touch.

"They'll get Doctor Satan, too," he thought frantically. There's no reason why they should pursue me and not him."

But he knew as he thought that there was a reason.

The lean tall figure in the red cloak, and these warped creatures of after-life, were of the same stuff. Satan could command them, not be destroyed by them, because he thought as they did and lived as they had lived before death took them.

"Take him!" he caught Satan's soundless command to the hideous gray shapes. "Take his soul! Hold it here, that on earth his body may be forever a lifeless shell, with soul and intelligence gone!"

And then the gray shapes were on Keane, and he was a wavering form in a monstrous sea.

There was no pain. He saw claw-like hands rip into him, and saw the likeness of his body shredded from him as bits of cloud are shredded from the main cloud bank by a screaming wind. But there was, of course, no pain.

However, there was mental agony far exceeding any physical pain. He had no way of being told it, but he knew the truth: If these clawing hands managed to rip away entirely the thought-mantle that clothed his spirit, if they managed to strip him of his conception of himself, then he could never go back the way he came. He would be really dead, with no link between him and the hulk of himself that sat before the empty water glass on the ebony desk.

"Take him!" Doctor Satan was exhorting the host he would assuredly join when it was his turn really to die. "Strip his soul! Keep him here!"

No real substance, but mist-stuff that could be shredded and torn as misty veils are torn! Keane struggled in the hideous current of writhing, clawing, venomous forms. Doctor Satan was near him. He got to the red-cloaked form.

He had but half an arm left, though like a man in a nightmare, he could look at it and be appalled and yet feel no pain. But the hand remained on this arm, the whole underside of which had been clawed away. That hand drove for Satan's throat, and found it.

Perhaps it was because Keane was not really dead, and that hence his materialization had a shade more actuality than those of the writhing things about them. Perhaps it was that his hate of the man, whose cruel joke it was to act as Lucifer as well as costume himself in Luciferian manner, was strong enough to take some tangible form here in a place of intangibility. At any rate, Keane's one crippled hand did more damage than all the clawing hands of all the clawing things that tore at him.

Like a ball of mist on a mist-column, Satan's head wavered and seemed about to leave its body as Keane's hand grasped at the shadowy throat.

"Take him!" Satan exhorted, frenziedly, fearfully, to the crawling throng. "Take him—"

His own red-gloved hands were wrenching and tearing at Keane's mangled wrist. But they could not tear it away.

"Take him—"

Something was happening to Keane.

Suddenly, impossibly, he was beginning to feel pain. It was as though Keane's body was being broken and every atom of flesh on it was crushed. As the pain swept down on him in ever-increasing waves, the horrible gray shapes faded from his perception—as did the red-clad form of Doctor Satan. The luminous gray nothingness in which he had moved for an unguessable length of time (it might have been a minute or a year or a century) began to fade too.

There was Satan's thwarted, raging command, "Take him—" There was a last vengeful tightening of his hand on Satan's throat. Then, the pain mounted over everything else and robbed him of consciousness….

A VOICE WAS calling to him. A girl's voice, frantic, urgent.

"Ascott! Ascott!"

He tried to open his eyes, and could not for a moment. He was shuddering, and felt clammy with perspiration. He had just undergone some terrible ordeal, but for a little while longer he was spared memory of it.

"Ascott! Darling—"

He knew that voice. Yes… the Voice of Beatrice Dale… yes….

With an enormous effort he opened his eyes. He saw the polished ebony of his desk-top within inches of his face; saw his hands.

His hands! He gasped, and stared at them as memory returned. But his hands were all right. He had them both, and neither was torn or mutilated. Nor were his arms.

"Nightmare!" he muttered.

But he knew better than that. He had undergone an actual experience in an actual place: the land of the dead. Now—

He sat up. He had been slumped over his desk with his hands supporting his head while his intelligence roamed afar from his body under the influence of Marxman's antidote. But now he sat up—and saw Beatrice's white face.

"Ascott!" Thank God. You've been unconscious—dead, from all appearances—for an hour over the twelve the drug was supposed to stop working! I was going to call a doctor, the police, anything! But now—"

"Now, I'm all right," said Keane, breathing heavily. "All right—now—nightmare I went through."

Beatrice bathed his clammy face, gave him adrenalin, ministered to him with all the affection she kept from expressing verbally for him. And then, when he was breathing normally and, while pale, seemed all right again, she said:

"Did you—did you find Doctor Satan, Ascott?"

Keane's nostrils thinned.

"I did. I got him in time. And—he almost got me. He calls himself Doctor Satan—and there is a hell, Beatrice, and at his command I was almost kept in it! I wonder… Many a circumstance is shaped apparently by coincidence, and many a mortal unconsciously acts in a way to bear out literally the conceptions of religion. An actual hell…. I wonder if our red-cloaked friend really could be an incarnation of the evil force we've always called Satan, though he himself thinks he is only acting a part?"

"Drink this," said Beatrice, handing him a cup of coffee with the practicality of the female. "Ascott, did Doctor Satan come back to life too?"

"I'm afraid he did," sighed Keane.

"Then everything was useless? Satan can return whenever he pleases, and get the secrets of the dead as he did before?"

Keane shook his head.

"That, at least, I think we can stop. There is a hell, and creatures in it like maimed demons. Then it follows that there must be beings in the land of the dead who were decent in life and are so in death. And it also must follow that they outnumber the maimed."

He stared at the coffee, making no effort to drink it.

"I was almost kept from returning to life by the things from hell. I think Doctor Satan might be kept from returning to life by the decent dead. Anyway, I'm going back, now, to see my father and band the dead against Satan if he should ever return.

Go to Marxman's assistant and get another dose of the antidote."

"For God's sake, Ascott—"

Keane stared at her. His eyes were as grim as death, and as impersonal.

"Get more of the drug, please, Beatrice."

Beatrice Dale's lips parted, closed again without uttering words. She turned and left him.

THE DEVIL'S DOUBLE

IT WAS THE middle of an early summer afternoon in Louisville. The sun bathed the streets with hot gold. People thronged the main avenue. Women shoppers streamed in and out of the stores; men hurried on business; traffic rolled in orderly haste.

The middle of a prosaic afternoon. All seemed as it should be....

The town car turned onto the avenue from a side street. It was a big foreign car, speaking of great wealth. Its curtains were drawn.

The town car stopped before a building which was under construction. The sidewalk here was railed off to prevent pedestrians on the walk from being struck by falling bricks. But as the town car halted, a man appeared from the interior of the unfinished building. He walked unobtrusively past the car.

As he passed, one of the curtains over the car windows was raised. A shaking hand came out with a newspaper-wrapped package in it. The man from the building took the package. He walked back into the building again.

The town car's motor raced preparatory to going away. But before it could get into motion, another car with curtained windows swung onto the avenue. This did not stop anywhere. It slowed a little near the town car, but that was all.

However, in the short time of its slowing, it discharged a passenger. Of the hundreds on the avenue, only a few noticed the car, a big blue sedan. Of these few, only two or three saw the passenger get out. At first, that was!

A prosaic street, crowded with prosaic people going about their commonplace affairs....

And then, seemingly all at once, they began to stare at the discharged passenger. Once they had seen, they craned their necks to look again, shocked out of all commonplace, living by what their eyes were regarding.

The person who had come from the blue sedan was a woman—a girl, rather, scarcely more than twenty. She was tall, maturely curved, strikingly lovely. She had dark hair and great dark eyes, and skin so fair that it looked snow-white in contrast to the blackness of her hair and eyes.

She had descended from the car, run a few paces to get her balance as she hit immovable ground from a moving object, and then stood still in the middle of the avenue, with surprised drivers jamming their brakes to keep from running her down.

For an instant she continued to stand there, in the middle of the street, as if dazed, with traffic a twin river around her. Then cars began to stop on each side of her, and cars and staring crowds began to ring her in.

"What's the matter with her?" a woman snapped. "Is she walking in her sleep?"

"Might be, at that," a man snickered beside her. "Looks like she's got a nightie on."

Dazedly the beautiful girl looked around at the crowds. And it could be seen that the nightgown simile was not far from the mark.

Sheer strips of some stuff swathed her body, were draped loosely around her legs. That was all she wore, the sheer stuff through which her form could be vaguely seen as through mist.

"What is she—a veil dancer?" snorted another man.

The traffic cop from the corner began to force his way to the block-up in the center of the square. Like a statue swathed in mist, the girl stood in the cleared space. And now the door of the town car opened and an elderly man stumbled out. His eyes were wide with horror. He staggered toward the girl, hands outstretched as though groping his way.

Suddenly the girl moved. She poised one slippered foot and from the folds of gauze that covered her she drew a short, slim blade. Her voice raised in a shrill, eerie incantation, the words of which could not be distinguished. She waved the sword. She began to dance.

"A publicity gag," someone shouted. "She's a sword-dancer after a newspaper write-up."

The crowd laughed and yelled agreement. Some fool began to beat time to the girl's slow rhythmic steps by clapping his hands. But horror was growing on the face of the elderly man from the town car. And on the face of the cop, as he came nearer through the crowd, was amazement and something like awe.

"It's Jane Ivor," he panted suddenly. "By the saints—Jane Ivor!"

The dancing girl whirled more rapidly, more wildly. Her great dark eyes glittered with lurid fires. She performed her sword dance in the middle of the city's main street with more abandon.

"That's the girl," shouted the man who was clapping time. "If publicity's what you want, you'll get it."

The girl seemed not to hear him—seemed not to hear or see anybody. Her supple left hand tore at her breast, and a strip of the gray gauze enfolding her came loose and floated to the ground, exposing her smooth white shoulders.

"Now you're going to town!" laughed the man who clapped. "More, more!"

Jane Ivor—" panted the traffic cop, tearing his way forward with ever less ceremony.

"My daughter!" groaned the elderly man from the town car, fighting the heedless mob between him and the girl.

The girl began to sing more wildly. And now the crowd stilled a bit as a few words could be distinguished in her chant, and as more and more of the swathing gauze was torn from her body. People began looking at one another inquiringly.

"Satan... my master..." some of the words of the girl's chant sounded. "Devil... worship...."

The swathing gauze was nearly all on the street now. And a woman cried out a bit as the meaning came home to all. No publicity seeker would go quite so far. No girl would dare such censure in a mere quest for notoriety.

"Let me through, damn you!" shrieked the elderly man, fighting at the heedless ranks still between him and the girl.

"Get out of the way, you dumbbells," raged the cop, beginning to use his night stick. Jane Ivor—let me get to her!"

There was stunned silence, in which the girl's chant sounded louder, more weird than ever. Then, like a concerted echo, the crowd repeated the name.

"Jane Ivor! Jane Ivor!"

A young man in the outer fringe of the crowd gasped.

"Good God! It is Jane Ivor! Most beautiful deb in the city! Daughter of John Ivor, the distilling magnate! Kidnapped a week ago, along with her kid brother! And now she comes back—like this!"

In the cleared spot on the avenue now danced a girl with moonight hair and eyes, who wore nothing but frayed, high-heeled slippers. Her eyes were frenzied as she waved the slim sword above her head and chanted. And now the words of the incantation were only too clear.

"Satanic Majesty, I worship you. You, the Devil, are my master. Death to your enemies!"

THE CROWD, COMING through heedless laughter and growing confusion to something like terror, gave back before the girl's shimmering blade. That sword was obviously razor-sharp, and she was slashing it around with horrifying abandon.

"The Devil's my master! Death to his enemies!"

The pirouetting white figure circled the ring of cars and people shutting it in. And then a man yelled.

"My God!—look at her eyes!"

The girl's black eyes seemed about to start from her head. Wild white formed a rim around the pupils.

"She's mad! Get her before she kills somebody!"

"Satan is my master! I worship the Devil—"

Screaming now, the crowd that had been laughing rolled back from the girl. The man who had been clapping time, ashen-faced, led the rush. Several other men, with the traffic cop beside them, leaped for her.

"Back!" she screamed, slashing with the sword. "You are enemies of Satan! I will kill all enemies of the Devil!"

"Jane," cried the elderly man, breaking at last through the milling crowd. "Jane—my own daughter—"

"Back—I'll kill—"

The elderly man, sobbing, gasping, fell back from the keen blade that had darted toward his heart.

"Jane—don't you know me? It's Dad!"

"Back—"

The traffic cop sprang at her. Like a tigress she stepped away, blade flashing. The cop's face turned sickly as the blade grazed his cheek. And then, the others were on her, horrified, deathly afraid of the blade in her mad fingers, but risking their lives to catch the lovely maniac before others in the crowd died to the bite of the blade.

"Enemies of the Devil! Enemies of the Devil!"

Her shrill voice was a clarion call, a bugle note of madness. But they got her at last, hands gripping her white flesh firmly, though as compassionately as possible.

The elderly man approached her as she struggled in the grip of the men, who tried to cover her writhing white body with their coats.

"Jane," he groaned, "Look at me, recognize me! It's John Ivor, your father, Jane."

The girl only gazed at him out of great eyes in which the whites were lunatic rings around the pupils, and tried to gouge his face with taloned fingers.

"Jane Ivor!"

"Released by the kidnappers—but insane!" the young man breathed. "Wait till I get that story into the paper! Insane heiress back from kidnap hell to do nude sword dance in the main street!

He ran for a phone. And the knot of men holding Jane Ivor, once the city's most popular debutante, went with her to the town car which still stood beside the half-completed building, and put her in it with her white-faced father.

2.

THE AIR WAS tense, still, in the best private room of Louisville's finest hospital.

Four people were in that room. One, tied with webbed linen to the iron bed, was Jane Ivor. The second was her father, who sat with fingers gripping the edge of his chair till they showed white in the reflected sun-glare from the cream-colored walls. The third was the chief of staff of the hospital, an internationally known psychiatrist. The fourth was a figure such as might have stepped out of a nightmare or a masquerade ball.

This figure was tall, spare. It was cloaked from head to heels in a red garment that enveloped it utterly. Over its face was a cloth mask, also red. On its hands were red rubber gloves, and hiding the head and hair was a red skull-cap from which projected two knobs in mockery of Lucifer's horns.

Keen eyes blazed through the eyeholes of the mask. Steel-gray eyes, icily calm.

The girl with the mad eyes writhed on the bed against the bonds. But her struggles were patently to get to the weird red figure, although in her eyes was stark horror of it.

"Satan," she whispered. "Master, I must serve you."

The figure uttered words which made the red mask move a bit over shrouded lips.

"Yes. I am Satan. And you must serve me. You hear?"

"I hear and I obey," whispered the girl.

"Jane—" faltered John Ivor, in a cracked voice.

The red-garbed figure held up a stern hand. The fingers of that hand seemed shielded in fresh blood as the sunlight caught the smooth red rubber of its glove.

John Ivor, Louisville's richest citizen, bit his lips for silence. The red mask moved with more words.

"You must serve me, even though, perhaps, I be not Satan after all."

For an instant the wildness in the girl's eyes faded a very little. Perplexity, fear, took its place.

"But you are Satan. You told me so, many times. And you told me I must serve you."

"That is true," the red-clad figure droned. "But I may have deceived you. Would it matter if I had deceived you?"

The girl said nothing for an instant. The light of perplexity was still stronger in her lovely eyes, still was robbing the light of madness that had originally showed there. And as it did so, the doctor and the father leaned tensely forward; for perplexity is a thing of sanity, not madness.

"Would it matter if I had deceived you, and was not Satan after all, but only a man?" the red-clad figure said.

The girl answered indirectly.

"You are Lucifer. You told me so. And you told me I must obey you, and kill your enemies…."

"I am sure it would make no difference to you if I were only a man, instead of Satan incarnate," said the masked lips smoothly.

"But you are Lucifer—"

It was almost a scream that came from the girl's lips. But again, there was a subtle difference from that scream and the mad laughter that had come from her lips before.

"Watch," commanded the red-garbed one quietly.

He took off the red rubber gloves, revealing long-fingered hands that were almost inhumanly powerful, but which yet were indisputably human. He removed the skull-cap and mask from his face.

And that face, like the hands, was indisputably mortal. It was a strong face, with level gray eyes under coal-black brows; and with a high bridged, patrician nose over a long, firm chin.

The girl half rose in spite of her bonds. Here eyes were wide and glazed as they glared at the revealed face. Her cheeks were white with nerve shock.

"You are a man," she whispered in a strangled voice. Then more loudly: "A man! You are only a man! Then I need not serve you! Oh, God, you're not Lucifer, and you have no power—"

Her words stopped as though cut with the sharp sword she had waved an hour before. She dropped back to the bed. The doctor rose quickly, and the father gasped.

"She has fainted," said the man in red quietly. "That is all." "A tremendous nerve-shock, but she will be all right. And when she comes to, she will no longer be mad. The discovery as far as she is concerned, that the dread master she thought she must serve is only mortal, will restore her sanity."

The doctor stared at him.

"I can almost believe you, Mr. Keane," he said slowly, "though when Miss Ivor was brought in here I would have sworn nothing could ever cure her madness. Who are you, that you know the mind so well, and know so well the exact thing to do to cure her?"

Ascott Keane shrugged powerful shoulders.

"It doesn't matter who I am." He turned to John Ivor. "We'll leave her here in good hands for a little while," he said. "Shall we go to your home?"

"Yes," breathed the father of the girl who had been mad, "Yes. Anything you say. You have saved my girl. Now, If you could only do something for my boy—"

"That's what we shall talk about," said Ascott Keane.

IN JOHN IVOR'S home on the boulevard, Keane and Ivor faced each other in a quiet library room. The phone has just rung, and word came from the hospital that Miss Ivor had regained consciousness and was indeed sane, though broken by some terrible experience she had gone through and of which she refused to speak. John Ivor's face was still pale, and his hands still trembled; but in his eyes there was a measure of relief.

"Thank God for your arrival!" he said brokenly. "If there is anything I can do to—"

Keane waved his hand.

"Forget that. I'm a wealthy man myself, perhaps richer than you are. Tell me everything about the kidnapping. I think I know most of it, but tell me anyway."

John Ivor sighed brokenly.

"It's hard to speak of it. A week ago today my daughter, Jane, and my son, Harold, started for the country club. Jane was going to play tennis with some friends, and Harold had a golfing engagement. They left—and did not come back."

"At six-thirty, an hour after they should have returned, I phoned the club. They had not gone there. No one had seen them, or knew anything about them. I wasn't too much worried, however, till my man came to me with a plain envelope and said there was a message in it left by some man who refused to wait for an answer.

"I opened the envelope and took out the message. It was the one that has been shown in the papers: an announcement that Harold and Jane had been kidnapped and were being held for ransom, the amount of which and place of delivery would be given later.

"I still wasn't sure the letter was anything but the grim prank of some moron, but then the police phoned that they had just found Jane's wrecked roadster. It was in the ditch. And in the car—Ivor's voice cracked—"was a man's handkerchief saturated with chloroform, and my daughters racket. With the racket were Harold's golf clubs.

"That night I got a note demanding that I pay one million dollars for the return of my boy and girl. I was to give the money at two in the afternoon, a week from that day, to a man who would receive it at a certain building under construction, where there would be no one on the sidewalk to try to stop him.

"I went to the police with everything. I knew it was risky, but so often kidnappers kill their victims anyway, and go on with their plans as if the victims were still alive, that I thought it more risky to keep the thing to myself."

Keane nodded.

"All as I have read for myself," he said. "Go on."

Ivor bit his lips.

"That much you have read. But there are two things you haven't read—which no one knows about yet."

"One is that I paid the ransom money today, Just before my girl was pushed from the blue sedan. The other—"

Ivor mopped his forehead with a trembling hand.

"I didn't have a million in cash where I could get to it. That's a terrific sum, Mr. Keane. I could only get half a million. So, I wrapped that up in newspaper, and gave it to the man who came to my town car for it.

"Half a million, Mr. Keane. And the kidnappers gave me back my daughter—half of the pair they kidnapped!"

He stared beseechingly, fearfully at Keane.

"No one knew I was going to pay only half the ransom. Yet they came in the sedan with only my girl—somehow knowing in advance that I hadn't the full sum with me!"

He paced the library, while Keane watched him.

"If that were all there was to it, I might think the return of half what I lost, in trade for half the sum demanded, was a coincidence. I might think that the kidnappers were playing the usual double-crossing game—expecting the full million but hoping to get still more by returning only my daughter. But there is more. I found this note in my pocket, thrust there by someone in the crowd, a little while after we'd got to the hospital."

He handed a crumpled bit of paper to Keane, who read:

> John Ivor: When you deliver the other half-million, you shall get your son back. Meanwhile, your daughter's madness shall be your punishment for not giving the full sum in the first place.

The note was unsigned.

"You see?" Ivor said almost pleadingly. "Days ago, the kidnappers knew I was going to give only half the ransom, though not a soul on earth but myself knew that!" He jerked around. "Have you any explanation for that?"

Keane's long fingers touched softly.

"An excellent one," he said. "You wouldn't understand, however. All I will say is that it only confirms my knowledge of the kidnapper.

Ivor gasped. "You know who he is?"

Keane nodded.

"Then—my God, man!—the police—"

"Can do nothing, if it's the person I think it is. Think! Know! The kidnapper is Doctor Satan himself. The huge sum asked made me think so in the first place, which is why I came to Louisville from New York when I first read of the affair. The diabolically induced madness was another indication. 'The Devil is my master. I serve Satan.' I knew who had inspired that delusion, all right! Now, the apparent magic by which the kidnapper knew you were going to pay only half the demand. Doctor Satan read your mind, my friend.

"Doctor Satan?"

"So the name means nothing to you! I wish it didn't to me." Keane sighed wearily. "He is a man who performs crime for the sheer, icy love of it—a devil if ever there was one. Your daughter in her delusion about having been in contact with Satan himself, was not so far wrong, my friend!"

He strode toward the door.

"Don't tell the police or anyone else my name or my connection with this," he warned. "I want to work alone. Give me twenty-four hours to try to track this man down and rescue your boy."

He nodded and was gone; a man, Ivor thought, like a steel blade; a man to inspire hope when all hope was lost, as he had inspired it in that bizarre and still inexplicable cure of Jane Ivor....

"BUT OF COURSE it was apparent at once what had happened," said Keane a few minutes later.

He was talking to a tall, lovely girl with deep blue eyes and reddish hair, in her hotel suite. The girl was Beatrice Dale, secretary, companion, right-hand man.

"Knowing that Doctor Satan was behind this, we could guess at the source of the girl's madness. Doctor Satan was seen by her only in his crimson costume, of course. In that costume he subtly and deliberately induced madness in her. Therefore, her cure suggested itself: Dress as Satan did, and unmask before her, letting her see that the being she thought the Devil incarnate was only a man after all."

Beatrice was frowning a little. She nodded impatiently.

"Yes, I see how the cure would suggest itself. But why did Doctor Satan drive her mad in the first place?"

Keane signed. "It was in line with his usual process: A reign of terror among wealthy citizens—then demands for money. Satan kidnapped Jane and Harold Ivor intending from the first to send them back to society incurably and horribly mad. With that as a precedent, no other father would hesitate a minute to part with a fortune to spare madness in his own child!"

Keane's icily calm gray eyes grew colder yet with bitter anger.

"No one knows it yet, including the police—but eight rich men in the city have received notes from Doctor Satan. Each note demands a sum varying from two hundred thousand to five hundred thousand dollars. Each note threatens kidnapping and induced insanity for the child of that man if the money is not paid on demand! Jane and Harold Ivor are but the first of many victims—if we can't stop that red-robed devil!"

Beatrice Dale faced him, cheeks a little pale, a light in her eyes that Keane had never yet really observed.

So again you go after this man," she murmured. "Ascott, be careful. I feel—this time—that you may not come back—"

Keane's rare smile flashed out.

"Save your sympathies for Satan, Beatrice. This time, he will be killed, and our work completed!"

3.

AT TEN O'CLOCK of the night when Jane Ivor had amazed and then horrified Louisville by doing her mad dance in the open street, a tall man in an enveloping topcoat approached the unfinished building where Ivor had delivered half a million dollars from his town car.

The man had his coat buttoned and the rim of his hat down over his face, though the night was warm. He carried a bundle under his arm.

At the building, on the deserted walk, the man paused. Light from across the street shone on his ice-gray eyes for an instant.

Ascott Keane.

Across the street were many people. Before the building there were none. Back from the empty sidewalk yawned the cavernous entrance of the brick shell.

Steps sounded from down the walk. Keane tensed a little and looked at his watch. It was three minutes after ten. In his pocket was a note—one of the eight extortion notes sent to the city's eight leading citizens. The note read:

> If you do not want your son kidnapped and returned a hopeless lunatic, you will deliver four hundred thousand dollars at five minutes after ten tonight at the address given below.

The given address was that of the unfinished building. The signer of the note was Doctor Satan.

Four minutes after ten. The approaching footsteps, slow, leisurely, came yet closer. Keane looked toward them.

For an instant Keane was startled and disappointed. For the maker of the steps was a uniformed policeman. He had expected anything but that; had expected an accomplice of Satan, perhaps disguised as a tramp, perhaps dressed as a sleek and respectable citizen....

"Disguise," breathed Keane. "But that doesn't necessarily mean as tramp or business man...."

Eyes wide with the thought, he stared harder at the approaching policeman. And then his eyes narrowed and his jaw tensed.

The policeman's eyes were glazed, drugged-looking. He was walking like something moved by a spring—or like a person moving in his sleep. His wide, staring eyes were fixed on Keane as though they didn't really see him.

"My God!" whispered Keane, as the full extent of Doctor Satan's scheme burst home to him. "He's using the police as his messengers now! This man is hypnotized—perhaps drugged first! But what more efficient way of collecting extortion money could he devise than to have a patrolman in full uniform, apparently only walking his beat, pick it up?"

The policeman came nearer, glazed eyes fixed on Keane's face. He slowed as he got to Keane, as if waiting for something.

Keane extended the bundle he carried.

"Have you come here for this?" he said, staring at the man's drugged, vacant eyes.

"Perhaps," the policeman spoke. His voice was thick and pitched in a monotone. "What is in the package?"

"That which will keep Malcolm Tibbet's boy from sharing the fate of Jane Ivor," said Keane.

"The word?" said the policeman.

Keane was staring into those drugged eyes with all the power of his will, now. And, as a result of his concentrated gaze, those eyes were flickering a bit.

"The word is 'immunity'," said Keane, quoting the password given in the letter.

For a moment the policeman hesitated. And Keane knew that his brain was struggling to catch the message of the master mind that had hypnotized him. Where was that message coming from? Keane had to find out, and do it through this man.

"'Immunity' is the correct word," the man said monotonously. "Give me the package...."

His voice trailed off as Keane continued to stare at him, hypnotically, powerfully. His eyes widened and grew perplexed. Slowly but surely Keane's brain was hammering down the wall of hypnosis induced by Doctor Satan previously. Keane realized, when the man was free of Satan's spell and not entirely under his own!

"The package—" the policeman reiterated vaguely. And then his eyes, clearing more and more, blinked as he stared around him, for an instant in full possession of his faculties.

"Hey, what the hell! What am I doing here? Who are you? What's this package you got?"

He stepped a swift pace back from Keane, hand driving for his gun.

"This is the joint where Ivor was to have handed over the kidnap dough! Now you're here with a bundle! By God, you must be one of the guys—"

HIS GUN WAS half drawn before Keane's eyes completed their work. He stood rigidly still in that attitude, gun half out of its holster, face hostile, staring at Keane.

Keane spoke.

"You will do what I command," he said.

The man's breathing had become regular again. His eyes were glazed once more; but not, this time, from the hypnosis of Doctor Satan!

"I will do what you command."

"You were sent here for this package. Who sent you?"

"A man in red, with a red mask."

"Where did you meet him?"

"He was in a blue sedan. He stepped out of it as I came near. He looked at me a long time, and then told me what to do."

"Where were you to deliver the bundle you got from the man who brought it to this building?"

"To the blue sedan, at the same corner."

He named an intersection toward the eastern limit of the town. Keane's fists clenched. Would Doctor Satan be in that sedan again? If so, he was going to meet him in less than fifteen minutes! And this time—"

Keane felt of a small, egg-shaped thing he carried gingerly in his coat pocket. Bullets, knife-blades, clubs—these ordinarily lethal weapons could not be used on Doctor Satan. He had means of protecting himself against such crude weapons. But this thing he had in his pocket! That, Keane thought, spelled death for the man!

"We'll go to the blue sedan," he said to the policeman. My car is down a block. Come with me to it."

THE DEVIL'S DOUBLE

A DARK INTERSECTION, with an abandoned factory on one corner throwing black shadow. In the shadow, a blue sedan—the car from which Jane Ivor had been pushed that afternoon.

Keane gripped the egg-shaped thing in his pocket. Then he cursed in his heart as he drew near the sedan with the cop. For there was only one person in the car, and that one was a man on whose face was stupid cruelty, who sat at the steering wheel.

Doctor Satan himself had not come; he had merely sent a casual accomplice to get the money. Keane's quest of the red-garbed devil who engaged in crime for the love of it as some men hung big game in Africa, was not to be so easily ended.

The man at the wheel of the sedan eyed the two doubtfully as they drew near. Obviously he had been expecting only the uniformed patrolman; his fingers clutched the gear-shift lever uncertainly when he saw Keane too. But he waited till Keane got to the car. And that was his mistake.

Keane's eyes bored into his as they had drilled into the cop's. The man blinked uneasily, tried to turn his head as instinct warned him of some danger he could not understand.

"You were to receive a package from this man," said Keane, indicating the policeman. His voice was level, quiet, soothing.

"Yeah," said the driver of the sedan. "But where did you come from?"

"I'm the one who took it to the building. I'm to go with you to your master with it."

The man's lips tightened.

"Oh, no, you're not. You—"

He stopped. His eyes were helplessly held by Keane's.

"You can't—" he mumbled.

His face became stony, his eyes unwinking. Keane got into the car beside him. Then he turned to the policeman, and made a pass with his hand before the other's heavy face.

"Drive!" he snapped to the man at the wheel.

The command was given none too soon. With the passing of Keane's hand across his face, the cop came out of his trance. He saw Keane, really, instead of through a hypnotic mist. He remembered seeing him before, in connection with some suspicious place or happening that he couldn't quite spot at the moment.

"Halt!" he roared, as the car jumped forward.

"Faster," said Keane to the staring driver.

Gun shots sounded from behind. The policeman was trying to shoot the tires of the blue sedan. But they left him behind and sped on, toward the city limits.

"You will drive me to your master," Keane said to the man he had enslaved momentarily to his will.

"I will drive you to my master," the man repeated.

THIRTY MILES THEY went, from the limits of Louisville. They got to a farmhouse that was a tumbledown ruin. Behind it there was a barn, in even worse shape.

The man turned into the drive of the vacant place. He got out of the car. Keane followed. The man went into the barn.

There he walked directly to a mound of hay. There was a bit of wood at the edge of the mound. The man grasped this and pulled it. The hay mound turned, as though resting on a turntable. A square hole was revealed in the barn floor with steps leading down.

"Where does this go?" demanded Keane.

"It strikes a short tunnel that leads into a cave. I don't know where the cave ends. I think it is a far part of the Mammoth Cave system. Anyhow, I know it goes for a long, long way. And somewhere back in it, my master, Doctor Satan, stays."

Keane took a deep breath. He had trailed Satan to many different lairs, but none of them promised to be as appropriate as this. It was fitting that a man masquerading as Lucifer should have his haunt in the bowels of the earth—near Hell, if there were such a place.

The man who had driven him walked down the steps and touched a projecting stone. The hay mound above slid into place, leaving them in thick darkness,

"Now?" said Keane.

The man pointed. Keane felt his arm go up, looked in the direction of its extended finger. Far ahead, he saw a pin-prick of light.

He turned to the man.

"You will sleep," he said quietly, his hand on the man's arm.

"I will sleep," was the somnolent answer.

Keane felt the man lowering himself to the rock floor of the crude tunnel they were in. He felt him lie down, heard no further movement. Alone, he started toward the pin-prick of light far in the distance—and toward whatever weird place Doctor Satan had fixed down here as his lair.

"A lair near Hell," Keane muttered as he felt his way along toward the distant light. "Please God I can send you to Hell tonight."

4.

THE TUNNEL DOWN which Keane walked grew constantly lighter. As it lightened, it turned faint rose-colored from the oddity of the light ahead. And now Keane heard a faint roaring from that same light.

He got nearer, and saw that the light across the tunnel ahead of him was not constant; it flickered and twisted, like a great yellow serpent.

Then he saw the nature of it.

Up from the rock floor roared a column of flame at least two yards across. It disappeared through an orifice in the rock ceiling, stretching from floor to top like a solid column, save it twisted and writhed constantly like the fiery serpent it resembled.

Keane stopped. The rock beneath him was trembling with the fury of the pillar of fire. The heat blasted at his face twenty feet away. It was a door to what lay beyond the tunnel more forbidding than any portal of steel. "Natural gas," he muttered.

But a guess as to the nature of the column did not help him pass it. That stopped him, for the moment. But, he reflected, there must be a way to tame the pillar. People passed along there. They couldn't do that if the flame persisted constantly.

He thought of going back and getting as guide the man he had left in hypnotic slumber at the tunnel mouth. But that was not necessary. Even as he thought that, he heard the roar of the pillar diminish a little, felt the rock shake less violently under his feet.

The fiery column was dying down. It burned less brightly as he watched it. It sank till he could see the leaping crest of it top under the low ceiling.

And over that crest he saw a man's head, on the other side. It was a head to induce nightmares. Like a naked skull it was, with unbelievably little flesh to clothe it. In deep eye-sockets, drugged eyes peered forth.

The flame died down still lower. Keane saw the man's body, as skeletal as the head. And as the emaciated body was more and more revealed by the subsiding of the flames, Keane shrank back into a niche in the wall to be out of sight. He opened the "bundle he had brought with him.

From the bundle he took the costume he had worn in the hospital to restore Jane Ivor's sanity; red cloak, red mask, red skull-cap, red gloves-point for point a costume matching Doctor Satan's own as Keane remembered it from former encounters.

He donned cloak and gloves, started to put on the mask.

But by now the pillar of fire had sunk below the floor level, down into the hole from which it sprang. It left only a ragged orifice like the mouth of a well in the rock floor. The opening was only about six feet across. Keane, looking around the corner of his small alcove, saw the emaciated man with the drugged, staring eyes, leap this hole and start walking down the tunnel toward where he hid.

There was no time to don the mask and skull-cap. The man was abreast of the niche before Keane could get them on. He stared at Keane in the lessened light of the lowered flame. His mouth opened for a shout.

Keane felled him with a blow to the jaw. There was neither time nor need for subtler measures. He caught the falling, thin body and lowered it to the floor just out of the way of the tunnel itself. Then he put on the mask and the skull-cap and with the two projecting knobs a mocking imitation of Satan's horns.

Tall and spare, with the red robe arrogantly draped over his broad shoulders, he stalked toward the hole into which the flame had sunk—an exact replica of Doctor Satan himself. Already the roar of the fiery pillar was increasing again, and he saw the tip of the flames as it started to rise once more to bar the tunnel.

He leaped the two-yard opening. Heat seared him for an instant, threatened to set fire to his robes even in the half-second of his jump. But he got to the other side....

Behind him the fire column rose to the ceiling in its full strength. His way back was cut off. Before him—

Keane looked, and gasped aloud.

He was in a great, low cave, extending before him farther than the eyes could penetrate. Stalagmites, like withered, warped bodies, thrust up from the floor. Stalactites dripped from the low ceiling. Among the stalagmites half a dozen figures moved; figures no less warped and distorted than the limestone pillars around them.

Keane's eyes narrowed as he looked at them. He had guessed that Doctor Satan had more accomplices here than he normally used in his devilish business; the layout of the place had indicated that. But he had not reckoned on so many, and he had not dwelt on the possible caliber of the accomplices.

Doctor Satan must have scoured the underworld to get these men who were smoothing the floor of the cave, storing supplies, in general working to make of it a permanent and sumptuous base for their diabolical master. Keane had never seen such seamed, degenerate, evil countenances! Why, with the red light from the flame pillar flickering over the weird cavern, and over their twisted bodies, they looked like demons in a real Hell!

Now two of them glanced toward him, and shouted aloud. They straightened, and the others straightened with them. At attention, like ghouls parading before the Devil himself, they waited the orders and coming of the one dressed in Lucifer's red robe.

ARROGANTLY, IMITATING DOCTOR SATAN'S stride, Keane went toward them. And he saw again, in every eye, the glazed look he had seen in the eyes of the policeman and the man who looked like a walking skeleton. Doctor Satan was taking no chances of disaffection or insubordination among the rabble he had chosen to set his evil underground house in order. He had made each of them a slave to his hypnotic will.

"Somewhere back in... the cave system... my master, Doctor Satan, stays."

So had said the man Keane had come to the caves with. Keane, not glancing at the murderous-looking men who stood at attention, stalked past them and toward the far end of the big cave. But as he went, his mind wrestled with a thought as breathtaking as it was monstrous.

So much like a real Hell, this place looked! So much like actual, inhuman demons appeared the dregs of criminal humanity working in it!

Doctor Satan masqueraded as Satan. Yes, but was it all masquerade? Was it not conceivable that—Lucifer being only a personification and title for the evil passions of men—Doctor Satan was actually Lucifer, or as near to it as a being could ever

THE DEVIL'S DOUBLE

be?

Keane shrugged the thought aside. True or fanciful, it was beside the point; the point being the destruction of the master criminal who had given rise to it.

He got to the end of the big cave at last, and squeezed through a rock opening barely large enough to admit his lean but powerful body, into another smaller cave. And with his entrance into this he instantly leaped sideways and behind a big stalagmite. For in this second cave was everything he had come here to find.

Tensely, cautiously, he peered around the concealing rock cone....

TO ONE SIDE of the cave, which was roughly circular and about fifty feet in diameter, was a legless giant who supported his torso on muscular arms as big as most men's thighs. The man's stupid, cruel eyes blinked toward the center of the cave. This was Bostiff, Satan's main lieutenant in crime since Keane had blasted his other lieutenant, Girse, out of existence. He was looking at two figures in the center of the place.

One of these was a boy of nineteen or so, dressed in expensive clothes which were now wrinkled and stained. The boy's face expressed terror beyond that tolerable to sanity. His wild eyes glared at the figure that faced him with the fascination in them expressed in the eyes of a small animal hypnotized by a snake.

And this other figure was that of Doctor Satan himself.

Tall and arrogant it towered over the boy, who was Harold Ivor, brother of the girl who had been left, a maniac, on the main street of Louisville. It was garbed in red from head to foot and, point for point, was as like the red-clad figure of Keane, concealed behind the stalagmite, as a reflection of that figure in a mirror.

Only in one detail did the two identical figures differ. The eyes peering through the holes in the mask covering Keane's face were steel-gray. The eyes of the figure towering over the boy were black, lurid, infernal.

"Who am I?" Doctor Satan rasped to the boy.

Harold Ivor, panting, glaring helplessly into the arrogant black eyes, replied: "You are Lucifer."

"You truly believe that?"

"I truly believe that."

Keane, behind his concealing pillar, felt glacial rage flood through him. He had got here just in time to witness Doctor Satan's method of driving his victims mad. He had turned Jane Ivor into a maniac. Now he was doing the same to Harold Ivor. Then the boy would be released in the town as Jane had been—a second horrible object-lesson as to what happened to the children of the rich if their parents did not pay to prevent it.

"Whom do you serve?" rasped Doctor Satan to the lad.

"I serve you, Satanic Majesty. And I will kill your enemies."

There was a silence, while the black eyes of the masked figure stared into the glazed, mad eyes of the boy.

"Bostiff," Doctor Satan said.

The legless giant swung his body toward his master, using the calloused backs of his hands as feet.

"Take him to his prison. Another session like this and he will be ready for release."

"Yes, master."

Bostiff seized the boy's hand, propelled him toward an opening in the cave. He dragged himself after. The two went through the opening.

The red-robed figure in the center of the cave was alone. The red-robed figure behind the stalagmite near the door, drew up to its full height, then stepped out of its place of concealment.

Doctor Satan had been staring at the opening through which Bostiff had gone with Harold Ivor. Now he whirled like an uncoiling spring, and stared at Keane. And in his black eyes was a sudden madness of surprise, hate and rage.

THE DEVIL'S DOUBLE

Keane drew near him. He stood before Satan, and the result was fantastic.

Two Satans stood there; two Lucifers, clad in red, red-masked, with Luciferian horns. The Devil and his double! Crimson twins, with death in the eyes of each.

Then Doctor Satan stepped toward Keane with right hand clenched.

"Keane!" he grated. "Again! At every turn I find you—squarely in my path! But this time that path shall lead ahead without obstacles, to limitless power."

"No, said Keane softly, "this time the path shall be blocked if my dead body must be used to block it!"

5.

DOCTOR SATAN TOOK a step nearer the figure so closely resembling his own. His black eyes played sardonically over Keane's red cloak.

"So," he grated, "in order to get past my men you imitated my trappings. You made a mockery of the masquerade it amuses me to wear."

Keane shrugged.

"It seemed the easiest way. I was sure you had many serving you here. I didn't want to kill them. It seemed easier to get past them by trickery."

"And having passed them," said Doctor Satan, "what then?"

Keane's mask stirred to the deep breath he drew.

"This," he said softly. "A thing I think even you are unfamiliar with, Doctor Satan. You will learn of it shortly. And it will be the last thing you ever will learn about!"

His hand went under the red cloak. It came out of his pocket with the weapon he had carried from the hotel—his one weapon, on which he was staking everything.

He opened his fingers and let Doctor Satan see the egg-shaped thing lying on his palm. It was smooth, perhaps two and a half inches long by two inches through. It seemed to be made of gray vitrum.

"Long ago," Keane said, "there were inquiring minds more versed in their own science than our present-day scientists, with their research laboratories and fine equipment, are in theirs. That was the science of Black Art. This is one of the results. I found it in the ruins of a Druid monastery in England."

Doctor Satan stared at the thing in Keane's hand. And as he stared, his black eyes lost their arrogance and became filled with the shadow of dawning fear.

"Where did you… get your knowledge of what this is?" he breathed, voice thick. "Why, it is… it is the—"

He stopped, and a silence like that of the grave held the cavern.

"It is the Blue Death of Saint Sartius," said Keane. "It was first used in Rome. Then its secret was forgotten till the black ages, when a Druid monk rediscovered it. I have read records of the death of everyone in a certain town in England. The records stated that an odd sort of plague was responsible, but intimated that death was caused by some of these."

His fingers clenched over the vitreous shell.

"Sarlfolk," whispered Doctor Satan hoarsely. In his black eyes was a fear he had never shown before. "I have read the records, too. The town of Sarlfolk—depopulated overnight and never occupied again—But that can't be the Blue Death you hold in your hand! Its secret was again lost when England was still a wilderness with men like animals populating it."

Keane's masked lips moved in a bleak smile. He raised the egg-shaped thing in his hand.

"You'll find out," he said.

And he threw the thing with all his force at the feet of Doctor Satan!

SATAN SCREAMED. IT was the first scream of terror that had ever come from the shielded, perpetually hidden lips. He leaped back from the object that had burst like a tiny bomb save that no explosion accompanied it. But quick as he was, he had acted too late.

Keane had thrown it so that it burst to pieces between him and the only two openings from the cave—the one into which Bostiff had taken Harold Ivor, and the one through which Keane had come. And with the instant of its bursting, the vitreous egg had emitted that which rose as a barrier to those exits.

From the broken shell a bluish, heavy mist rose rapidly and moved toward Satan as though acting with a will and intelligence of its own.

Another scream tore from Satan's shielded lips. He was probably the only man on earth, aside from Keane, versed enough in the occult to know what terror it was that crawled toward him. But he knew well enough!

The bluish mist spread with the rapidity of flame devouring straw. It poured from the broken shell like a rolling wall. And it formed in a half-circle around Satan, forcing him back toward the rock wall of the cavern.

In Keane's eyes was the glitter of triumph long delayed.

"You'll know now some of the anguish you've caused others," he said savagely. "You'll know some of the torment endured by the men you've killed—some of the mental torture being undergone at this moment by the parents of the children you threatened. I could feel sorry for anyone facing the Blue Death of Saint Saritius, but not for you."

There was a shuffling sound at the entrance through which Bostiff and Harold Ivor had gone. Bostiff had reappeared. He swayed in the doorway, eyes glinting with brute surprise as he saw two red-robed figures where only one had been before, and with fear as he saw without understanding the blue fog that was rolling toward the one he recognized instinctively as his master."

"To me!" Doctor Satan screamed. "Bostiff—"

The legless giant turned, snarling, toward Keane. Then he turned back obediently toward Satan and began hitching his body toward the blue fog on his hands.

"No!" breathed Keane in something like horror as the legless man hitched forward. But he did not utter the word aloud. Bostiff was as evil as his master, limited only by his own thick-wittedness. He deserved death as well as Satan.

Bostiff reached the edge of the blue fog, paused, then groped a little into it.

A scream suddenly came from his distorted lips. And the fog, touching him, underwent an instant change.

From being a sort of mist, it became a clinging, viscous shroud. Bostiff began wrenching and tearing at it as it poured itself swiftly over and around him. The viscous shroud grew more opaque, palpably harder. It was as though the legless man were suddenly encased in frosted blue glass.

His hoarse shouts died in volume. Through the blue opacity his staring eyes, like the eyes of a man caught under ice and swimming desperately under water to find the hole he fell through, peered out.

"Master! Save me!"

The shout could barely be heard. And in any event Doctor Satan wasn't listening. Nor could he have done anything if he had.

The blue mist had reached him now. It circled him closer as he crouched against the rock wall as though trying to force his body into it. It touched his face....

Doctor Satan's hands were up, fingers extended in a cabalistic sign. His lips were moving the red mask over his face as they chanted a ritual not heard by human ears for fifty generations.

And as he watched, perspiration studded Keane's face under his mask. The blue fog was slowing a little. Was it possible that

Satan could evade this death?

But the fog, halting for a moment with the cabalistic signs and the incantation, surged forward again. Incredibly, the mist-like stuff grew what seemed to be horrible tentacles. The shreds of them wrapped around Satan's red-sheathed arms and dragged them down.

A few yards away, Bostiff was now only a cocoon of a thing lying moveless on the floor. Even his ghastly, staring eyes could not now be seen. The fog portion that had wrapped around him had hardened like the vitrum of which the shell of the egglike object containing it had been made. Keane repressed a little shudder. Such a fearful death!...

Doctor Satan was down now. Over him, as it had over the legless man, the blue mist was becoming a viscous, sticky sheath. But Satan had stopped screaming. Keane saw his black eyes glisten through the mask with fearful intensity of thought.

Next moment Keane found out what the thought had been directed at.

A man stepped through the narrow portal into the first cave off the flame. Another man followed, and another. Six men lined before the opening and began to advance on Keane. Slaves of Satan's hypnotic will, they had been called silently, from this distance.

KEANE EXCLAIMED ALOUD, though not in fear of his own safety; the summoning of these comparatively stupid mortals was a futile last gesture, as Satan must have known in his extremity. The thought that wrenched the cry from Keane's lips was the fear that by sheer numbers the men might defeat the death, he had brought here for the red-robed fiend he had struggled against so long.

The Blue Death could surround and kill only a limited number of bodies! True enough, the ancient records hinted that the Blue Death had killed all the inhabitants of the old town of Sarlfolk. But if that were so, a great deal more of it must have been released than had been carried here in Keane's egg!

The deadly blue mist would attack every moving thing within range save the being that directed it! But it took a definite amount of it to kill. It now surrounded two forms. If it divided to surround six more—would there be enough to kill them all?

For once in his life, Keane wished he had a gun. In his deadly resolve to overcome Doctor Satan at all costs, he would have shot these men, because their dead bodies would not have drawn aside any of the fatal mist. But he had no gun, and he could not attack six men bare-handed. Biting his lips, he could only watch what took place.

Meanwhile the six men, hypnotized by Doctor Satan and acting blindly according to his will, sprang at Keane. With an athlete's quickness, he dodged their concerted rush. Two of them plunged into the Blue Death, already rolling toward them. One, laying hands for an instant on Keane, he flung into the ominous fog. The other three started to attack a second time, and stopped like ice-sheathed statues as the Blue Death reached them.

Keane's breath came between his clenched teeth in a ragged hiss. Eight bodies were cased in the viscous blue stuff which the mist became when it touched flesh! They lay like cocoons on the rock floor, some motionless, some feebly writhing, but all things of horror and despair.

Keane went to the form which still showed a little reddish through the blue coat over it—the form of Doctor Satan.

Terror-filled, dulling black eyes stared at him through the fearful sheath. Red-gloved hands raised a little, crackling the blue stuff that cased them, in a final gesture of malediction. Then they fell and the black eyes closed.

"THANK GOD!" BREATHED Keane, voice harsh and cracked.

The fight was over. He was sure. To make doubly sure, he would have liked to strangle that stark form; to have clubbed its head in. But he dared not touch the blue shell. That would have meant death for him, though he himself had released it.

He went to the opening through which he had seen Harold Ivor taken. The boy was beyond, in a small cave like a prison room. He was cowering against the wall, and he shrieked and threw up his hands as Keane entered in his red masquerade.

Keane dragged off his mask, and threw back his red hood. The boy stared as Jane Ivor had stared.

"You're—you're a man?" he sobbed. "You're not—"

Keane smiled, and in that smile was a gentleness that erased the fear from the boy's face.

"I am not Satan," he said. "There is no Satan—at least, none to frighten you any more.

As Jane Ivor had done, her brother, Harold, swayed in the beginning of a fainting fit from shock. But he had not been as far driven in madness, yet, as his sister had been. He reeled from the shock, but he did not lapse into unconsciousness. And after a moment he came to Keane, trembling hand outstretched.

Keane grasped it.

"Come," he said. "We'll leave here. We'll leave this Hell, and the demons in it, and its master—all dead—"

But then, as he got to the door, a hoarse shout was wrung from his lips. He leaped to the spot where Doctor Satan had been lying, eyes wide with a shock of astonishment that almost unnerved him.

The spot where Doctor Satan had lain was empty. His blue-sheathed form was no longer there. And over the bodies of the seven who had served him, the blue casing was a little thicker.

"Damn him," raged Keane, trembling fists raised. "Damn him!!"

Satan had gathered the remnants of that icy, terrific will of his while Keane was away with the boy, and had, out of his own fragmentary knowledge of Saint Sartius' Blue Death, contrived somehow to divert its hardening shell from his own body and onto the others that lay near by.

That was obviously what had happened. But, sick with defeat when victory had been tasted, Keane refused entirely to believe it till he got to the anteroom cavern with Harold Ivor.

The flaming pillar was down. Someone had just passed this way and had hurdled the well-mouth opening from which the fire hissed.

Had that someone hurdled it feebly, barely dragging his body up the opposite edge? Keane thought so. For on the far edge of the small abyss was a single, torn, red glove.

But, feebly or not, Doctor Satan had escaped from the caves. Again he had cheated with death to which Keane had driven him closer than he had ever been before in his satanic existence.

The flame pillar was already rising again.

"You must jump that hole," Keane said to the boy.

He set the example. The youth followed. Clinging to Keane's hand, Harold Ivor went with him down the outer tunnel.

The concealed trap-door above was open, as Satan had left it, too hard-pressed and weak to bother to shut it after him. Under the door the man Keane had hypnotized after his use as guide had been no longer needed, lay stretched on the floor. Eyes open and blank, he slept the sleep from which there is no awakening save by the action of the one who induces that sleep.

Keane started toward the man, then stopped. He was a human rat. The emanations from his hazed mind caught by Keane's superhuman psychic perception whispered that he was at least once a murdered, perhaps twice or thrice.

Face bleak, Keane went on past him with the shuddering boy. He left the man sleeping there....

Outside, in the driveway of the abandoned farm, the blue sedan was gone. Keane bit his lips as he visioned the swaying, raging figure in red at its wheel, speeding off somewhere into the night—to strike at humanity again when he had recovered.

Somberly, with his shoulders drooping, Keane started toward

town with the boy. He had stopped the reign of terror in Louisville—but his real work was not yet done.

MASK OF DEATH

ON ONE OF the most beautiful bays of the Maine cost rested the town that fourteen months before had existed on an architect's drawing-board.

Around the almost landlocked harbor were beautiful homes, bathing-beaches, parks. On the single Main Street were model stores. Small hotels and inns were scattered on the outskirts. Streets were laid, radiating from the big hotel in the center of town like spokes from a hub. There was a waterworks and a landingfield; a power house and a library.

It looked like a year-round town, but it wasn't. Blue Bay, it was called; and it was only a summer resort....

Only? It was the last word in summer resorts! The millionaires backing it had spent eighteen million dollars on it. They had placed it on a fine road to New York. They ran planes and busses to it. They were going to clean up five hundred per cent on their investment, in real estate deals and rentals.

On this, its formal opening night, the place was wide open. In every beautiful summer home all lights were on, whether the home in question was tenanted or not. The stores were open, whether or not customers were available. The inns and small hotels were gay with decorations.

But it was at the big hotel at the hub of the town that the gayeties attendant on such a stupendous opening night were at their most complete.

Every room and suite was occupied. The lobby was crowded.

Formally dressed guests strolled the promenade, and tried fruitlessly to gain admission to the already overcrowded roof garden.

Here, with tables crowded to capacity and emergency waiters trying to give all the deluxe service required, the second act of the famous Blue Bay floor show was going on.

In the small dance floor at the center of the tables was a dancer. She was doing a slave dance, trying to free herself from chains. The spotlight was on; the full moon, pouring its silver down on the open roof, added its blue beams.

The dancer was excellent. The spectators were enthralled. One elderly man, partially bald, a little too stout, seemed particularly engrossed. He sat alone at a ringside table, and had been shown marked deference all during the evening. For he was Matthew Weems, owner of a large block of stock in the Blue Bay summer resort development, and a very wealthy man.

Weems was leaning forward over his table, staring at the dancer with sensual lips parted. And she, quite aware of his attention and his wealth, was outdoing herself.

A prosaic scene, one would have said. Opening night of a resort deluxe; wealthy widower concentrating on a dancer's whirling concentrating on a dancer's swirling bare body; people applauding carelessly. But the scene was to become far indeed from prosaic—and the cause of its change was to be Weems.

AMONG THE PEOPLE standing at the roof-garden entrance and wishing they could crowd in, there was a stir. A woman walked among them.

She was tall, slender but delicately voluptuous, with a small, shapely head on a slender, exquisite throat. The pallor of her clear skin and the largeness of her intensely dark eyes made her face look like a flower on an ivory stalk. She was gowned in cream-yellow, with the curves of a perfect body revealed as her graceful walk molded her frock against her.

Many people looked at her, and then, questioningly, at one

another. She had been registered at the hotel only since late afternoon, but already she was an object of speculation. The register gave her name as Madame Sin, and the knowing ones had hazarded the opinion that she, and her name, were publicity features to help along with the resort opening news.

Madame Sin entered the roof garden, with the assurance of one who has a table waiting, and walked along the edge of the small dance floor. She moved silently, obviously not to distract attention from the slave dance. But as she walked, eyes followed her instead of the dancer's beautiful moves.

She passed Weems' table. With the eagerness of a man who has formed a slight acquaintance and would like to make it grow, Weems rose from his table and bowed. The woman known as Madame Sin smiled a little. She spoke to him, with her exotic dark eyes seeming to mock. Her slender hands moved restlessly with the gold-link purse she carried. Then she went on, and Weems sat down again at his table, with his eyes resuming their contented scrutiny of the dancer's convolutions.

The dancer swayed toward him, struggling gracefully with her symbolic chains. Weems started to raise a glass of champagne abstractedly toward his lips. He stopped, with his hand half-way up, eyes riveted on the dancer. The spotlight caught the fluid in his upraised glass and flicked out little lights in answer.

The dancer whirled on. And Weems stayed as he was, staring at the spot where she had been, glass poised half-way between the table and his face, like a man suddenly frozen—or gripped by an abrupt thought.

The slave-girl whirled on. But now as she turned, she looked more often in Weems' direction, and a small frown of bewilderment began to gather on her forehead. For Weems was not moving strangely, somehow disquietingly, he was staying just the same.

Several people caught the frequency of her glance, and turned their eyes in the same direction. There were amused smiles at the sight of the stout, wealthy man seated there with his eyes wide and unblinking, and his hand raised half-way between table and lips. But soon those who had followed the dancer's glance saw, too. Weems was holding that queer attitude too long.

The dancer finished her almost completed number and whirled to the dressing-room door. The lights went out. And now everyone near Weems was looking at him, while those farther away were standing in order to see the man.

He was still sitting as he had been, as if frozen or paralyzed, with staring eyes glued to the spot where the dancer had been, and with hand half-raised holding the glass.

A FRIEND GOT up quickly and hastened to the man's table.

"Weems," he said sharply, resting his hand on the man's shoulder.

Weems made no sign that he had heard, or had felt the touch. On and on he sat there, staring at nothing, hand half-raised to drink.

"Weems!" Sharp and frightened the friend's voice sounded. And all on the roof garden heard it. For all were now silent, staring with gradually more terrified eyes at Weems.

The friend passed his hand slowly haltingly before Weems' staring eyes. And those eyes did not blink.

"Weems—for God's sake—what's the matter with you?"

The friend was trembling now, with growing horror on his race as he sensed something here beyond his power to comprehend. Hardly knowing what he was doing, following only an instinct of fear at the unnatural attitude, he put his hand on Weems' half-raised arm and lowered it to the table. The arm went down like a mechanical thing. The champagne glass touched the table.

A woman at the next table screamed and got to her feet with a rasp of her chair that sounded like a thin shriek of fear. For Weems' arm, when it was released, went slowly up again to the same position it had assumed when the man suddenly ceased becoming an animate being, and became a thing like a statue clad in dinner clothes with a glass in its hand.

"Weems!" yelled the friend.

And then the orchestra began to play, loudly, with metallic cheerfulness, as the head waiter sensed bizarre tragedy and moved to conceal it as such matters are always concealed at such occasions.

Weems sat on, eyes wide, hand half-raised to lips. He continued to hold that posture when four men carried him to the elevators and down to the hotel doctor's suite. He was still holding it when they sat him down in an easy chair, bent forward as though a table were still before him, eyes staring, hand half-raised to drink. The champagne glass was empty now, with its contents spotting his clothes and the roof garden carpets, spilled when the four had borne him from the table. But it was still clenched in his rigid hand, and no effort to get it from his oddly set fingers was successful....

THE FESTIVITIES OF the much-heralded opening night went on all over the new-born town of Blue Bay. On the roof garden were several hundred people who were still neglecting talk, drinking and dancing while their startled minds reviewed the strange thing they had seen; but aside from their number, the celebrants were having a careless good time, with no thought of danger in their minds.

However, there was no sign of gayety in the tower office suite atop the mammoth Blue Bay Hotel and just two floors beneath the garden. The three officers of the Blue Bay Company sat in there, and in their faces was frenzy.

"What in the world are we going to do?" bleated Chichester, thin, nervous, dry-skinned, secretary and treasurer of the company. "Weems is the biggest stockholder. He is nationally famous. His attack of illness here on the very night of opening will give us publicity so unfavorable that it might put Blue Bay in the red for months. You know how a disaster can sometimes kill a place."

"Most unfortunate," sighed heavy-set, paunchy Martin Gest, gnawing his lip. Gest was president of the company.

"Unfortunate, hell!" snapped Kroner, vice president. Kroner was a self-made man, slightly overcolored, rather loud, with dinner clothes cut a little too modishly. "It's curtains if anything more should happen."

"Hasn't the doctor found out yet what's the matter with Weems?" quavered Chichester.

Kroner swore. "You heard the last report, same as the rest of us. Doctor Grays has never seen anything like it. Weems seems to be paralyzed; yet there are none of the symptoms of paralysis save lack of movement. There is no perceptible heart-beat—yet he certainly isn't dead; the complete absence of rigor mortis and the fact that there is a trace of blood circulation prove that. He simply stays in that same position. When you move arm or hand, it moves slowly back to the same position again on being released. He has no reflex response, doesn't apparently hear or feel or see."

"Like catalepsy," sighed Gest.

Kroner nodded and moistened his feverish lips.

"Just like catalepsy. Only it isn't. Grays swears to that. But what it is, he can't say."

Chichester fumbled in his pocket.

"You two laughed at me this evening when I got worried about getting that note. You talked me down again a few minutes ago. But I'm telling you once more, I believe there's a connection. I believe whoever wrote the note really has made Weems like he is—not that the note was penned by a crank and that Weems' illness is coincidence."

"Nonsense!" said Gest. "The note was either written by a madman, or by some crook who adopted a crazy, melodramatic name."

"But he predicted what happened to Weems," faltered Chichester. "And he says there will be more—much more—enough to ruin Blue Bay far ever if we don't meet his demands—"

"Nuts!" said Kroner bluntly. "Weems just got sick, that's all. Something so rare that most doctors can't spot it, but normal just the same. We can keep it quiet, and have him treated secretly by Grays. That'll stop publicity."

He rapped with heavy, red knuckles on the note which Chichester had laid on the conference table. "This is a fraud, a thin-air idea of some small shot to get money out of us."

He turned to the telephone to call Doctor Grays' suite again for a later report on Weems' condition. The other two bent near to listen.

A breath of air came in the open window. It stirred the note on the table, partially unfolded it.

"… disaster and horror shall be the chief, though uninvited, guests at your opening unless you comply with my request. Matthew Weems shall be only the first if you do not signify by one a.m. whether or not you will meet my demand…."

The note closed as the breeze died, flipped open again so that the signature showed, flipped shut once more.

The signature was: Doctor Satan!"

2.

AT TWO IN the morning, two hours and a half after the odd seizure of Matthew Weems, and while Gest and Kroner and Chichester were in Doctor Grays' suite anxiously looking at the stricken man, eight people were in the sleek, small roulette room of the Blue Bay Hotel on the fourteenth floor.

The eight, four men and four women, were absorbed by the wheel. Their bets were scattered over the numbered board, and some of the bets were high.

The croupier, with all bets placed, spun the little wheel, and all watched. At the door, a woman stood. She was tall, slender but voluptuously proportioned, with a face like a pale flower on her long, graceful throat. Madame Sin.

She came into the room with a little smile on her red, red lips. In her tapering fingers was held a gold-link purse. She did not open this to buy chips, simply walked to the table. There, with a smile, two men moved over a little to make a place for her.

"Thank you so much," she acknowledged the move. Her voice was as exotically attractive as the rest of her; low, clear, a little throaty. I am merely going to watch a little while, however. I do not intend to play."

The wheel stopped. The ball came to rest in the slot marked nineteen. But the attention of those at the table was divided between it and the woman who was outrageous enough, or had sense of humor enough to call herself Madame Sin. In the men's eyes was admiration. In the women's eyes was the wariness that always appears when another woman comes along whose attractions are genuinely dangerous to male peace of mind.

"Make your plays," warned the croupier dispassionately, holding the ball between pallid thumb and forefinger while he prepared to spin the wheel again.

The four couples placed bets. Madame Sin watched out of dark, exotic eyes. She turned slowly, with her gold-link purse casually held in her left hand; turned so that she made a complete, leisurely circle, as though searching for someone. Then, with her red lips still shaped in a smile, she faced the table again.

The croupier spun the wheel, snapped the ball into it. The eight players leaned to watch it....

And in that position they remained. There was no movement of any sort from any one of them. It was as though they had been frozen to blocks of ice by a sudden blast of the cold of outer space; or as though a motion picture had been stopped on its reel so that abruptly it became a still-life, and with all the actors in mid-move and with half-formed expressions on their faces.

A tall blond girl was bent far over the table, with her left hand hovering over her bet, on number twenty-nine. Beside her a man had a cigarette in his lips and a lighter in his left hand which he had been about to flick. Two other men were half facing each other with the lips of one parted for a remark he had begun to make. The rest of the eight were gazing at the wheel with arms hanging beside them.

And exactly in these positions they remained, for minute after minute.

During that time Madame Sin looked at them; and her smile now was a thing to chill the blood. You couldn't have told why. Her face was serene-looking as ever, and there were no tangible lines of cruelty in evidence in her face. Yet she looked like a she-fiend as she stared around.

She walked to the croupier, who stood gazing at his wheel, with his mouth open in the beginning of a yawn.

Down the hall came the clang of the elevator doors, and the sound of laughter and voices. Madame Sin glided toward the door. There she paused, then went purposefully back to the table. She went swiftly from one to another of the frozen, stark figures in their life-like but utterly rigid positions, then back to the door.

Smiling, she left the room, passing five or six people who were about to enter it for a little gambling. She was almost to the elevator shafts when she heard a woman's scream knife the air, followed by a man's hoarse shout that expressed almost as much horror as the scream had done.

Still smiling, utterly composed, she stepped into an elevator—and the elevator boy shivered a bit as he stared at her. He had not heard the scream, did not know that anything was wrong. He only knew that something in this lovely woman's smile sent cold fingers up and down his spine.

MASK OF DEATH

IT WAS A grim, white-faced trio that sat in the conference room of the Blue Bay Hotel at eleven next morning.

Chichester nor Gest nor Kroner—none had a moment's sleep all night. They had been in Doctor Grays' suite with Weems when a shivering man—a well-known young clubman, too, which was unfortunate—stumbled up to tell of the dreadful thing to be seen in the roulette room.

With horror mounting in their breasts, half knowing already what they would see, the three had gone there.

Nine more, counting the croupier, in a state like that which Weems was in! Nine more people with all life, all movement, arrested in mid-motion! Ten now with some kind of awful paralysis gripping them in which they had not moved or seemingly breathed—ten who were dead by every test know to science, but who, as even laymen could see at a glance, were yet indubitably alive!

"Blue Bay Development is ruined," ground out Kroner. It had been said a dozen times by every one of the three; but the words made the other two look at him in frantic denial just the same.

"If we can keep it quiet—just for a little while—just until—"

"Until what?" snapped Kroner. "If we only had an idea when this mysterious sickness would leave these people! We could stall the news perhaps for a day, or even two days—if we could have some assurance that at the end of twenty-four or forty-eight hours they'd be all right again. But we haven't. They may be like that for months before they die—may even die in a few hours. Grays can't tell. This is all beyond his medical experience. So it seems to me we might as well make public announcement now, face ruin on the resort development, and get it over with."

Chichester spoke, almost in a whisper.

"This Doctor Satan, whoever he is, gives us assurance in his note. He says that if we pay what he demands, the ten will recover, and everything will be all right."

"And if we pay what he demands, we'll be ruined just the

same as though we'd been killed by publicity," objected Gest.

Kroner glared at the wizened treasurer.

"I'm surprised you'd even suggest that, Chichester. But you've not only suggested it—you've pled for it all night long. Do you get a cut from Doctor Satan or something?"

"Gentlemen," soothed Gest, as Chichester half rose from his chair. "We're in too serious a jam to indulge in petty quarrels. We've got to decide what to do—"

"I move we call the police," growled Kroner, "I still can't believe that any human being could induce such a state of catalepsy, or living death, or whatever you want to call it, in other human beings. Not unless he's a wizard or something. Nevertheless, in view of this threat note from Doctor Satan, there may be a definite criminal element here that the cops should know about,"

"Let's wait on the police," objected Gest. "We have already done better than that in summoning this Ascott Keane to help us."

Chichester's dry skin flushed faintly.

"I still say that that was a stupid move!" he snapped. "Ascott Keane? Who is he, anyhow? He has no reputation for detective work or any other kind of work, A rich man's son—loafer—dilettante. What we should have done was contact Doctor Satan after his first note… after Weems was stricken. Then we would have saved the nine in the roulette room, and at the same time saved our project here."

"You'd pay this crook our entire surplus?" snarled Kroner, "You'd give him a million eight hundred thousand in cold cash, when you don't even know that he has had a hand in what ails the ten?"

"Its worth a million eight hundred thousand to save our stake in Blue Bay," said Chichester obstinately. "As for Doctor Satan's having a hand in the horrible fate of Weems and the rest—he told you beforehand that it would happen, didn't he?"

"Please," sighed Gest, as for a second time the florid vice-president and the wizened treasurer snarled at each other.

"We—"

The door of the office suite banged open. The assistant manager of the hotel staggered into the room. His blue eyes were blazing with excitement. His youngish face was contorted with it.

"I've just found out something that I think is of vital importance!" he gasped. "Something in the roulette room! I've been in there all night, as you know, looking around to see if I could find poison needles fastened to table or chairs, or anything like that, and quite by chance I noticed something else. The maddest thing! The roulette wheel! It's—"

He stopped.

"Go on, go on!" urged Kroner. "What about the roulette wheel? And what possible connection could it have with what happened to the people in that room?"

He stared at the young assistant manager, as did Gest and Chichester, with his hands clenched with suspense.

And the assistant manager, slowly, like a falling tree, pitched forward on his face.

"My God—"

"What happened to him?"

The three got to him together. They rolled him over, lifted his head, began chafing his hands. But is was useless. And in a moment that was admitted in their faces they looked at each other.

"Another victory for Doctor Satan," whispered Chichester, shuddering as though with palsy. "He's—dead!"

Gest opened his mouth as though to deny it, but closed his lips again. For palpably the assistant manager was dead, struck down an instant before he could tell them some vital news he had uncovered. He had died as though struck by lightning, at just the right time to save disclosure. It was as though the being who called himself Doctor Satan was there, in that office, and had acted to protect himself!

Shivering, Chichester glanced fearfully around. And Gest said: "God—if Ascott Keane were here—"

3.

DOWN AT THE lobby door, a long closed car slid to a stop. From it stepped two people. One was a tall, broad-shouldered man with a high-bridged nose, long, strong jaw, and pale gray eyes under heavy black eyebrows. The other was a girl, equally tall for her sex, beautifully formed, with reddish brown hair and dark blue eyes.

The two walked to the registration desk in the lobby.

"Ascott Keane," the man signed. "And secretary, Beatrice Dale."

"Your suite is ready for you, Mr. Keane," the clerk said obsequiously. "But we had no word of your secretary's coming. Shall we—"

"A suite for her on the same floor if possible," Keane said crisply. "Is Mr. Gest in the hotel?"

"Yes, sir. He is in the tower office."

"Have the boy take my things up. I'll go to the office first. Send word up there what suite you've given Miss Dale."

Keane nodded to Beatrice, and walked to the elevators.

"Secretary!" snorted the key clerk to the head bellhop.

"What's he want a secretary for? He's never done any work in his life. Inherited umpteen million bucks, and plays around all the time. Wish I was Ascott Keane."

The head bellhop nodded. "Pretty soft for him, all right. Hardest job he has is to clip coupons...."

Which would have made Keane smile a little if he could have heard, for the clerk and the bellhop shared the opinion of him held by the rest of the world; an opinion he carefully fostered. Few knew of his real interest in life, which was that of criminal detection.

He tensed as he swung into the anteroom of the office suite. Gest, one of the rare persons who knew of his unique detective work, had babbled something of a Doctor Satan when he phoned long distance. Doctor Satan! The mention of that name was enough to bring Keane instantly from wherever he was, with his powers pitched to their highest and keenest point in an effort to crush at last the unknown individual who lived for outlawed thrills.

As soon as he opened the door, it was apparent that something was wrong. There was no one sitting at the information desk, and from closed doors beyond came the hum of excited voices.

Keane went to the door where the hum sounded loudest and opened that.

He stared at three men bending over a fourth who lay on the floor, stark and motionless—obviously dead! Keane strode to them.

"Who are you, sir?" grated Kroner. "What the devil—"

"Keane!" breathed Gest. "Thank God you're here! There has just been a murder. I'm sure it's murder—though how it was done, and who did it, are utterly beyond me."

"This is your Ascott Keane?" said Kroner, In a slightly different tone. His eyes gained a little respect as they rested on Keane's light gray, icily calm eyes.

"Yes, Keane—Kroner, vice president. And this is Chichester, treasurer and secretary."

Keane nodded, and stared at the dead man.

"And this?"

"Wilson, assistant manager. He came in a minute or two ago, saying he had something of the utmost importance to tell us about the players in the roulette room...."

Keane nodded. He had been told of that just before he took

a plane for Blue Bay. Gest swallowed painfully and went on:

"Wilson had just started to explain. He said something about the roulette wheel, and then fell dead. Literally. He fell forward on his face as though he had been shot. But he wasn't. There isn't a mark on his body. And he couldn't have been poisoned before he came in here. No poison could act so exactly, striking at the precise second to keep him from disclosing his find."

"Doctor's report?" said Keane.

"Grays, house physician, is on his way up now. We sent the information girl to get him. Didn't want to telephone. You know how these things spread. We didn't want the switchboard girls to hear of this just yet."

Keane's look of acknowledgement was grim.

"The publicity, of course. We'll have to move fast to save Blue Bay."

"If you can save it, now," muttered Chichester.

The door opened, and Doctor Grays stepped in, with consternation in his brown eyes as he saw the man on the floor.

They left him to examine the body, and the three officials told Keane all the details they knew of the strange tragedy that had overtaken Weems and, two and a half hours later, the nine in the roulette room.

They returned to the conference room. Grays faced them.

"Wilson died of a heart attack," he said. "The symptoms are unmistakable. His death seems normal...."

"Normal—but beautifully timed," murmured Keane.

"Right," nodded the doctor. "We'll want an autopsy at once. The police are on their way here. They're indirectly in our employ, as are all in Blue Bay; but they won't be able to keep this out of the papers for very long!"

"Where are Weems and the rest?"

"In my suite."

"I'd like to see them, please."

In Doctor Grays' suite, Keane stared with eyes that for once had lost some of their calm, at the weird figures secluded in the bedroom. This room was kept locked against the possibility of a chambermaid or other hotel employee coming in by mistake. An unwarned person might well have gone at least temporarily insane at the sudden sight of the ten in that bedroom.

In a chair near the door sat Weems. He was bent forward a little as though leaning over a table. He stared unwinkingly at space. In his hand was still a champagne glass, raised near his lips.

Standing around the room were the nine others, each in the position he or she had been in when rigidity overtook them in the roulette room. They stared wide-eyed ahead of them, motionless, expressionless. It was like walking into a waxworks museum, save that these statuesque figures were of flesh and blood, not wax.

"They're all dead as far as medical tests show," Grays said. There was awe and terror in his voice. "Yet—they're not dead! A child could tell that at a glance. I don't know what's wrong."

"Why don't you put them to bed?" said Keane.

"We can't. Each of the ten seems to be in some kind of spell that makes it impossible for his body to take any but that one position. We've laid them down—and in a moment they're up again and in the former position, moving like sleep-walkers, like dead things! Look."

He gently pulled Weems' arm down, Slowly, it raised again till the champagne glass was near his lips. Meanwhile the man's eyes did not even blink. He was as oblivious of the touch as if really dead.

"Horrible!" said Chichester. "Maybe it's some new kind of disease."

"I think not," said Keane, voice soft but bleak. He looked at a night table, heaped with jewelry, handkerchiefs, wallets, small change. "That collection?"

"The personal effects of these people," said Gest, wiping sweat from his pale face.

Keane went to the pile, and sorted it over. He was struck at once by a curious lack. He couldn't place it for an instant; then he did.

"Their watches!" he said. "Where are they?"

"Watches?" said Gest. "I don't know. Hadn't thought of it."

"There are ten people here," said Keane. "And only one watch! Normally at least eight of them would have had them, including the women with their jeweled trinkets. But there's only one…. Do you remember who owned this, and where he wore it?"

He picked up the watch, a man's with no chain.

"That's Weems' watch. He had it in his trousers pocket."

"Odd place for it," said Keane. "I see it has stopped."

He wound the watch. But the little second hand did not move, and he could only turn the winding-stem a little, proving that it had not run down.

The hands said eleven thirty-one.

"That was the time Weems was paralyzed?" said Keane.

Gest nodded. "Funny. His watch stopped just when he did!"

"Very funny," said Keane expressionlessly. "Send this to a jeweler right away and have him find out what's wrong with it. Now, you say your assistant manager was struck dead just as he said something about the roulette wheel?"

"Yes," said Gest. "It was as though this Doctor Satan were right there with us and killed him with a soundless bullet just before he could talk."

Keane's eyes glittered.

"I'd like to look over the roulette room."

"The police are here," said Grays, turning from his phone.

Keane stared at Gest. "Keep them out of the roulette room for a few minutes."

He strode out to the elevators…

HIS FIRST CONCERN, after locking himself into the room where nine people had been stricken with something which, if it persisted, was worse than any death, was the thing the assistant manager had mentioned before death hit him. The roulette wheel.

He bent over this, with a frown of concentration on his face. And his quick eyes caught at once a thing another person might have overlooked for quite a while.

The wheel was dish-shaped, as all roulette wheels are. In its rounded bottom were numbered slots, where the little ivory ball was to end its journey and proclaim gambler's luck.

But the little ball was not in one of the bottom slots!

The tiny ivory sphere was half up the rounded side of the wheel, like a pea clinging alone high up on the slant of a dish!

An exclamation came from Keane's lips. He stared at the ball, what in heaven's name kept it from rolling down the steep slant and into the rounded bottom? Why would a sphere stay on a slant? It was as if a bowl of water had been tilted—and the water's surface had taken and retained the tilt of the vessel it was in instead of remaining level!

He lifted the ball from the sloping side of the wheel. It came away freely, but with an almost intangible resistance, as if an unseen rubber hand held it. When he released it, it went back to the slope. He rolled it down to the bottom of the wheel. Released, it rolled back up to its former position, like water running up-hill.

Keane felt a chill touch him. The laws of physics broken! A ball clinging to a slant instead of rolling down it! What dark secret of nature had Doctor Satan mastered now?

But the query was not entirely unanswered in his mind. Already he was getting a vague hint of it. And a little later the hint was broadened.

The phone rang. He answered it.

"Mr. Keane? This is Doctor Grays. The autopsy on Wilson

has been begun, and already a queer thing has been disclosed. It's about his heart."

"Yes," said Keane, gripping the phone.

"His heart is ruptured in a hundred places—as though a little bomb had exploded in it! Don't ask me why, because I can't even give a theory. It's unique in medical history."

"I won't ask you why," Keane said slowly. "I think—in a little while—I'll tell you why."

He hung up and strode toward the door. But at the roulette table he paused and stared at the wheel with his gray eyes icily blazing.

It seemed to him the wheel had moved a little!

He had unconsciously lined up the weirdly clinging ball with the knob on the outer door, as he examined it awhile ago. Now, as he stood in the same place, the ball was not quite in line. As if the wheel had rotated a fraction of an inch!

"Yes, I think that's it," he whispered, with his face a little paler than usual.

And a little later the words changed in his brain to: I know that's it. A fiend's genius…. This is the most dangerous thing Doctor Satan has yet mastered!"

He was talking on the phone to the jeweler to whom Weems' watch had been sent.

"What did you do to that watch?" the jeweler said irritably.

"Why?" parried Keane.

"There doesn't seem to be anything wrong with it. And yet it simply won't go. And I can't make it go."

"There's nothing wrong with it at all?"

"As far as I can find out—no."

KEANE HUNG UP. He had been studying for the dozenth time the demand note Doctor Satan had written the officials:

Gentlemen of the Blue Bay Development: This is to request that you pay me the sum of one million, eight hundred and two thousand, five hundred and forty dollars and forty-eight cents at a time and place to be specified later. As a sample of what will happen if you disregard this note, I shall strike at once at one of your guests, Matthew Weems, within a few minutes after you have read this. I guarantee that disaster and horror shall be the chief, though uninvited, guests at your opening unless you comply with my request. Matthew Weems shall be only the first if you do not signify by one a.m. whether or not you will meet my demand.

DOCTOR SATAN.

Keane gave the note back to Blue Bay's police chief, who fumbled uncertainly with it for a moment and then stuck it in his pocket. Normally a competent man, he was completely out of his depth here.

One man with a heart that seemed to have been exploded internally; ten people who were dead, yet lived, and who stood or sat like frozen statues....

He looked pleadingly at Ascott Keane, whom he had never heard of but who wore authority and competence like a mantle. But Keane said nothing to him.

"An odd extortion amount," he said to Gest. "One million, eight hundred and two thousand, five hundred and forty dollars and forty-eight cents! Why not an even number?"

He was talking more to himself than to the president of Blue Bay. But Gest answered readily.

"That happens to be the precise sum of the cash reserve of Blue Bay Development."

Keane glanced at him sharply. "Is your financial statement made public?"

Gest shook his head. "It's strictly confidential. Only the bank, and ourselves, know that cash reserve figure. I can't imagine how this crook who signs himself Doctor Satan found it out."

4.

THE HOUSE WAS serene and beautiful on the bay shore. The sun beat back from its white walls, and glanced in at the windows of the rear terrace. It shone on a grotesque figure there; a man with the torso of a giant, but with no legs—a figure that hitched itself along on the backs of calloused hands, using muscular arms as a means of locomotion.

But this figure was not as bizarre as the one to be found within the house, behind shades drawn to keep out any prying eyes.

Here, in a dim room identifiable as a library, a tall man stood beside a flat-topped desk. But all that could be told of the figure was that it was male. For it was cloaked from heels to head in a red mantle. The hands were covered by red rubber gloves. The face was concealed by a red mask, and over the head was drawn a red skull-cap with two small projections in mocking imitation of Lucifer's horns.

Doctor Satan!

In the red-gloved hands was a woman's gold-link purse. Doctor Satan opened it. From the purse he drew a thing that defied analysis and almost defied description.

It was of metal. It seemed to be a model in gleaming steel of a problem in solid geometry; it was an angular small cage, an inch wide by perhaps three and a half inches square. That is, at first it seemed square. But a closer look revealed that no two corresponding sides of the little cage were quite parallel. Each angle, each line, was subtly different.

Doctor Satan pointed it at the library wall. The end he pointed was a trifle wider than the end heeled in the palm of his hand. On this wider end was one bar that was fastened only at one end. The red-covered fingers moved this bar experimentally, slowly, so that it formed a slightly altered angle with the sides.

The library wall was mist, then nothingness. The street outside was not a street. A barren plain stood there, strewn with rocky shale, like a landscape on the moon.

The little bar was moved back, and the library wall was once more in place. A chuckle came from the red-masked lips; a sound that would have made a hearer shiver a little. Then it changed to a snarl.

"Perfect! But again Ascott Keane interferes. This time I've got to succeed in removing him. An exploded heart…."

He put the mysterious small cage back in the gold-link purse, and opened the desk drawer. From it he took a business letterhead. It was a carbon copy, with figures on it.

"Bostiff…."

On the rear terrace the legless giant stirred at the call. He moved on huge arms to the door and into the library….

In his tower suite, Keane paced back and forth with his hands clasped behind him. Beatrice Dale watched him with quiet, intelligent eyes. He was talking, not to her, but to himself; listing aloud the points uncovered since his arrival here.

"A few second after talking with Madame Sin, Weems was stricken. Also, the lady with the odd name was seen coming from the roulette room at about the time when a party entered and found the croupier and eight persons turned from people into statues. But she was nowhere around when Wilson died in the conference room."

He frowned. "The watches were taken from all the sufferers from this strange paralysis, save Weems. By whom? Madame Sin? Weems' watch is absolutely in good order, but it won't run. The ball on the roulette wheels stays on a slant instead of rolling down into a slot as it should when the wheel is motionless. But the wheel doesn't seem to be quite motionless. It apparently moved a fraction of an inch in the forty-five minutes or so that I was in the room."

"You're sure you didn't touch it, and set it moving?" said Beatrice. "Those wheels are delicately balanced."

"Not that delicately! I barely brushed it with my fingers as I examined the ivory ball. No, I didn't move it. But I'm sure it did move...."

There was a tap at the door. He went to it. Gest was in the corridor.

"Here's the master key," he said, extending a key to Keane. "I got it from the manager. But—you're sure it is necessary to enter Madame Sin's rooms?"

"Very," said Keane.

"She is in now, said the president. "Could you—just to avoid possible scandal—inasmuch as you don't intend to knock before entering—"

He glanced at Beatrice. Keane smiled.

"I'll have Miss Dale go in first. If Madame Sin is undressed or—entertaining—Miss Dale can apologize and retreat. But I am sure Madame Sin will be unaware of intrusion. In spite of the conviction of your key clerk that she is in, I am quite sure that, at least figuratively, she is out."

"Figuratively out?" echoed Gest. "I don't understand."

"You will later—unless this is my fated time to lose in the fight I have made against the devil who calls himself Doctor Satan. Are Chichester and Kroner in the hotel?"

Gest shook his head.

"Kroner is in the Turkish bath two blocks down the street. Chichester went home ten minutes ago."

"Madame Sin will be unaware of intrusion," Keane repeated enigmatically and with seeming irrelevance.

He turned to Beatrice, and the two went to the woman's room.

KEANE SOFTLY CLOSED Madame Sin's hall door behind him after Beatrice had entered first and reported that the woman was alone and in what seemed a deep sleep. At first, with a stifled scream, she had called out that Madame Sin was dead; then she had pronounced it sleep....

Keane went at once to the central figure of the living-room; the body of Madame Sin, on a chaise-lounge near the window. The woman was in blue negligee, with her shapely legs bare and her arms and throat pale ivory against the blue silk. Her eyes were not quite closed. Her breast rose and fell, very slowly, almost like the breathing of a chloroformed person.

Keane touched her bare shoulder. She did not stir. There was no alteration of the deep, slow breathing. He lifted one of her eyelids. The eye beneath stared blindly at him, the lid went nearly closed again at the cessation of this touch.

"Trance," Keane said. "And the most profound one I have ever seen. It's about what I had expected."

"I've seen her somewhere before," said Beatrice suddenly.

Keane nodded. "You have. She is a movie extra, working now and then for the Long Island Picture Company. But I'm not much interested in this beautiful shell. For that's all she is at the moment—a shell, now emptied and unhuman. We'll look around. You give me your impressions as they come to you, and we'll see if they match mine."

They went to the bedroom of the apartment. Bedroom was like living-room in that it was impersonal, a standard chamber in a large hotel. But this seemed almost incredibly impersonal! There was not one picture, not one feminine touch. In the bath there were scarcely any toilet articles; and in the closet there was only an overnight bag and a suitcase by way of luggage, with neither of them entirely emptied of their contents.

"One impression I get is that these rooms have not been lived in even for twenty-four hours!" said Beatrice.

Keane nodded. "If Madame Sin retreated here only to fall into sleep and did not wake again till it was time for her to venture out, the rooms would have just this look. And I think that is exactly what she has done!"

Beatrice looked deftly through Madame Sin's meager wardrobe. Keane searched dresser and table and bureau drawers. He wasn't looking for anything definite, Just something that might prove the final straw to point him definitely toward the incredible goal he was more and more convinced was near.

He found it in the top of the woman's suitcase.

His fingers were tense as he unfolded a business letterhead. It was a carbon copy, filled with figures. And a glance told him what it was.

It was a duplicate of the financial statement of the Blue Bay Development Company—that statement which was held highly confidential, and which no one was supposed to have seen save the three Blue Bay officials, and a bank officer or two.

Keane strode to Madame Sin's phone, and got Gest to the wire.

"Gest, can you tell if Kroner and Chichester are still out of the hotel?"

Gest's voice came back promptly. "Kroner is here with me now. I guess Chichester is still at his home on Ocean Boulevard; at any rate he isn't in the hotel—"

"Ascott!" Beatrice said tensely.

Keane hung up the phone and turned to her.

"The woman—Madame Sin!" Beatrice said, pointing toward the still, lovely form on the chaise-lounge. I thought I saw her eyes open a little—thought I saw her look at you!"

Keane's own eyes went down a bit to veil the sudden glitter in them from Beatrice.

"Probably you were mistaken," he said easily. "Probably you only thought you saw her eyelids move…. I'm going to wind this up now, I think. You go back to your suite, and watch the time. If I'm not back here in two hours, go with the police to the home of Chichester, the treasurer of this unlucky resort development. "And go fast," he added, in a tone that slowly drained the blood from Beatrice's anxious face.

5.

CHICHESTER'S HOME SAT on a square of lawn between the new boulevard and the bay shore like a white jewel in the sun. It looked prosperous, prosaic, serene. But to Keane's eyes, at least, it seemed covered with the psychic pull that had come to be associated in his mind with the dreaded Doctor Satan. He walked toward the blandly peaceful-looking new home with the feeling of one who walks toward a tomb.

"A feeling that might be well founded," he shrugged grimly, as he reached the porch.

He could feel the short hair at the base of his skull stir a little as he reached the door of this place he believed to be the latest lair of the man who was amused to call himself Doctor Satan. And it stirred still more as he tried the knob.

The door was unlocked.

He looked at it for several minutes. A lock wouldn't have mattered to Keane, and Satan knew that as well as Keane himself. Nevertheless, to leave the door invitingly open like this was almost too obliging!

He opened the door and stepped in, bracing himself for instant attack. But no attack of any kind was forthcoming. The front hall in which he found himself was deserted. Indeed, the whole house had that curiously breathless feeling encountered in homes for the moment untenanted.

Down the hall was an open double doorway. Keane stared that way. He himself could not have told how he knew, but know he did, that beyond that doorway lay what he had come to find. He walked toward it.

Behind him the street door opened again, very slowly and cautiously. An eye was put close to the resultant crack. The eye was dark, exotically lovely. It fastened to Keane's back.

Keane stared in through the doorway. He was gazing into a library, dimmed by drawn shades. He entered it, with every nerve-end in his body silently shrieking of danger.

The street door softly closed after admitting a figure that moved on soundless feet. A woman, with a face like a pale flower on an exquisite throat. Madame Sin.

Her face was as serenely lovely as ever. Not by a line had it changed. And yet, subtly, it had become a mask of beautiful death. Her eyes were death's dark fires as she moved without a sound down the hall toward the library. In her tapering hands was the gold-link bag.

IN THE LIBRARY, Keane stood with beating heart over two stark, still bodies that lay on the thick carpet near a flat-topped desk. One was wizened, lank, a little undersized, with dry-looking skin. It was the body of Chichester. At first it seemed a corpse, but then Keane saw the chest move with slow, deep breaths, as the breast of the woman back at the hotel had moved.

But is was not this figure that made Keane's heart thud and his hands clench. It was the other.

This was a taller figure, lying on its back with hands folded. The hands were red-gloved. The face was concealed by a red mask. The body was draped by a red cloak. From the head sprang two little knobs, or projections, like Lucifer's horns. Doctor Satan himself!

"It's my chance," whispered Keane. "Satan—sending his soul and mind and spirit from his own shell into that of others— Madame Sin, Chichester. Now his body lies here empty! If I killed that—"

Exotically beautiful dark eyes—with death in this loveliness—watched him from the library doorway as he bent over the red-robed figure. Sardonic death in lovely eyes!

"No wonder Gest thought that Wilson was killed in the

conference room, just before he could tell of the roulette wheel, as if Doctor Satan had been there himself! Satan was there! And he was on the roof garden earlier, and in the roulette room! A trance for the woman, the crowding of Satan's black spirit into her body—and she becomes Madame Sin, with Satan peering from her eyes and moving in her mantle of flesh! A trance for the unfortunate Chichester—and Satan talks with Gest and Kroner as the Blue Bay treasurer, and can strike down Wilson when he comes to report! Chichester and Madame Sin—both Doctor Satan—becoming lifeless, trance-held shells when Satan's physical shell, lying in a coma at his feet, to be killed at a stroke! His deadly enemy, the enemy of all mankind, delivered helplessly to him!

"But if I do kill the body," Keane whispered, "will I kill the spirit too, or banish it from the material world so that humanity won't again be troubled? Satan's spirit, the essential man, is abroad in another body. If I kill this red-robed body, will it draw the spirit out of mortal affairs with it? Or would it simply deprive it of its original housing so that I'd have to seek Satan's soul in body after body, as I have till now sought him in the flesh in lair after lair? That would be—horrible!"

He drove away the grim thought. It was probable that with the death of his body. Doctor Satan in entirety would die, or at least pass out of mortal knowledge through the gateway called death. And the mechanics of forcing him through that gateway was to kill the body.

Behind him, Madame Sin crept closer and closer on soundless feet. Her red lips were set in a still smile. The gold-link purse was extended a little toward Keane. Her forefinger searched for the movable bar that changed angles of the queer, metal cage within.

Keane's hand raised to strike. His eyes burned down at the red-clad figure of the man at his feet, who was mankind's enemy. Behind him, Madame Sin's finger found the little bar....

It was not till then that Keane felt the psychic difference

caused by the entrance of another into a room that had been deserted save for himself. Another person would not have felt that difference at all, but Keane had developed his psychic perceptions as ordinary men exercise and develop their biceps.

With an inarticulate cry he whirled, and leaped far to the side.

The wall behind the spot where he had been disappeared as the gold-link bag continued to point that way. The woman, snarling like a tigress, swung her bag toward Keane in his new position.

But Keane was not waiting. He sprang for her. His hands got her wrist and wrenched to get the gold-link purse away from her. It turned toward her, back again toward him, with the little bar moving as her hand was constricted over the thing in the purse.

It was a woman's body he struggled with. But there was strength in the fragile flesh beyond the strength of any woman! It took all his steely power to tear from her grasp the gold-link purse with its enclosed device. As he got it, he heard the woman's shrill cry of pain and terror, felt her sag in his arms. And then he heard many voices and stared around like a sleepwalker who has waked in a spot different from that in which he had begun his sleep—a comparison so exact that for one wild moment he thought it must be true!

He was in a familiar room.... Yes, Doctor Grays' room at the Blue Bay Hotel.

The people around him were familiar.... There was Gest. There were Kroner and Doctor Grays, and—Beatrice. There were the Blue Bay chief of police, and two men.

But the limp feminine form he held in his arms was Madame Sin, the fury he had been fighting in Chichester's library! And in his hand was still the gold-link bag he had wrenched from her!

The woman in his arms stirred. She looked blankly up at

him, stared around, a cry came from her lips.

"Where am I? Who are you all? What are you doing in my room? But this isn't my room?"

Her face was different, younger-looking, less exotic. She wasn't Madame Sin, she was a frightened, puzzled girl.

Keane's brain had slipped back into gear, and into comprehension of what had happened.

"Where do you think you are?" he said gently. "And what is your name?"

"I'm Sylvia Crane," she said. "And I'm in a New York hotel room. At least I was the last I knew, when I opened the door and the man in the red mask came in...."

She buried her face in her hands. "After that—I don't know what happened—"

"Nor do any of us," quavered Gest. "For God's sake, Keane, give us some idea of what has happened here, if you can!"

IT WAS OVER an hour later when Beatrice and Keane entered the door of his suite. It had taken that long to explain to the people in Doctor Grays' rooms. Even then the explanation had been but partial, and most of it had been frenzied and stubbornly disbelieved even though proof was there.

Keane's shoulders were bowed a little and his face wore a bitter look. He had thwarted Doctor Satan in his attempt to extort a fortune from the resort. But once more his deadly enemy had got away from him. He had failed.

Beatrice shook her head.

"Don't look like that. The fact that you're here alive is a miracle that makes up for his escape. If you could have seen yourself, and that girl, when the police brought you back from Chichester's house! As soon as they set you down in the doctor's rooms, you and the girl came together. You fought again for her purse, as you say you started to do in Chichester's house ten hours ago. But you moved with such horrible slowness! It was like watching a slow-motion picture. It took you hours to raise your arms, hours to take the purse from her hand. And your expression changed with equal slowness.... I can't tell you how dreadful it was!"

"All due, as I said, to this," Keane sighed.

He stared at the little metal cage he had taken from the purse.

"The latest product of Doctor Satan's warped genius. A time-diverter, I suppose you might call it."

"I didn't understand your explanation in Grays' rooms, after you'd brought those people out of their dreadful coma," said Beatrice.

"I'll try again."

Keane held up the geometric figure.

"Time has been likened to a river. We don't know precisely what it is, but it seems that the river simile must be apt. Very well, we and all around us float on this river at the same speed. If there were different currents in the same river, we might have the spectacle of seeing those nearby move with lightning rapidity or with snail-like slowness as their time-environment differed from ours. Normally there is no such difference, but with this fantastic thing Doctor Satan has succeeded in producing them artificially.

"He has succeeded in working out several sets of angles which, when opposed against each other as this geometric figure opposes them, can either speed up or slow down the time-stream of whatever it is pointing at. The final angle is formed by this movable bar in its relation to the whole. By its manipulation, time can be indefinitely retarded or hastened. He utilized the bizarre creation in this way:

"In New York he contacted a quite innocent party by the name of Sylvia Crane. He hypnotized her, and forced his spirit into her body while hers was held in abeyance. Then 'Madame Sin' registered here. She made acquaintance with Weems. On the roof garden, she pointed the infernal figure at him, with the little bar turned to retard time. The result was that Weems suddenly lived and moved at immensely retarded speed. It took about twenty-four hours for his arm to raise the champagne glass to his lips, though he thought it took a second. Our actions were so swift by comparison that they didn't register on his consciousness at all. He confessed after I'd brought him out of his odd time-state with the device, that he seemed to raise his glass while in the roof garden, and start to lower it when he found himself abruptly in Doctor Grays' bedroom. He didn't know how he got there or anything else. It was the same with the nine in the roulette room. They came back to normal speed only a second or two after being retarded in the roulette room. But it was hours to us, and meanwhile they seemed absolutely motionless.

"How on earth did you ever get a hint of such a thing as this?" said Beatrice.

"Weems' watch gave a pointer. It was all right, the Jeweler said, but it wouldn't run. Well, it did run—but at a speed so slow that it could not be recorded. The roulette wheel was another. The ivory ball did not roll down the side of the wheel because the wheel was rotating with infinite slowness after being retarded by the same thing that made the people look like frozen statues. Satan, as Madame Sin, couldn't do anything about the wheel. But he—'or she'—could and did take the watches from all concerned, to guard against discovery that way. However, there was no chance to get Weems' watch; there were always people around."

"You said Doctor Satan moved in the body of Chichester as he did in the girl's body."

"Yes, I got a hint of that when I observed that Chichester and Madame Sin never seemed to be in evidence at the same time. Also because the exact sum of Blue Bay's cash reserve was so readily learned. Again when Wilson was killed in a room where only the three officials sat. He was killed by Chichester, who was at the moment animated by Satan's soul. He was killed, by the way, by a speeding-up of time. The rest were retarded and suffered nothing but nerve shock. Wilson was killed when the speed of his time-stream was multiplied by a million: you can stop a heart without injuring it, but you can't suddenly accelerate a heart, or any other machine, a million times, without bursting it. That's why his heart looked as though it had blown up in his chest."

Keane stopped. The bitter look grew in his eyes.

"This failure was wholly my own fault," he said in a low tone. "I knew when I found the duplicate financial statement in Madame Sin's rooms that it was a trap to draw me to Chichester's home. Doctor Satan would never have been so careless as to leave a thing like that behind inadvertently. Knowing it was a trap, I entered it, and found Satan's soulless body. If I'd destroyed it immediately… But I didn't dream that Madame Sin would follow me so quickly."

Beatrice's hand touched Keane's fleetingly. He was looking at the geometric figure and did not see the look in her eyes.

"The world can thank heaven you're alive," she said softly. "With you dead, Doctor Satan could rule the world—"

There was a knock at the door. Gest was in the hall.

"Keane," he said. "I suppose this will sound like a small thing after all you've done. You've saved us from bankruptcy and saved Lord knows how many people from a living death from that time-business you tried to explain to us. Now there's one more thing. Workmen in Chichester's home tell us that they can't build up one of the walls in the library, which is non-existent for some reason. There the room is, with one wall out, and it can't be blocked up! Do you suppose you—"

Keane nodded, with a little of his bitterness relieved by a smile.

"I remember. The time-diverter was pointed at that wall for an instant as the girl and I struggled. Evidently, it was set for maximum acceleration, to burst my heart as it did Wilson's. It got the library wall, which is gone because in the point of the future which it almost instantly reached, there is no library or home or anything else on that spot. I'll bring it back to the present, and to existence again, so you won't have a physical impossibility to try to explain to nervous guests of Blue Bay Resort."

"And after that," he added to himself, "I'll destroy this invention of Hell. And I wish its destruction would annihilate its inventor along with it—before he contrives some new and even more terrible toy!"

PAUL ERNST

WRITING WEIRD TALES

Paul Ernst was a sailor during the war, after, in the advertising business till 1926, then discovered that he had a "knack" of writing weird tales. Speaking of himself Mr. Ernst says he has sold nearly three hundred gems of literature to over fifty magazines, including Weird Tales, Strange Tales, Astounding Stories, Amazing Stories, Ghost Stories. *Among the many types of horror stories he has written are detective, love, sex, adventure, pseudo-scientific, gangster and travel stories. Mr. Ernst is thirty-three years of age.*

FIRST, YOU SHIVER.

The weird tale from first to last is the account of a shudder. Your reader is supposed to feel apprehensive with paragraph one, clammy with paragraphs two, three and four, and cold at the pit of his stomach when the climax smashes upon him.

For the reader to get this out of your horror story you must first put it in. Hence the initial shiver.

One good way to induce the opening shudder is to begin with the ending. Present your hero as a nervous wreck, picking at his tremulous lips and starting at shadows. Then go ahead and tell how he got that way.

Another method is to open with description, This is heresy with most fiction forms, but in the horror yarn a purely descriptive opening may be very effective. As far as that goes, description can be a vibrant, exciting bit of business. For example:

... In former times a cemetery existed there.... The earth,

which had been glutted with corpses for more than a century, literally perspired with death; and it had been necessary to open a new cemetery at the other end of town, The old cemetery, long abandoned, had been covered with dark, thickset vegetation.... This rich soil, in which gravediggers could no longer delve without turning up human remains, possessed a formidable fertility. The tall weeds which overtopped the walls after the spring rains were plainly visible from the high road, while inside the place had the appearance of a deep, somber sea studded with large blossom of sinister brilliancy.... The vegetation, in its vigorous growth, had rapidly assimilated the decomposing matter in the old cemetery; while the fever rising from the human remains had been greedily absorbed by flowers and fruits, so that the only odor one could detect, in passing by this accumulation of putrefaction, was the rank, noxious odor of gilly flowers....

Would this, penned by friend Zola, be a food opening for a horror tale, or would it not?

WITH YOUR STORY off to a shuddery start, you proceed to get your hero into the most bizarre predicaments, and distress him with the most nightmare creations it is in your power to invent. The more inconceivable the better—if you can make the incredible appear like gospel truth.

There, incidentally, is a wreck-strewn rock. Your weird story must be convincing above all else. This is not too easily accomplished but it must be done.

There are several methods of achieving plausibility. One is by the use of extra-dignified phraseology here and there. A fractured tibia, for instance, is better than a busted leg as a result of a brush with occult powers. Another method is to pause now and then and doubt your own story. Yes, these things seemed to have happened, but they couldn't have, of course. Not really. Proclaim the impossibility of your yarn loud enough and the reader will soon brand you a liar and start believing the narrative.

The real test of a story's convincingness comes with the climax. Here your character and the nightmare creation he is pitted against go through their most poignant battling. But the battling must be consistent, chill-inducing, as well as exciting. There is no set rule, but usually it is poor form for your ghost to black your hero's eyes, and usually your magician is not very bright if he lets himself get shot. Supernatural beings should be just that: super-natural.

Possibly the best horror climax is that in which the action is only half apprehended by the reader. No climax at all, in the action sense of the word. There is the approach of action, the promise of terrible and swift destruction, the swoop of a menacing, shapeless Thing of evil all the more deadly for being sensed rather than seen. Finally, eerie, incredible (but entirely believable) disaster.

After that, stop your story in a hurry. In weird tales more than in most stories an anticlimax is to be avoided. A few brief sentences insuring that the reader's concluding thought will be: "Well, it 'could' have happened, at that." No more.

Doesn't sound like an easy, foolproof outline on which to build numberless weird tales, does it? Sorry. In the writing of horror fiction there is no formula, as far as I know.

However, in conclusion, I'll try to be more specific.

Suppose we had been clever enough to invent Zola's cemetery for our opening shiver. Now let's go on with the vegetable description and place in the center of the ancient boneyard a single, scarlet flower on a naked, distorted stalk. The bloom is beautiful but sinister, gigantic but graceful, unlike any other flower whatsoever.

To this deathly bloom a botanist, a mild, unworldly man, has beaten a path. (A few botanical terms, in telling what he is an authority of will give plausibility.) He goes every day to study it in spite of warnings of the country-people. (The most terrible things have happened to the foolhardy in that cemetery!) Particularly is he warned against going there in the full of the moon. But it happens that his blood-red flower takes nourishment only at night. (More atmosphere. He has found skeletons of rodents near the naked stalk. A mongrel dog, which he tied to the stalk one afternoon, was a deflated bag of skin next morning. The posy is a meat-eater, it seems.) In spite of repeated warnings, our botanist goes to spend a night watching the flower which roots literally in death.

The vigil starts with the botanist fighting down silly premonitions of disaster. Bah! Only superstition! Of course there is no danger. (Oh, no?) The climax is approached. Botanist against flower. The botanist's mounting terror, which he still fights against, is given a boost by the realization that the blossom is now exuding a sickly fog, a sort of miasma of death. (Not a bad title.) He is rapidly paralyzed. Finally, unable to move, although his brain remains horribly alert and clear, he is taken prisoner by the flower. The leafless stalk winds about his throat. The red bloom sways toward him in the ghastly moonlight. The flower presses its hideously beautiful petals almost in a caress against his cheek....

Next morning he is found in a rather used condition.

All of which illustrates one last Don't in the writing of horror fiction. That is, don't use old stuff. The above plot happens to fall into a class so hackneyed that even a swell story developed from it would probably not sell.

Be original, start with a shiver, and end with a climax that will send the reader to bed with the lights on.